Welcome to Gabby
hilarious and spicy
world – praise for

'Gabby is **one of the f**
Sarah Millican

'The sort of story **you want to climb inside so you can hang out with all the characters**. Hilarious, warm and kind!'
Louie Stowell, author of the *Loki* series

'A perfect mix of **thrilling, sexy and funny**, all set in an alternate sixteenth century London' Poppy Kuroki, author of *Gate to Kagoshima*

'A terrific book with a big beating heart. **Every page sizzles** and the cast of eccentric characters keeps you hooked'
T. L. Huchu, *The Library of The Dead* series

'I absolutely loved it! **Danger, excitement and kissing –** it's got the lot' Lucy Porter

'Hutchinson Crouch's London is dark, dangerous and very funny. **A chuckle on every page guaranteed**' Mark Stay, author of *The Witches of Woodville* series

'Funny, **joyous**, subversive' Joanne Harris, author of *Broken Light*

'Magic. Gabby has created a world of mythological and supernatural lore that's **completely unique**' Sara Gibbs, author and comedy writer

'A spectacular romp through Elizabethan London, with all the wit you'd expect from a writer with comedy talons as sharp as Crouch's. A **hugely imaginative** read!' Rose Biggin, author of *The Belladonna Invitation*

CURSED IN THE LOST CITY

Cursed, Book Two

GABBY HUTCHINSON CROUCH

Farrago

First published in the United Kingdom by Farrago in 2025
Farrago, an imprint of Duckworth Books Ltd
1 Golden Court, Richmond, TW9 1EU, United Kingdom
www.farragobook.com

A catalogue record for this book is available from the British Library

Book design by Danny Lyle

Printed and bound in Great Britain by Clays Ltd, Elcograf S.p.A

The authorised representative in the EEA is Easy Access System
Europe, Mustamäe tee 50, 10621 Tallinn, Estonia.

Paperback ISBN: 9781788425414
eISBN: 9781788425421

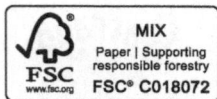

MIX
Paper | Supporting
responsible forestry
FSC® C018072

For my family

CHAPTER ONE
TOAST

London: city of dreams, theatre, fashion, passion and, occasionally, plague. The city so great they built it twice, with the newer subterranean metropolis of Deep London housing dragons, magicals and the undead directly beneath its older, more flammable, human-centric counterpart city on the surface. Even though the peace between humans and magical kind had been kept for hundreds of years by separating the Upperside and Deepside Londons, with two different monarchs and two different sets of laws, still dragons, vampires, zombies and the like regularly traversed through the tube network to enjoy the thrills of the Upper city's theatres and bars. Indeed, they were legally free to do so, as long as they had an up-to-date passport and remembered not to kill or eat anybody on the surface. So too were humans free to take the tube down Deep and gasp in wonder at the vast, candlelit, carved cavern of a city that sprawled all the way from Deep Blackheath to below Camden. It's just that humans were far less likely to take the trip down Deep, because to do so was to run the risk of getting swiftly – and legally, by Deepside rules – exsanguinated.

There was still a very good chance of getting exsanguinated in Upper London, mind you, by ordinary humans with big knives. Just ask Lazare de Quitte-Beuf, who only a month previously was stabbed to death in an alley. It had hurt like the blazes, and frankly had ruined all of his well-laid yet thus far unsuccessful plans of becoming a famous actor, not to mention his second best doublet. He had awoken from death as some strange new type of being, incapable of dying, and with – for reasons that remained elusive to him – a huge pair of leather wings, which really didn't help with his difficulty in landing roles. It really wasn't fair. Vampires had wings, and vampires could get work just fine, but Lazare wasn't a vampire, nor a zombie nor a ghoul. He didn't know what he was for certain, except 'hugely inconvenienced'.

He was, at least, currently hugely inconvenienced in a beautifully carved embassy building in Deep London, filled with well intentioned, if not particularly effectual, púca, brownies and goblins. And he was at least amongst friends in this gorgeous palace to diplomacy. And there was a pretty little trolley covered in breakfast foods.

'Brekkie?' asked Grubble, a púca ambassador, rightly proud of his little trolley.

'Is there any paperwork on that trolley?' asked a voice that sounded like someone had taught a headache how to speak. Fang, the owner of said voice, regarded Grubble's trolley with all the cheerful patient goodwill of a man with a desperate hangover thirst being presented with an assortment of dry crackers. 'Safe passage to Redthroat's palace, perhaps?'

'Fang,' sighed Nell, 'we only decided to seek counsel with Redthroat last night; she's all the way off in the Lost City of Llanelli—'

'Which isn't actually lost,' interjected Fang.

'Which – yes, technically, but the point is, it may as well be because it's walled off to humankind—'

'Which technically we aren't anymore,' continued Fang, nodding to Lazare's wings.

'Yes, fine, clever dick,' Nell told him irritably, 'but it's still a walled-off hyper-exclusive magical enclave.'

'It's a fifteen-year waiting list to live there for Deep London dragons alone,' agreed Grubble. 'Longer for fae-folk, worse still for undead. The paperwork just for visitors' permits takes ages.'

'The postman alone takes days to get to Wales,' Nell added. 'It'll be a long wait, trust me.'

It was understandable that Nell would know of Welsh matters, since she was from Carmarthen. It was also understandable that Fang was itching to speak with the dragon queen Redthroat, since he was on a quest. Well. They were all on a quest together, really, but it had been Fang's idea to go on the quest in the first place, and… the quest hadn't exactly 'failed' as such, it was just that Lazare could see how Fang might view their quest as a failure thus far. Fang and Nell were like Lazare: cursed at the point of death, turned to things rich and strange by a fae spell of immortality, cast without malice, by accident, by a child.

The source of their curse, the centre of their quest, sat in Fang's lap, clinging to him like a kitten to its mother. Tem. Half-fae, half-human, small and sad and big-eyed, by Lazare's

3

best guess no more than five or six years old. Tem the tiny, Tem the orphaned, Tem the rejected, Tem the most magically powerful being Lazare had ever crossed paths with, allowed Fang to pass her small triangles of thickly honeyed toast to munch listlessly upon.

'So, for all those reasons and more, there's no paperwork for breakfast,' Grubble told them. 'It's mostly toast and kippers.'

'Kippers?' called Lazare's dragon friend Amber excitedly, already on the bottom shelf of the trolley, rooting around for fish. Nobody chided Amber for doing so. Frankly, thought Lazare, she needed the calories. He was fairly certain dragons were supposed to be bigger than three feet long.

'We may as well get comfy here for a bit,' said Nell. 'We might not even need to go all the way to bother the mighty dragon queen; we've got contacts here in Deep London now, don't we, Grubble?'

'Er...' panicked the púca.

'Nell,' sighed Fang, 'it's a dead end down here. We tried to take Tem home, and we failed. The fae can't help her.'

'Technically it's more that they *won't* help her,' Amber interjected, crunching through fish bones, 'because they're a bunch of arrogant dicks – no offence, Tem sweetheart.'

'What's a dick?' asked Tem. Fang huffed angrily at Amber.

'The fae aren't the be all and end all down here,' Nell told the group. 'There must be others we can ask.'

'Yeah,' said Amber, 'but Queen Redthroat's all ancient and wise and full of magical miracles, so she'll get this curse off you lot with a flick of her claw, I reckon.'

'Ancient and wise, yes, glory to Redthroat,' added Nell swiftly. 'But Llanelli's miles away – a city state within a different country. We'd need to get to Wales, do a load of paperwork to be allowed past the walls of Llanelli. We'd need our passports – it'd be a faff.' Nell gestured around herself with a sausage. 'We're in a magical city already; let's just ask around.'

'Don't you have a shop to run?' asked Fang.

'I can nip up on the tube at opening hours,' Nell argued. 'I'm just saying, what's the rush? Your room here's nice, isn't it?'

Lazare glanced down at his plate. Yes. Yes, the guest suite he shared with Fang here was nice. The wallpaper was exquisite. And, only the night before…

Lazare's memory flashed, unbidden, with graphic images. His hands on Fang's thighs, desperate lips seeking his with an all-consuming hunger, dark eyes bright with need. And then, pain, choking, a freezing river, those same eyes tortured and lifeless, those same lips slack and blue.

Lazare looked up again, found himself making awkward eye contact with Fang, and hurriedly turned his gaze to Grubble instead.

'The room,' he told the púca as smoothly as he could muster, 'is sublime.'

Nell flourished her sausage some more. 'And we're safe here…'

'Oh yes, that reminds me,' added Grubble. 'No paperwork, but I do have a diplomatic warning for you – you're not safe here at all.'

Tem whimpered. Fang shot to his feet, clutching the child, a thin shower of toast crumbs falling from him as he moved. 'What?'

'Could you not have led with that, Monsieur?' added Lazare, also getting to his feet, a now-familiar panic clutching at his heart and lungs.

'Is he back?' whispered Tem urgently. 'Is he still chasing us?'

Grubble held out his little furry hands in an attempt to placate the fretful group. 'The alchemist who attacked you last night is still very dead. But that's part of the problem. He was an Upper London citizen, so we had to inform Queen Elizabeth's court, and her lot have already been asking *loads* about you three.' He nodded to Lazare, Fang and Nell. 'Her chief Royal Guard's already demanded a permit to arrest you. Since you're not undead, Queen Redthroat's protection doesn't extend to you if you killed a human down here.'

'We didn't kill him,' blurted Nell. '*He* killed *us*. Repeatedly, in Fang's case!'

Tem whimpered again. Lazare's heart still hammered at the memory.

'But if they suspect you're tied to it,' continued Grubble, 'we have an extradition treaty for foreign suspects. We'd even be obliged to extradite the Welshwoman. But,' he added brightly, 'we would at least send a note of apology to the Welsh king for your imprisonment and torture, so that's something.'

Fang clutched Lazare's shirt. 'We have to go.'

'Let's get back to my shop,' added Nell in agreement.

'If Elizabeth's guards are looking for you, you're *definitely* not safe in Upper London,' reminded Grubble matter-of-factly. 'Her swans and ravens will try to swoop you the second you leave the tube.'

'Really not helping,' railed Fang, dragging Lazare away from the table.

'What I mean is,' Grubble continued, 'if the plan was still to head to the Lost City of Llanelli, you could just take the Emfor tunnel? It's direct and underground.'

In spite of the danger, Nell shuddered. 'Urgh. Not the Emfor.'

'We needs must go to Nell's shop, Monsieur,' Lazare told the púca. 'If we are to travel, we need our passports. Particularly since we are, as you put it, "foreign".'

'We've evaded Elizabeth's bird guards before,' Fang reminded Grubble. 'I'm sure we can get to Nell's shop without incident.'

'Thank you for breakfast,' squeaked Tem, stopping Fang in his tracks.

Fang gnawed at his lower lip guiltily. 'Thank you for your help and hospitality,' he told Grubble awkwardly.

'S'all right,' replied the púca. 'Sorry it had to end like this. I don't think I'm very good with people.'

'Sir,' Lazare reminded him hotly as they left, 'you are literally a diplomat!'

CHAPTER TWO
DUCKIES

A hurried cart-ride to Deep Southwark's tube later and they were all climbing up the winding tube slope to the Upperside opening, hiding behind a large black dragon to avoid the gaze of any beady bird eyes watching the exit. Lazare was bathed in the cold, grey daylight of Upper London. God's Nose, he'd missed natural light. He wanted to take a moment to bathe in its dingy delights, but the others pressed straight on with a quiet anxiousness. The tube was busy enough for them to be able to evade the two ravens they spotted stationed nearby. They slipped from behind the larger dragon to a group of hooded vampires.

Fang pulled the hood of his new cloak up over his own head, which Lazare supposed was meant to help Fang pass as just another vampire out on a trip. It probably would have looked more convincingly vampiric had the new cloak not been one of Lazare's cast-offs, and therefore a particularly lurid shade of green. As little as it made the man look like a vampire, Lazare felt the new cloak rather suited Fang. He looked very handsome with a pop of colour – well, Fang managed to look ridiculously handsome even in rancid bin-clothes and a thick layer of grime, but he looked even better framed in parakeet green, and it was nice to see Lazare's gift had been accepted with grace. Chartreuse cloak and all, the group hurried away as fast as they could inconspicuously manage, to the relative shelter of the narrow alleyways of Upper Southwark, with Tem scooped up in Fang's arms, and Amber straining to keep up on her stumpy legs.

'Not far to my shop from here,' Nell told the child and the struggling dragon encouragingly.

Tem, who had recently discovered the joy of shops, prompted largely by Fang's inability to say no to her requests for inexpensive new ribbons and dollies, nodded. 'Do you sell toys, Nell?'

'Er,' replied Nell, a little flustered. Lazare knew that technically Nell did sell toys, but they were special toys for those experiencing 'marital difficulties', and were kept in a curtained-off alcove that was most definitely not for the perusal of children.

'Nell sells something better than toys,' Fang said hurriedly. 'She sells coffee. Kids like coffee, right?'

'I don't know what that is,' replied Tem.

'You might prefer chocolate,' Nell told her, with an air of relief. 'I sell that too, but you're cute, so I'll let you have some for free.'

'I don't know what chocolate is, either.'

'We won't be staying long,' Fang added. 'Then we'll go to the dragon queen.'

''Cause she can help us,' said Tem, sounding unsure.

Fang nodded at her, his expression also seeming unsure. It did nothing to allay Lazare's concern that Fang's 'dragon queen' idea was rather clutching at straws – just an excuse to run again, as was Fang's habit.

'And we need passports,' continued Tem seriously, still clutching the document the púca ambassador had given her before they'd left the Deepside Embassy. 'Because "up top is a foreign country"?'

'Yep. And so's Wales,' Nell told her. 'Sort of. It's a different country for humans, but dragons and so on see it as part of Deep England. Or rather, they see Deep England as an extension of Wales. It's complicated. There was a war and then a peace treaty and then three hundred years of trying to make the treaty work on a practical level, so stuff got fudged, lines got blurred.'

'Wales is King Llewellyn's country and also a utopian home for all magicalkind, except for the large areas of land gifted to Redthroat for walled-off exclusive magical use, out of the Welsh king's gratitude for their help in the war, which are even *more* utopian than the normal utopia,' puffed Amber. 'Deep England's a sort of dragon annexe except for when it's not. Britain, innit. It's all a lovely mishmash except for Scotland.'

'What's Scotland?' asked Tem.

Amber visibly bristled. 'You don't want to know.'

'I do want to know!'

'Scotland was fine until their king decided he hated witches and magicals,' Nell told her. 'It's all gone a bit bad up there.'

Tem looked frightened. 'We're not going up there?'

The others shook their heads, and none of them gave voice to the silent worries that had been growing every time news of King James of Scotland's latest magical purge reached their city – worries about an ailing, heirless Tudor queen, and her family tree, and the possibility of power being passed to the dangerously hateful by pure accident of birth.

'Don't worry about Scotland,' Fang told the child. 'Think about getting your curtsey right when you meet Queen Redthroat. That'll be nice, won't it?'

Tem nodded, with the expression of a child as delighted by the thought of meeting a queen as she was by the thought of getting to meet more dragons, and Lazare wondered – not for the first time – whether Fang put in extra effort to always say the right thing to Tem, or whether saying the right thing was second nature to him, and he had to concentrate more effort into saying the *wrong* thing to everybody else. Fang certainly knew how to always say the wrong thing to Lazare. Lazare supposed it was intended to make him feel less attached to Fang, out of some sort of misguided kindness. It didn't work.

The group came to an intersection between alleys and a wider street. They all looked around carefully for Royal Guards and, seeing none there, scuttled for the closed-in shelter of the next alleyway, only for a now-familiar sound of street violence to inform them that doing so hadn't been the best way to avoid trouble after all. Several yards down the alley, three armed muggers were crowding around a small, frightened, balding man. There was no question of the group turning back and leaving the poor wretch to be attacked. Fang simply set Tem on Amber's back, who flew the child up to the safety of the eaves, and wordlessly the immortal trio approached the muggers.

'This is but paper,' growled one of the muggers, throwing sheets of folio from their victim's bag. 'Where's the good stuff? The gold?'

Another mugger tried to prise a ring off the little man's finger.

'No, please, sir, that is my wedding ring,' cringed the man in an odd accent that Lazare immediately recognised.

'This paltry thing?' sneered the second mugger. 'He mocks us, boys. He's a poet! All poets are nobs, everyone knows that. And yet his only jewels are a single earring and the wedding ring of some bumpkin lad?'

'We're not all nobs,' protested the victim, 'and I married young; it was all we could afford. Please! I'm sure if you stop crowding me, we can reach an amicable arrangement…'

'He's trying to trick us,' cried the third mugger, waving the paper in the victim's face. 'Bloody lying poet. How can someone be "more lovely than a summer's day"? Summer days are magical; my old mum's birthday is July – are you saying some sexy man is nicer than my old mum's birthday?'

'No, I just—'

'It's always the same silver-tongued rhetoric with you lot, isn't it?' interrupted the first mugger. 'Well, how good are you going to be at that with an actual silver tongue? After we've cut your real tongue clean out of your lying mouth?'

'No,' whimpered the victim, 'please? I need my tongue for so many things…'

'I can vouch for that,' announced Lazare, making his group's presence known to the muggers. 'I once saw this man stress-drink a whole bottle of sack in thirty minutes flat.' He nodded at the victim. 'Morning, Bill.'

'Lazare?' Bill Shakespeare gasped, looking at Lazare and his group with wide, frightened eyes. 'Please, I want no trouble – if you could fetch Sly or Cowley perhaps they could raise some funds for these gentlemen and… and why are the walls melting?'

The walls were melting because of Fang. Fang was also the reason why at that moment, Bill's face was collapsing in on itself with putrefaction. The muggers let go of Bill and stepped away from him as a terrified and repulsed instinct.

'Witchcraft,' wailed the second mugger. 'The Scottish king warned us of this in his book about the evils of magic; the sooner the English court heeds his words, the better!' The mugger tried to run away, but the first mugger grabbed his shoulder.

'Hold it, lads,' the first mugger ordered. 'Some of the other Custard boys warned me of this witchcraft. It's just an illusion.' He poked Bill's nose, which was indeed still there, along with the rest of his face. 'It's that Turk,' he told them, nodding his head in Fang's direction as Fang tried his best to look like he wasn't casting multiple illusions. 'He's got some sort of warped version of fae glamour; he can cast illusions of pestilence and rot. He was doing it all last week, ran circles round the Custard gang *and* the Hapenny boys.'

Oh, *merde*. Lazare had rather hoped that with the earlier arrests of many of the Hapenny and Custard street gangs, as well as the death of the man who had ultimately been controlling both factions, the criminal organisations might have collapsed. Obviously, that was wishful thinking – for starters, it had only been a day, and secondly, just because a secret criminal overlord's been eaten alive in a tunnel by hungry vampires, that doesn't mean all the other members of the crime syndicate are going to pack up the whole business and go, 'Well, then, better retrain as a farrier, I suppose.' These muggers were carrying on as normal, as would many of Upper London's rival street gangs, and the only long term effect of the gang's prior skirmishes with Lazare and his friends was that the criminals were now forewarned and forearmed against the immortals' magical powers. At least, up to a point.

'Get that Ottoman sod,' screamed the third mugger, and all three criminals lunged at the same time for Fang. Fang balled his fists and centred his weight, as if the silly arse was about to fight them all single-handed, which obviously wasn't going to happen while Lazare had a say in the matter. Lazare opened his wings, grabbed Fang under the armpits and, with one flap, lifted both himself and the other man ten feet into the air. Fang gave a small squeak of surprised irritation. Lazare would just have to deal with the inevitable lecture on non-consensually lifting Fang out of danger later. For now, he was satisfied that if he flung Fang against the alley's wall, the other man would be able to vault right over all three muggers' heads and land behind them, staying in the fight while gaining the upper hand. He did so, and Fang was able to run a few steps along the wall using the momentum Lazare had given him before breaking his fall by landing on the first mugger's shoulders, crossing his ankles around the other man's neck as he continued to let gravity do its work on his body, thus hoiking the mugger backwards by the throat. The mugger toppled fast, spinning more than ninety degrees in the air, a helpless foot catching one of his accomplices in the jewels as he kicked out automatically, before slamming onto the cobbles with his back and head, and with Fang still twisted around him. It would have looked really cool, thought Lazare, had Fang not also seriously winded himself doing that.

'I'm not Turkish,' wheezed Fang, flat on the ground, and half-beneath the now unconscious first mugger. 'I'm from the Great Ming.'

'Am I...' struggled the kicked mugger, doubled over and clutching his walloped crotch, '... supposed to care... what a ming is?'

'It's Cathay, innit,' the third mugger informed him. 'East Asia.'

'*Thank* you,' replied Fang.

Lazare and Nell held back. Was the fight over? It felt like the fight might already be over.

The second mugger's face, already contorted by pain, twisted into a mask of hate. 'Coming round here with your filthy foreign witchery,' he screamed, rushing at Fang. The third mugger, apparently out of some sort of panic reflex, responded to this by stabbing Lazare in the neck. Ow. Spoke too soon – the fight wasn't over after all.

'Duckies!' screamed Nell, pulling open her bodice, and the alley changed again.

Time slowed down. The alley was turning, twisting in a slow and beautiful dance. Lazare was somehow watching himself over his own shoulder as Nell danced the knives right out of the muggers' hands, and Nell's duckies bounced in slow motion and, once, the Lazare that was no longer Lazare, but a different Lazare, might have desired her, but now the very thought was hilarious to the Lazare standing behind his own shoulder. He stood and laughed at Nell, his sister-friend, his cellmate in the prison without death, cursed like him and Fang, cursed and bound by love, it was so *funny*, why was it so funny all of a sudden? Blood ran down his shoulder merrily merrily as a silly hot colourful stream. Nell danced around the muggers, who clutched one another, laughing, crying, kissing as they fell into a puddle of mugger to the floor, and Bill grabbed Lazare, Bill the sadface poet, weep-laughing, shedding folio like an autumn oak sheds dry and crumpled leaves.

'Such stuff as dreeeeeeeams are made on,' Bill sang into Lazare's ear, a thousand miles away, 'the gooooorgeous paaaaalaces, the solemn temmmmmplesssssss.'

Nell. Their beautiful dancing secret weapon. She'd only been cursed last night, so none of the street gangs would have had the time to learn of her powers yet. The pharmacist had become the pharmacy. Her very body was capable of exuding all the potions known to or invented by her. And whatever chemical concoction exuded from the valley of her breasts made Lazare feel like a feather floating on a breeze of warm laughter.

Nell danced, and lifted Fang up to his feet, and Fang was eyes and hair and cheekbones and the most beautiful man that Lazare had ever seen, a wounded angel in filthy rags, nature's art putting Da Vinci and Michelangelo to shame, and Lazare wanted to hold Fang so tight that he would go *inside* him, not in that way, but also yes, in that way, he wanted to make Fang cry out his name, he wanted to taste more of the desperate, white-knuckled kiss they had briefly shared last night against the expensive wallpaper of the embassy suite before it had all turned bad. Fang had clung to him like a drowning man clinging to ballast.

Drowning.

Drowning.

Fang had been tortured by the man who had orchestrated their shared curse. Lazare had been forced to watch Fang get violently drowned, over and over. They had all been forced to watch, even the child, and since then Lazare's memory had continued the torturer's work, replaying the scene again and again, and every time he remembered, he felt ill. The alchemist screaming at Fang to break as he pushed his head underwater. Fang had not broken. Perhaps Fang was already so broken that being drowned several times in a row made little difference to the deep fissures within his psyche, but Lazare... witnessing it had cracked his mind, his heart, his liver like cheap pottery. He couldn't bear it. He couldn't bear to see Fang hurt again. He was going to have to see Fang hurt again. Fang was always getting hurt, damn him. Look at him, he was clutching his ribs in pain right now, even as he smiled vacantly up at the eaves, his pupils huge and dark and lovely as a midwinter midnight.

An annoying, sensible voice within Lazare urgently told him that he needed to get them all out of there. Nell's potion was wearing off. He was no longer floating. His neck was bleeding really quite badly, and although it wasn't going to kill him, for obvious reasons, he was now aware that it really hurt. The world wasn't funny anymore. Their powers weren't funny anymore. Fang's reverse glamour had the power to make anything look ugly except for himself, and that wasn't funny.

17

It wasn't funny that Fang wanted people to think he was ugly. Saw himself as ugly. A magical spirit, a huli jing, had fallen in love with Fang when he was a young lad back in Cathay, and she'd been slaughtered for it, and he blamed himself – was only even in London because he had run half the world away from the guilt, which still pursued him. That wasn't funny, not at all. Fang and Lazare had only met because they had both been cursed by a tormented, orphaned, lost little slip of a girl, still watching the bloody violence in the alleyway even now from the eaves with only a runt of a dragon for protection. That wasn't funny. The floating feeling had entirely left him, now. He noticed the others had stopped smiling, crying and laughing as he and Nell helped Bill and Fang to safety. The muggers still in the alleyway had also stopped smiling. He and Nell sped up. As they turned in to a wider, busier street, Amber flew back down from the eaves with Tem still on her back, joining them. Tem looked as worried as Lazare had thought she might. They deposited a still woozy Bill in a nearby tavern, grabbed some rags to mop up the blood from Lazare's rapidly healing neck wound and continued towards Nell's shop without stopping again.

The floatiness had turned into a horrible leaden heaviness, as if he'd just got out after a long swim. Fang was still the most beautiful man Lazare had ever seen. He still wanted to crawl inside Fang and chase the ghosts from all his corners. Lazare was, for the first time in his twenty-nine years, utterly in love. And that wasn't funny at all.

It was actually quite shit. And his neck *really* hurt.

Lazare was on a quest to help Tem and break her spell, not merely in the name of gallantly doing the right thing by the girl. He was on a quest because… because he didn't know what else he could do, right now. Even though breaking Tem's spell likely meant condemning himself to return to death. Maybe he was better off dead than existing like this, haunted by the pain and suffering of death, of watching someone he loved suffering death again and again, never released by it, never finding peace in it. Maybe he was better off dead than this… chimera, neither one thing nor another, wrong whichever which way one looked at him. This failure. The heaviness worsened, and Lazare couldn't be sure anymore that it was just an effect of Nell's drugs wearing off.

And he was so consumed by the heaviness of it all as they hurried the last half a mile to Nell's shop that he didn't raise his head to notice the huge raven in the queen's livery, watching them from a roof.

CHAPTER THREE
THE WORLD, NOT AT WAR

'**P**assports,' announced Fang as Nell let them into the shop.

'Kettle,' Nell corrected him.

'Seriously?'

'I need to get everything here shut up safe for the next few weeks,' Nell explained, filling the kettle. 'Might take an hour or so. I'm not sure; I've never left the shop before. But there's definitely time for a hot drink. I promised Tem chocolate, and I expect you lads want coffee? You always want coffee.'

'We do love coffee,' conceded Lazare, dabbing at his neck.

'Especially after the alley,' added Nell. 'Clear your heads?'

Amber lit the stove with a single puff. 'What *was* that down there?' she asked Nell. 'I saw you lot fighting the muggers and then you pulled your bodice open and everyone started giggling.'

'Maybe because duckies are silly?' asked Tem quietly. 'They're all wobbly.'

'I gave you all the list this morning,' Nell told them, putting the kettle on the stove. 'I stayed up half the night cataloguing what bits of me expel which potion. Pores between my breasts release a really strong dose of that euphoria vapour I developed. That's why I shouted "duckies"; I was trying to warn you. Did I do all that work for nothing?'

Fang ignored the wadded-up, unread list in his pocket. 'Don't call people's breasts "silly" please, Tem,' he chided the child gently.

"Kay, Daddy,' replied Tem and, like everyone else in the room, Fang decided to also ignore her use of the D word. He wasn't her daddy; it was going to cause issues getting her home to the fae if she was going to keep referring to him as her daddy, but... he'd deal with that problem later.

'It's fine,' said Nell, preparing the chocolate. 'My duckies *are* silly. I like them that way. You lads can make your own coffee; Amber, help yourself to dried frogs. I need to work out what on earth I'm supposed to pack for Wales.'

Lazare started preparing coffee. 'Do you not go back to visit and restock? Aren't a load of your products Welsh?' He pointed to a small engraving on the pestle in front of him. 'This thing says "*Gwneud yng Nghymru*".'

'Mam brings stock when she comes by to see the sights and catch a show,' Nell explained. 'I haven't been back since I moved here.' She paused, then added hurriedly, 'No time to close shop usually, you see. This is a special case.'

'You've never been back to Wales?' asked Fang, in rather a more judgemental tone than he'd intended.

'You've never been back to the Ming!'

'That's different,' argued Fang.

'Sorry, could we backtrack to the "catch a show" thing?' Lazare asked. 'Are... are there not theatres in Wales?'

'Not really – not in Carmarthen, anyway. We have poetry recitals? It's kind of similar?'

Lazare looked utterly aghast. 'But... what do your actors do?'

Nell shrugged. 'Mummers' play at Christmas – you know, Queen Redthroat slaying the beastly Sir George, "he's behind you", that sort of thing? Besides that, mostly what non-London theatre folk do is move to London, like you did, and Bill did, and, well, loads of people, really.'

Lazare's expression remained a mask of horror at the whole 'lack of theatres' thing. 'What strange and backwards worlds will this quest take us to?'

'Oi,' replied Nell. 'Wales is *not* backwards; it's a magical utopia and the seat of the mighty and benevolent dragon queen.'

'Redthroat may be the only one who can end the curse so the fae will let Tem go home,' Fang sighed. He briefly considered reminding Lazare that he didn't need to come, but swiftly decided against it. Of course Lazare would come. Lazare was under the ridiculous mistaken belief that he was somehow in love with Fang, which was nonsense, obviously. Obviously!

It wasn't love. Fang had been in love; love was pain and blood and suffering. This was... well, admittedly, it was a little bit painful; he *had* just been tortured by drowning the night before and he *did* keep getting punched, kicked and stabbed, but that was kind of par for the course for Fang just generally.

Admittedly, Lazare was an incredible kisser. Admittedly, when Lazare had pushed him against the wall the night before and returned Fang's kiss with a forceful fury, the white-hot rage of his mouth had sung to Fang's own anger and sadness, and every blood vessel in Fang had jangled with a sensation he hadn't felt in many years. Admittedly, at the time, he'd desperately wanted to carry on with the kiss, and beyond. He'd wanted Lazare to scoop him up and throw him onto the bed and gently mock his dirtied, threadbare clothes as he removed them with those expressive, elegant, workshy actor's fingers. He'd wanted to see Lazare's big, warm, brown eyes sparkling with fond mischief from on top of Fang – the soft curls of his excessively groomed beard brushing Fang's cheek. Wanted to hear that silly French accent in his ear – whispering something like 'Oh, you can do better than that,' or 'Well now, *that's* shut you up, hasn't it?'

Admittedly, even now in the cold light of day, a poisoning and multiple drownings later, Fang was still thinking about that kiss, and about how much he would quite like to give it another go, actually properly finish it this time, against a wall, or in a bed – hell, if there were nobody else here right now, Nell's sales counter would do. Just to get rid of the tension. For Lazare's sake as much as his own, although... admittedly...

Admittedly, Lazare was terribly pretty. Fang didn't mind the wings at all. After all, his former fiancée, the love of his life, had been a huli jing, complete with pointed fox ears and tail; he wasn't one to turn his nose up at the occasional odd body part on a person. If anything, the wings enhanced Lazare's striking prettiness and general Lazareness. Lazare managed to carry around ten foot, buff-brown leather wings and yet still somehow be mostly legs and teeth. The bright yellow hose and stockings Lazare flaunted those long legs about in were ludicrous to Fang. They made Lazare look like some silly tropical bird. And the cocky grin that flashed those shining teeth was laughably superficial. Lazare was ridiculous. And annoying. And caring – *too* caring; it was stifling, honestly, but it really wasn't worth even thinking about telling Lazare to stay in his precious London with his precious theatres. He was practically attached to Fang's hip by this foolish, foppish fancy of his, so there was no reason to waste energy in thinking about how badly Fang would miss him if he stayed behind, how the idea of his silly, preening parakeet of a companion not being there hit Fang like a punch to the stomach.

And, of course, Nell, Amber and especially Tem would miss Lazare horribly if he didn't come with them, and nobody would want to upset those three.

Another thought tried to enter his mind – that if this quest to have Redthroat undo the spell were to be successful, he and Lazare and Nell would simply be dead, and he would never get to see them ever again, and Tem and Amber would have to grieve. Fang slammed the door on the thought before it had a chance to so much as hang up its cloak.

Lazare handed Fang a cup of coffee. Fang took a deep whiff with a grateful half-smile in Lazare's direction – for the coffee, obviously. Nell's coffee was some of the finest and freshest in both Londons, but Lazare was particularly skilled in its brewing. Fang noticed that Lazare didn't smile back – barely looked at him, in fact. Just turned away. He'd done the same at breakfast in the embassy, Fang recalled.

'Chocolate!' Nell poured thick and spicy steaming chocolate into two cups and passed one to Tem.

'Blow on it,' warned Fang, tearing his attention away from the unusually avoidant Frenchman and back towards the child in his care.

Tem blew, then gave the drink a cautious sniff.

'It's from the Aztec Empire way out west,' Nell told her as she fussed about, putting stock away. 'Got a contact based out in Tlacopan. Always a good idea to hang around the docks seeing what explorers and traders you might bump into and take for drinks.'

'Yes,' said Fang, 'we all know what you're like for meeting people down the docks.'

'I happened to show Eztli a particularly cordial welcome to our damp little island,' continued Nell with some pride, 'told them all about how Welsh magicals thwarted the English invasion way back when, just like how Aztec magicals stopped *them* getting invaded by the Spanish. I'll let you draw your own conclusions as to how the rest of the night went, but the upshot is, I get to stock top-grade chocolate at mate's rates. Though I make it hot, Mayan style, and I add way more honey than the Aztec recipe calls for. Don't tell Eztli.'

'The people who make chocolate got invaded too?' asked Tem.

'An attempt was made, by the Spanish,' Nell explained, 'but they were defeated.'

'Does invasions happen a lot?' Tem continued.

'Unfortunately, yes,' sighed Fang. 'I come from an empire, I travelled through multiple empires to get here, the Upper English have tried making an empire several times – even the

Aztecs are an empire; they got to be one by invading other people's lands.'

'Why?'

Fang shrugged into his coffee. 'People see other people as useful things, to make them richer or more powerful, so they try to take them, and take their homes.'

'Like the alchemist did?'

Fang nodded at Tem, saddened that such a young child could have first-hand experience to make her understand such cruelty.

'That's the human world for you I'm afraid, kiddo,' said Amber, with a mouth full of dried frog. 'Always warring and whatnot.'

'Dragons and magicals have been involved in plenty of wars,' Fang reminded the dragon.

'Yeah, but usually only 'cause humans started it,' argued Amber. 'Go back to the old ways, I say – you got a beef with someone, just eat 'em. Far simpler.'

'Eat them?' fretted Tem.

'Only if you want to,' added Amber.

Fang interjected, trying to change the subject, 'Your chocolate is probably blown enough by now, Tem.'

Tem finished blowing on her drink and took a sip. Her eyes widened. 'I like chocolate.'

'Called it.' Nell smirked.

Tem took another slurp. 'I *love* chocolate!'

Captain Dame Isobel Honkensby was not an easily intimidated individual. This was hardly a surprise, what with her being the head of the Royal Guard and also a six foot magical hyper-intelligent talking swan. She was used to being treated with the sort of cowed respect one would expect when one is a massive, livery-bedecked, snow-white waterfowl with the strength to break an ogre's legs with a single flap of her wing and the authority, if she so wished, to have said luckless ogre dragged to the Tower for obstructing an officer of the law. Nevertheless, she was considerably unsettled at being commanded to the queen's counsel for the second day in a row, and even though she was the largest and physically strongest being in that chamber of only four people, she couldn't help but feel intimidated.

The queen stood, flanked as ever by her two cephalophore ladies-in-waiting. She was a small woman, although a long, wide dress and tall wig of shining auburn falsely added to her stature. Honkensby found herself folding her neck towards her chest, to shrink herself, adding to the unspoken mutually agreed fiction that Elizabeth was the biggest person in the room. Only the queen's thin face and hands poked out of the acres of silk and fake hair, and even those were thickly painted mercury-white. Not a barleycorn of the woman beneath the careful, sturdy construct of the queen was exposed, not for Honkensby's eyes.

'Well, Honkensby,' said the queen, 'what updates have you?'

Really not many at all, considering it had been less than a day since Honkensby had last been summoned by the monarch.

'We... are continuing to process Avis Hapenny and the other gang members in custody,' replied Honkensby, hoping she didn't sound too much like she was blathering on in a panic even though that was precisely what she was doing.

'One of the first priorities is to ensure that the remaining street gang members don't descend into factional gang warfare that would threaten the wellbeing of civilians. Er, we remain in close liaison with the Deep London Embassy; an alchemist from the Upperside was killed in a Deepside river last night. The attaché is adamant it was a vampire attack and has advised we push yet another public information campaign in Upper London reminding humans that if they venture Deep with no protective amulets they are legally defined as prey. I applied first thing to the embassy for a warrant to investigate the case myself, but have been warned it may take some days—'

'That's all well and good, Captain,' interrupted the queen, even though in fact, none of that information was particularly well or good, 'but what of the immortals? They were, last we spoke, hiding out in the Deep London Embassy, were they not? However, my ambassador just informed me that they have now left that place, along with that half-fae child whose kidnap you were investigating.'

'Yes. Um. Well, the Deep London Embassy stated that the individuals you speak of did not kidnap the child, but are in fact trying to return her to her home, although it seems they've hit upon a snag, and...'

'And where are they?' asked Queen Elizabeth. 'Are they still Deepside? Are they attempting to flee England?'

'I...' Honkensby started again, wincing away from the sharp eyes in that paint-white face. 'I have reason to believe that they knew the slain alchemist, and once a warrant has been granted, I can return Deepside and seek out their arrest over his killing. My ravens are watching the tubes and the streets in case they are foolish enough to try to return to Upper London. If they do so, I will personally see to it that they are brought to you. Whether they try to hide Deep or Upperside, they are trapped and will be caught.'

'What if they flee by other means?' asked Queen Elizabeth. 'Can we blockade the Emfor?'

Honkensby opened her beak silently. She absolutely could not blockade the Emfor, but she really didn't want to tell Her Majesty that her royal idea was a non-starter.

One of the cephalophores lifted her head to her neck and sighed. 'Bessie, be kind. You know full well the Emfor runs entirely through Redthroat's domain; the guards can't do a thing to it without sparking a major incident, which is the one thing you're trying to avoid, poppet.'

Honkensby ducked her head gratefully at the lady-in-waiting. 'Queen Anne is correct, I'm afraid, Majesty...'

'Just Lady Anne now, Captain,' replied Anne kindly. 'Bit of a demotion when the old you-know-what got chopped off.'

'You can still call me queen if you like,' said the other cephalophore.

'No she can't, Mary,' Anne told her. 'It'll get too confusing; we've been through this.'

'*Ferme ta gueule*,' muttered Mary.

'I can still speak French, you know,' hissed Anne.

'*Óinseach*,' added Mary, under her breath.

'And Gaelic!'

'So, they could, in theory, make it to Wales without even setting foot in Upper England,' concluded Elizabeth unhappily.

'Alas, yes,' admitted Honkensby.

'How's your Welsh?' asked the queen.

'Er... *ddim... yn... dda... cymraeg*,' struggled Honkensby.

'Well, it's going to have to do, Captain,' the queen told her. 'I must have my ambassadors tell Llewellyn's court to expect you, of course, as per our bilateral agreement.'

'Of course,' replied Honkensby, calm on the surface, panicking underneath. Having to chase fugitives across a border was bad enough, but being *expected* by another nation's bureaucrats was another. She'd be hampered from the second she crossed out of Upper England; she'd need to fill in twelve forms before she could even think about arresting her quarry in Wales. And Gruff would probably show up. God's Feathers, this was going to be a nightmare.

'I shall *not* be sharing the reasoning for these immortal fugitives' arrests, however,' continued Elizabeth, 'nor in fact shall I be sharing the information that they are immortals, so it's imperative you work with discretion once you're west of the border. The last thing we need is the King of Wales trying to force the secrets of eternal life out of those unfortunates. It's bad enough that word of their powers will have got to Redthroat.'

Honkensby bowed her head again, attempting to keep her demeanour as unruffled as possible in spite of the fact that she was actually extremely ruffled right now. How was she to go about arresting three immortals, a dragon and a fae child in Wales without causing a scene? She could barely speak Welsh. And she'd have to deal with stupid bloody Gruff. Why couldn't they just be in the streets of Upper London? That was Honkensby's comfort zone. They'd stand no chance if they were ambling about the streets of Upper London like the usual idiots; she'd be able to...

The huge wooden door to the chamber swung open heavily, and all eyes turned to a young raven constable, looking terrified in the doorway.

'A thousand apologies for the interruption, Majesties, Captain...'

'Only one Majesty, but go on,' said Anne.

'Sorry! Sorry! Of course! Sorry!' The raven turned to Honkensby. 'Just, you said to inform you immediately if the fugitives were spotted...'

The atmosphere of the room changed. Honkensby felt a flutter of hope and relief. 'You've found them?'

'We believe so. Upper Southwark.'

Oh, this was too good, they were just ambling about the streets of Upper London like the usual idiots. It was as if Honkensby's hatchday had come early. She turned urgently to the queen.

'You are excused, of course,' Elizabeth told her with a flap of her little white hands.

Honkensby nodded gratefully, and led the raven out of the chamber at speed.

The door slammed shut behind the birds, leaving Elizabeth with her undead confidants.

'And what *are* your reasons for wishing to arrest those immortals, Bessie?' Anne asked. 'I believe they've done nothing wrong.'

'And last I heard,' added Mary, 'not a one of them was Upper English, so you have no claim to any of them, certainly no more than Redthroat, Llewellyn, Henry of France or indeed the Wanli emperor.'

'I don't care for what you're insinuating, dear cuz,' replied Elizabeth.

'What are you going to do, behead me again?'

'I apologised for that already, Mary! I apologised a hundred times!'

'My head's still off, though, isn't it, "dear cuz"?'

'Bessie love,' said Anne over the burgeoning row, 'please tell me you don't intend to yourself "force the secrets of eternal life out of these unfortunates"? You know whatever afflicts these wretches, it's probably just another new form of being undead? Isn't one of them from Cathay? Where undeath was first accidentally created all those centuries ago?'

'Mummy,' sighed Elizabeth, 'you know I'm in a difficult situation…'

'And becoming undead would just make that worse, poppet. Undead are banned from human thrones…'

'It's immortality, Mummy! Not undeath!'

'What if it's the same thing? That really is no fun at all; take it from me and your cousin.'

'I don't do "fun", Mummy. I am Upper England…'

'Here we go,' sighed Mary, rolling her eyes. 'Acting like she's the only one of us who knows the pressures of monarchy. *Some* of us had to deal with that when we were but a wee baby…'

'And look where it got you, cuz.'

'Thanks to you.'

'Thanks to *you*.'

'Girls,' warned Anne.

'I'm getting old, Mummy. I don't know how much longer I have left, and when I die, so does the last of Father's line. While I feel no pity for that overstuffed arsecheek, the way he treated us all coming to naught, there is the issue of, well. Issue. And the lack thereof.'

'Bit late to be sorry about that,' interjected Mary.

'I wouldn't say I was sorry,' snorted Elizabeth. 'Pretty boys are fun in small doses, but I wouldn't want to have one put a whole person inside me.'

'Would it have killed you to have an heir, though?' Mary continued. 'I did, *and* he's the answer to your problems, so you are most very welcome.'

'Mary, your James *is* the problem.'

'He is a sweet sweet sweetie pie!'

'He is a tyrant, Mary! The way he treats magicals in Scotland! So many have fled south of the border that they're having to build a whole new city under Durham! Magical refugees I can live with, since they're primarily Redthroat and Llewellyn's problem, but as things stand, when I die, James of Scotland will have the strongest claim to my throne, and if he takes it, there will be war. Scotland and Upper England against Redthroat, against the very England that lies beneath our feet, and if you don't believe that Redthroat will call in favours from the Welsh, the Irish, the Icelandics, even the tribes and empires of the New World, then you are naive indeed. Three hundred years of peace, gone, turned into a war that could draw in the whole Atlantic, spread to engulf the rising tensions between Europe and the New World. All because I died with no heir but a cousin who has become obsessed with his hatred of magicals.'

'You seriously believe that just because my angel baby dumpling has reasonable concerns about the powers of witches and magical beings, that he would ignite an international war?'

'Mary, he banished his own mother as soon as he learned you were become undead! Forced his *mother* to throw herself on the mercy of the very woman who had signed your death warrant.' Elizabeth pointed her finger at Mary and spoke over her before she could interject again. 'The very woman whose friendship you betrayed. And I embraced you because you're still my cousin, and I know what it's like, when...' She trailed off, indicating towards her own poor headless mother. 'When someone has become so consumed by hate that he hurts his own family over it, there is no reasoning with him. When that person is a monarch, it becomes so very dangerous. Trust me. I would endure a fae curse if it means outliving James and keeping peace.'

She exhaled, and looked back at her two ladies-in-waiting, their heads held slack, their mouths agape.

'How was that?' she added. 'Was that convincing?'

'Yes,' replied Mary quietly.

'Good,' said Elizabeth, 'I'll use that speech on the immortals when Honkensby hauls them in, I'm going to have to use a lot of rhetoric to get them to give me their secret because you were right: none of them are English. If I torture it out of them, there'll be trouble with the embassies.'

'That's my girl.' Anne smiled. 'Making your case, appealing to their hearts instead of resorting to violence.'

'Oh, I'll absolutely have to resort to violence if a big speech doesn't work, Mummy,' added Elizabeth, 'I'd just rather not have to. You know what that French ambassador's like. Always speaking French, just to annoy me.'

'*Pourquoi ne devrait-il pas parler Français?*'

'Yes, Mary,' Elizabeth replied, 'exactly like that.'

CHAPTER FOUR
Go West

'Packing', as far as Fang was concerned, just involved him shoving his passport in one pocket and snacks for Tem in another, so he was done with his task almost immediately after getting back to Nell's shop. Lazare busied himself cleaning up his now barely present stab wound, and Fang helped Nell to carry stock into safe storage cupboards while the Welshwoman wondered aloud how many spare undergarments she'd need.

'I'm just saying, what if I have an accident?'

'Do you often have accidents?' asked Fang, huffing beneath a heavy crate of Gentlemen's Devices.

'Not since I ate that bad whelk back in '96. But what if I have an accident anyway and need spares? What if I have two accidents in a row?'

'Or you could pack a normal amount of underwear and not eat any whelks.' Fang put the crate in the cupboard.

'Do you think *I* have enough underclothes?' Lazare asked Nell.

Fang sighed. Nell was dithering and the dither had spread to Lazare. 'You have five bags of clothes, man.'

'Yes, but should I get more?'

'I can't believe you two are both technically travellers too,' huffed Fang. 'I'm amazed you both made it as far as London, even if it was only a couple of hundred miles. Take it from someone who's gone halfway across the globe – pack light, move fast. Emphasis on the "fast" aspect – you heard what Grubble said.' He turned to Nell. 'We should use that direct route he mentioned.'

'You want to use the Emfor?' asked Nell, sounding dismayed.

'It's faster and safer,' said Fang.

'Yeah, but it's *boring*,' Nell complained. 'It just goes on and on. Mam used it once, nearly crashed her cart 'cause she nodded off under Swindon. Never again.'

'Boring's good,' Fang argued. 'We could all do with more boring, right now. We were only in the Upperside streets for an hour and Lazare already got stabbed.'

'I'm fine, by the way,' added Lazare. 'I mean, obviously I am, I can't die. This shirt's probably stained, though.'

'Cold saltwater soak, vinegar if that doesn't work,' Fang advised him from his many years of experience in getting blood out of clothes.

'You got hurted,' mumbled Tem quietly into her chocolate.

'I'm fine, thanks to you,' Lazare reassured her, showing the child the almost fully healed thin scab on his neck. 'I was careless. Didn't think to protect my neck.'

'Well, we're Upperside now,' Nell told Fang. 'It was hard enough slipping past the guards at the tube entrance the first time. To get Deep for the Emfor we'd have to sneak past them *again*. Let's just hop on a cart headed west and ride through Upper England. It's easier, better views and more places to stop. The Emfor doesn't even have a decent privy break til Deep Reading, and that's *ages* away.'

'Since when did you start worrying about privy breaks?' Fang asked.

'Since we started looking after a small child,' Nell reminded him.

'I won't have to go so much if I don't drink,' said Tem, putting the half-drunk cup of chocolate down.

Fang picked it straight up again and set it back in her hands. 'We'll sort something out, poppet. Finish your chocolate. It'll make you strong. Probably.'

'Eztli said it was the drink of the gods,' concurred Nell, 'so I bet it's really good for the fae as well.'

Lazare continued to poke at his neck. His silly, long, soft neck with its ridiculous tender curves right at the level of Fang's mouth, as if on purpose. 'Perhaps a ruff would protect my throat?' said the silly dandy. 'Practical *and* fashionable, right?'

'Yeah,' called Nell, continuing to dither with stock, 'let's get you to a tailor. Ruffs for everyone!'

Lazare would look terrible in a ruff; he was too tall. Tall people, in Fang's opinion, shouldn't be allowed to wear ruffs because they were forever poking shorter people like himself in the eye, and it had nothing at all to do with Lazare having an incredibly nice-looking neck.

'We are fleeing London before we get arrested and tortured by a massive swan,' Fang told the others hotly. 'We don't have time to go clothes shopping!'

'I'm just saying,' Nell said, 'that if we *did* have time, perhaps we could get Tem some clothes that actually fit her?'

Tem looked up nervously at the mention of herself. The hand-me-down furs she was dressed in really were too big for her. The hat was always falling over her eyes, the sleeves kept covering her hands and no matter how often he tried to strap them up again, the britches and boots still fell down about once an hour. She never complained about them, and every time Fang asked if she was comfortable she'd tell him how warm and cosy the clothes were, but he was starting to get an inkling of the girl's personal tastes for how she wanted to dress, and it seemed to involve more ribbons and embroidered dragons, and fewer ancient, lumpy furs.

Fang knew that Nell knew that Fang knew this. He knew that she was deploying this so that she could hold off on leaving London. Unfortunately, it was working.

'Where's the nearest tailor?' asked Fang.

He would never find out where the nearest tailor was, because at that moment, the shop door was pecked in.

The sharp, dark beaks of two guard ravens made short work of the door as a familiar voice called from beyond.

'Open up, in the name of Queen Elizabeth,' cried Honkensby from outside, even though they were hardly able to open the door with two massive beaks pecking it in, now, were they?

Fang took no moment to explain this flaw in Honkensby's logic to her, nor did he take the time to tell her that no, he wasn't going to open up, actually; she had no right to arrest them, they had committed no crimes, they were just a bit weird, and last he'd checked, 'being a bit weird' was still legal in Upper England.

'You are under suspicion over the recent death of an alchemist,' called Honkensby. 'Where were you last night?'

Well, he *definitely* wasn't going to tell Honkensby that. Instead, he grabbed Tem, who in turn grabbed tight on to the tiny felt toy dragon she had rather sweetly named Little Amber. Nell grabbed her first-aid satchel and Lazare grabbed two of his five bags of clothes. Amber the dragon – or 'normal-sized Amber' if one wanted to differentiate between her and the dollie – glanced around for a moment, looking for something she could grab in her jaw and ended up taking Nell's bag of spare underthings, which Nell was about to leave behind after having made such a fuss in the first place.

'Argh, my door,' muttered Nell as she ushered them through to the back. 'I'm going to have to get Jago from the fish shop downstairs to fix that; I hate when I owe him a favour. Means I'm in no position to complain about the smell.'

'Big picture, Nell,' Fang reminded her.

'Yeah, yeah,' replied Nell, before muttering quietly, 'suppose if all goes to your plan, I won't be needing a front door anymore.'

Fang felt a pang of horrible guilt at that. He knew how much pride Nell took in her shop, how much joy she took from her life.

'I'm sorry, Nell,' he said quietly, and he meant it. 'If there were another way...'

Nell shook her head at him curtly. 'Now's not the time, you big wet mop.'

Nell opened up the window shutters in her back bedroom and allowed Lazare to fly her down the ten foot or so to the street below. Fang passed Tem to Amber so the dragon could fly the child down to the relative safety of the street, and then clambered down the wall. He dropped the last few feet to the cobbles, plucked Tem off Amber's back and they all ran – where to, he had no idea. Honkensby had found them, and from past experience that meant she'd have all the nearby tubes far too heavily guarded to slip past, this time. Wulfric had given them shelter before, but his inn was all the way out in Deptford, and they'd already led trouble to Wulfric's business very recently. The last thing Fang wanted was to get anyone else hurt by this mess. Even though Wulfric had seemed fine afterwards, he'd felt so guilty the other day when the guards had ransacked the tiny vampire's inn in their search for Fang and his group. What if something had happened to him? Wulfric was only a little guy. Yes, he was an ancient, powerful vampire and renowned businessman, but also he really was just a little guy. The vampire had his own problems and his own inn to run. Fang wasn't going to drag Wulfric into it this time.

'Fang! Lazare!' Wulfric's youthful face beamed down at them from a passing cart. 'You guys seem in a hurry – need a lift or something?'

What? How?

'No,' attempted Fang, but Lazare called over him.

'Yes please, *mon ami*!'

'Hop on, then!'

Wulfric's cart didn't stop, but that was probably for the best. It didn't need to stop for them to board it, after all.

40

Lazare scooped Nell up under the arms and deposited her on the speeding cart. Fang sprinted towards Wulfric, holding Tem out for the vampire to take her out of his hands, but instead Wulfric himself flapped out of the front seat, grabbed Fang by the tunic and hoisted him and Tem both into the air. Fang was generally not a fan of being grabbed and flown around by the various winged members of his social circle. He found it embarrassing and disconcerting enough when a tall handsome popinjay of a Frenchman did it. It was no improvement when it was done to him by a shockingly strong vampire with the tiny frame and guileless face of a ten-year-old boy. Wulfric dropped Fang and Tem in the cart before smoothly landing in the driver's seat.

'Well, well, well,' came a familiar voice, dripping with self-confidence and lasciviousness. Fang could hear the leer in the voice before its owner passed the reins to Wulfric and easily oozed over to sit right next to Fang – the smirking zombie of the late Kit Marlowe. Still annoyingly good-looking even as a zombie with an eyepatch, Kit claimed that after getting fatally stabbed through the eye in a bar fight he had been hurriedly turned, so as not to rob Upper London of her 'most celebrated playwright and greatest shag'. Rumour had it that in fact Kit himself had orchestrated the whole thing, paying a friend to kill and then reanimate him, thus using the loophole that the undead were subjects of Redthroat to wheedle his way out of a considerable tranche of criminal charges brought against him by the court of Queen Elizabeth. This struck Fang as far more likely. Kit was a man for whom consequences were things that happened to other people. This did not endear him whatsoever to Fang, who was a man that consequences happened to simply all of the time. For example, one consequence for Fang of Kit's continued undead existence was that every time they bumped into one another, Fang had to deal with the fact Kit had made it a mission to have sex with him.

It was a mission that clearly Kit was determined to continue, even on a cart rattling away from the Royal Guards. Completely ignoring that Fang had a small child with him, as well as Fang's annoyed expression, Kit leaned in close and ran a couple of fingers through Fang's long hair.

'Look what the bat dragged in.' Kit grinned.

'Vampires aren't bats,' Wulfric told Kit in the tone of voice of someone who's had to say this many times before.

'Kit!' Lazare's expression was a very particular combination of joy at seeing another old friend, gratitude for his help in their hour of need and extreme irritation at Kit's ongoing quest to seduce Fang. 'What are you lot doing here? How did you find us?'

'Well, we found you because you were in the middle of the road, sprinting away from Miss Nell's shop,' Wulfric told them. 'You in trouble, friends?'

'No,' lied Lazare.

'Oh come now,' replied Kit, his voice and smile slick as grease, 'no need to be coy. Nothing as attractive as being in a spot of hot water with the law. I should know.'

'We are simply trying to find swift passage to the Lost City of Llanelli,' Fang told them, 'so Tem here can go home.' It wasn't the whole truth, but it was enough of the truth for Fang not to feel too much of a bad influence for saying it in front of Tem.

Wulfric sucked through his sharp teeth. 'Weren't thinking of using the Emfor, were you? The Upperside entrance is swarming with guards right now for some reason. Massive tailbacks. Bit of a bone of contention – we were wanting to go west ourselves.'

'How come?' Nell asked. 'You two haven't said why you're haring around at breakneck speed; you must be doing twenty miles an hour.'

'It's we three, actually,' Kit told them, and indicated to the back of the cart. Bill Shakespeare, still looking rather worse for wear for the drugging, gave them a sheepish little wave. 'Found Billy-o here drooling in a pub, babbling that he had to get out of London. He does this every time he gets mugged: he gets scared and bolts for the tedium of Warwickshire for a couple of weeks. Honestly, you can take the glovemaker's son out of the provinces but you can't take the provinces out of him.'

'I had a letter this morning,' explained Bill, sounding hurt. 'My son is sick.'

'Oh, your son's always sick,' breezed Kit. 'You've been using that excuse since the plague, not to mention constantly pestering me and poor Wulfric to "fix" the little tyke. We're not doctors, Bill!'

'Kit, be kind,' called Wulfric over his shoulder.

'You definitely did get mugged today, though, did you not, my dear Willum?' Kit added, apparently ignoring the whole 'be kind' thing. 'It's written all over your frightened little face.'

Bill frowned, averting his eyes away from Fang, Nell and Lazare. Well, Fang certainly wasn't going to tell that smug sod Christopher Marlowe that Bill had not only been mugged, but Fang and his group had been the ones to rescue him.

'So, why exactly are you travelling with Bill?' Fang asked Kit, hoping that the poet wouldn't manage to turn a fairly hostile interrogation into something sexual. 'Is the great Marlowe abandoning his theatre troupes and his beloved Londons simply to lord it over a competitor all the way to Warwickshire?'

'Mr Fang!' Kit clutched his fist over his heart as if Fang had just stabbed him with his words. 'Myself and young Wulfric are helping out a beloved friend!'

'I'm considerably older than you,' Wulfric reminded him, 'and the only one of us who owns a cart. But, yes, Mr Fang, I really am helping out a friend in need.'

Bill opened his mouth to say something, then seemed to think better of it.

'At least,' continued Wulfric, 'in the ways that I *can* help.'

'And I owed him one after I poached Kempe for my theatre company,' smarmed Kit. 'It'll be nice to finally stop him banging on about that all the time.'

'I did *not* offer to forgive nor forget that, Christopher,' retorted Bill. 'I didn't even ask you to come; you just heard we were going via Oxford and jumped aboard.'

'A *lot* of astrologers in Oxford,' Kit confided in Fang with a waggle of his eyebrows and, honestly, Fang had no idea how or why Kit was trying to make out there was something particularly scurrilous about astrology.

'Astrologers?' Nell asked thoughtfully.

'Let me guess, Kit.' Lazare tried valiantly to squeeze himself in between Fang and Kit, to no avail, not for Fang's lack of trying. 'You wish to lie with an astrologer for a change.'

'Already had one, dear fellow,' Kit told him cheerfully. 'Simon Forman. Not a looker, but *what* a telescope. *And* he advised me that my humours were all out of whack. Fancied a bit more of that whole Mars ascending, Venus in retrograde stuff. They might be able to sort out my stiff shoulder joint.'

'Kit,' Wulfric told him, 'your shoulder's stiff because you're a zombie now.'

Kit ignored him. 'So yes, that's what *we're* all up to on a speeding cart bound west, and honestly, what a happy coincidence that we ran into you as you too were completely innocently heading west on foot at a full gallop for terribly normal reasons and definitely not because you're on the run from the law.'

Fang glanced down at Tem. She was staring up at him with big eyes and a confused expression. He was lying by omission, right in front of her; what sort of example was that supposed to set? He opened his mouth to set the record straight.

'Yeah, sorry, we're totally in trouble with the law,' admitted Amber before he could say anything.

'I knew it,' sighed Wulfric with a fond little shake of his head.

'They seemed to think we killed that alchemist last night,' added Amber pointedly. 'You know – the one *you* ate.'

'We'd hate to drag you into this again, Wulfric,' said Fang hurriedly. 'You've already bought us time and distance; if you wanted to let us off, we could safely sneak aboard a cart to Cricklewood or Finchley, and from there…'

'Tush pish,' said Kit, 'we offered you a ride, and a ride you shall have.' He shot Fang another meaningful gaze. 'It may be fraught, dangerous and leave you rather sore around the saddle, but it'll be one to remember, Mr Fang.'

'If I were the type of vampire to be squeamish about consorting with troublemakers and law-breakers, I would hardly spend as much time as I do with Christopher Marlowe,' Wulfric told them. 'Kit, put that Cathayan down; he's never going to tup with you.'

'Never say never, good Wulfric! 'Tis the capitulation of the coward.'

'Kit, he's got a child with him for pity's sake,' continued Wulfric.

'And I already said, that doesn't bother me,' Kit told Fang, not even glancing down at Tem. 'I'm very up for special cuddles with a dishy daddy, isn't that right, Bill?'

There was a pause. Everyone looked at Bill in the back. Even Wulfric spared a second to take his eyes off the road and shoot Bill a horrified glance.

Bill stared back at everyone, aghast. 'We agreed never to talk about that,' Bill told Kit through gritted teeth.

'Christopher, you need to stop,' snapped Wulfric.

'Give me one reason why!'

'You're being a *rabat-joie*,' Lazare told him quietly.

Kit looked – for possibly the first time – genuinely affronted at this. 'I'm not. Am I?'

'What's a rabbitjoy?' Tem asked.

'Someone who brings down the atmosphere of the party,' Lazare explained. 'A bore.'

Kit took a deep breath and gave Fang his personal space back. 'I apologise. Christopher Marlowe is many things: poet, lover, genius, rapscallion, spy... but never knowingly a bore.

Mr Fang, if I press my case too firmly, you have but to let me know.'

'I've been trying to tell you since we met,' said Fang. 'And it really isn't appropriate, in front of Tem.'

'Who is Tem?' Kit asked.

Fang pointed down at Tem incredulously.

'Am *I* a rabbitjoy?' worried Tem.

'Not in the slightest, young miss,' Kit told her. 'I can tell that your devastatingly pretty father loves you very much.' He handed Tem a flower, which stopped Fang from telling him that he was still being inappropriate, due to suddenly being perplexed over where on earth he'd pulled a flower from.

Tem seemed happy with the flower, and clambered into the back to show the others, and let Fang weave it into her messy plait of black hair. Wulfric slowed the cart a little and kept a more comfortable pace as they continued towards the western edges of Upper London. After a while, a small cat with a cropped tail crawled out from beneath the vampire's jacket and wandered over for a fuss, which surprised many of the cart's passengers as they hadn't realised he had a cat in his jacket.

'Wulfric,' asked Kit, 'are you made of cats?'

'That's Mimi,' called Wulfric over his shoulder. 'We're best friends. Long story. Mr Fang named her.'

'Aww,' squeaked Tem, and Fang didn't feel embarrassed at all.

They passed Cricklewood and Finchley, where they remained on the cart at the insistence of the vampire and the two playwrights. Wulfric cheerily informed them that they were making good time, and should get to Oxford a little after nightfall.

'I know a coaching house there,' Wulfric told them. 'Or those of you otherwise inclined can head off alone to find a bedmate for the night – mostly looking at you here, Kit.'

Kit nodded serenely. 'Indeed, I shall find an enthusiastic partner or three for tonight, and pitch woo towards Mr Fang no longer.'

'Thank you.'

'For now,' added Kit. 'I'm sure you'll come to your senses anon, and come that time' – he took Fang's hand – 'I look forward to consensually wrecking you, Mr Fang.'

'Wulfric,' called Lazare, 'he's doing it again.'

'Christopher Marlowe,' called Wulfric, 'do not make me turn this cart around! Because then *nobody* will get to tup with astrologers!'

CHAPTER FIVE
THE SECRET MIDNIGHT POETRY SOCIETY

Oxford was, to the best of Nell's description, 'full of fiddly bits'. This was saying something, bearing in mind she'd come from Upper London, which was fiddly all over, stuffed with narrow alleys and grand palaces jostling with humble shacks. Oxford was much smaller but similarly cluttered with little shops and houses, alongside what seemed at first to be grand palaces, but turned out to be university colleges, student dormitories and observatories.

'Is it me,' she muttered after passing yet another massive, fiddly building, 'or is this city about sixty per cent university?'

'It's not you,' Wulfric told her merrily. 'That's a pretty fair assessment.' He nodded at a coaching house ahead. 'Here we are! I'm going no further west, so here's where we part ways. It's a pretty easy journey to Wales from here, though. 'Nother few days, perhaps?'

Another few days. Another few days of slowly clopping towards the place she'd promised she'd never set foot in again, on a one-way journey to put a stop to Tem's spell, and Nell's new powers, and all her hard-won happiness. But what if that wasn't necessary after all? Redthroat the Invincible was so very powerful and kindly that it would be a crying shame to bother the mighty dragon queen with a matter as trifling as Tem's spell if the answers could first be found in the stars. Nell's knowledge of astrology was limited; she only consulted astrological texts when presented with a particularly difficult ailment that her usual potions and tinctures couldn't fix. Maybe the astrologers would have the answer to undoing the curse – or maybe, just maybe, the stars might have a different solution, one which allowed everyone to keep their freedoms and their lives. Maybe all the answers they needed were right here amongst the grand halls and fiddly bits of Oxford, and poor Tem wouldn't be subjected to a lengthy journey all the way to Wales. And neither would Nell. Yes, maybe they should just stay in Oxford. It was nice here; she liked it.

'I don't like it here.' Fang craned his head around, watching the streets and the skies for spying eyes. 'We should get Deep. Is there an entrance to the Emfor in town?'

'No tubes as far out as Oxford,' Wulfric told him. 'It doesn't have a Deep counterpart. You'd have to trek all the way to Swindon, and nobody goes to Swindon unless they really have to.'

'There's no Deep Oxford?' Lazare asked.

'Not many magicals live in Deep England,' Wulfric explained. 'There's a handful of interlinked Deep cities, and of those, Deep London's by far the biggest and most important.

The rest are just dug-out villages, really. Most British magicals settle in Wales.'

'Why?' asked Lazare.

'If you had the choice between being treated like the Welsh treat us – hailed as heroes, fresh air, plenty of food, proximity to the seat of power – or living under England like a second-hand citizen in a hole in the ground, getting harassed by giant swans, don't you think you'd move?'

'You didn't move, though,' reasoned Fang. 'Nor did Marlowe.'

'Yeah, well. I've got my pub,' blustered Wulfric. 'Couldn't leave my pub, could I? Or my regulars. And I've got my undead support group, and Deep London's pretty cool, as far as holes in the ground go.'

'And I have my theatre troupes and many, many lovers,' added Kit, lying with his eyes closed at the back of the cart. 'Wouldn't be fair to rob either London of my mighty quill or my mightier codpiece.'

'Oh, admit it,' said Nell, 'you two just really love London.'

'You haven't left London in years either,' Fang reminded her. 'Nor has Lazare.'

'I adore its theatre scene,' piped Lazare. 'I make no secret of that. The Swan and the Globe are the jewels of the world.'

'Thank you kindly,' replied Bill. 'The Globe *is* a beauty, is she not?'

Nell noticed Bill shoot a rare smug glance at Marlowe. As much as Kit ran rings around him in other areas, Bill at least had had the good business sense to invest in a bricks-and-mortar theatre house. To have a tangible place of business in the best city in the world, thought Nell, was quite the thing. She felt another pang of worry and sorrow for her poor, abandoned and pecked-in shop.

'If there's no Deep Oxford, though, then are there no magicals here at all?' Amber asked. 'Are they going to be OK with us? 'Cause even if we act all friendly and that, yer parochial little magic-free towns aren't necessarily going to be particularly happy about a load of undead, a dragon and a fae rolling into town.'

'Of course they will,' argued Nell. 'It's all astrologers.'

'I had a cousin once,' continued Amber, ignoring Nell, 'decided to hunt further afield, heard there was good eating in Gravesend. They turned him into shoes.'

'I don't want to be shoes,' panicked Tem.

'Nobody's turning anyone into shoes,' Fang told the child, holding her close and shooting the dragon an accusatory glare. 'I won't let them.'

'Nobody *wants* to turn you into shoes,' added Wulfric. 'Oxford is no Gravesend.'

'What does that mean?' asked Amber.

'It means that people in Oxford are all magically studious and wise,' Nell told the dragon.

Wulfric turned the cart in to the open stable doors of the coaching house. 'We'll see about that.'

What they saw, on disembarking and heading into the inn, was indeed a saloon bustling with students, scholars and astrologers. Fang even spotted a couple of alchemist robes amongst them, which made Tem cringe with fear and clasp tighter to him. He held her firm, surprised with himself that even though the alchemist who had tormented them was dead, the sight of men in similar clothes made his own heart hammer with alarm. There were no magicals in the inn; as the human drinkers and diners watched the entrance of Fang's group, with its dragon and vampire and zombie, with Lazare's awkwardly tucked-in wings, their eyes lit up with a curious, excited joy. Fang had seen those expressions before, but he couldn't quite put his finger on where.

'Wulfric,' cried the woman at the bar. 'You haven't changed a bit, you old devil!'

'You have, Jutte,' Wulfric greeted her. 'What's it been, ten years?'

'Give or take. Gained a grandchild, lost a husband, gained a ladyfriend and several more wrinkles, so overall it's been a positive.' Jutte nodded to Wulfric's party. 'Finally moving to Wales, then?'

'Just accompanying friends on a trip, like last time.'

'Well, I'm glad you popped by. Always keep pigs' hearts aside for wandering vampires and dragons, and my latest batch was about to go off.' Jutte glanced over at the group. 'Three, is it?'

'Two,' Lazare told her, showing her his non-vampire teeth.

'No, it's OK, you can give us three,' added Amber hurriedly. 'Me and Wulfric can split the extra one. In fact, if they're on the turn I will happily take a fourth off your hands.'

Jutte gave Amber the sort of gooey-eyed smile that the little dragon usually only ever got from Tem. 'Do you think you could manage five?'

'I will try my best,' replied Amber solemnly.

They sat, and found that it wasn't just Jutte who fussed over them. Within the first minute, Kit had an astrologer on each arm, which was a huge relief to Fang. Kit downed the first drink he was given, grabbed a slice of pork off an uncomplaining patron's plate and announced, 'Well, I'll be off, then.'

'OK, bye,' called Fang, before anyone could entreat him to stay.

'Come,' he told both astrologers, his mouth full of pork, 'bed with me and be my love, and we will all the pleasures prove...'

'That doesn't rhyme, Kit,' Bill said quietly.

'Yes it does; it's a half-rhyme.'

'It's a bit lazy.'

'Oh, shut up, Shakespeare, you do it too.'

And Kit was gone.

'Ah, he got me there,' sighed Bill. 'At least now I know he reads my poetry.'

Kit wasn't the only one getting a lot of attention from the other patrons. They flocked around Amber, Wulfric and Lazare and, as soon as they heard her Welsh accent, Nell. Fang realised where it was before that he'd seen those expressions the students wore around them. They were the excited smiles of townsfolk watching the circus rolling in.

'Don't mind them,' Jutte told Fang, putting down a big bowl of stew for those with human appetites. 'Magical studies is the most popular course at three different colleges round here, so they get all excited when an actual magical passes through. Not to mention the Welsh.'

Fang watched as Nell tried to ask four different students about astrology and curses, only to be asked various unconnected questions about the dragon queen's capital city of Llanelli in reply.

'You'd think they'd get less excited about the Welsh,' continued Jutte. 'There's plenty of foreigners here, students and the like. I came from the Low Countries to study and just never left. Plenty of Ottomans like yourself, too.'

'He's not Turkish, though,' said Lazare. 'He's from the Great Ming. Whole different end of Asia.'

A hundred pairs of eyes lit up at mention of the Ming Empire. Fang glared daggers at Lazare as the students and astrologers descended, questions about loong and huli jing and the old Emperor's accidental creation of the undead races mulching into one another as one big, imposing noise. Desperate to find some reason to ignore them all entirely, Fang turned his attention onto Tem, who was busily trying to pick bits of carrot out of her stew.

'Carrots are good for you,' he told her. 'If you eat some, I'll get you fruit toast and honey milk for pudding. Your favourite.'

'*God's Oksels*,' said Jutte, 'is that girl a fae?'

'A fae???' chorused the whole bar in delight.

Tem shrank into Fang, terrified by all the sudden attention.

Now it was the rest of Fang's group's turn to glare daggers at him. Oh, no. He'd really messed up.

It took a good hour or so of deflection on Fang's part to smooth things over and draw attention away from Tem once more. He'd had to go into a lot of detail with the students about the magical fauna, flora and history of the Great Ming. He'd had to try to be gregarious. And charming. It was awful. The others had swooped in to the rescue – whether that was to rescue him from the curious students or to rescue the students from his social awkwardness and tendency towards rudeness, Fang couldn't say.

Fang also couldn't say exactly how an initially tense evening of inquisition had turned into a night of raucous drinking songs, but Fang suspected that was the doing of Lazare. After all, it was Lazare who got up on the table, singing and clapping and stamping his feet while Nell got involved in a very intense talk with an attractive astrology professor, and Amber enjoyed belly rubs and a plate of pig hearts and trotters. Whether it was to rescue Fang and Tem from the students' queries, or simply because Lazare constantly craved the loving attention of an audience, or a little of both, Fang had to admit to himself, there were worse ways to round off an evening. Lazare did have a very pleasant singing voice, and, it seemed, an extensive knowledge of drinking songs from France, England and further afield at that. Fang watched as Lazare effortlessly picked up a song that Jutte taught him in Dutch. Only a week ago, Fang would have made good use of the distraction and slipped away to somewhere mercifully free from such rowdy merry-making, but now he sat and watched, bouncing Tem gently in his lap to the rhythm, and when the girl started shyly clapping along, well, at that point, how could he not join in? With the clapping, that was, not the actual singing. He hadn't gone completely mad.

'Sing "Do Nothing But Eat And Make Good Cheer",' called Bill.

'I don't know it,' cried Lazare from his table. 'How does it go?'

'Oh come on, man,' whined Bill.

Nell plonked herself next to Fang. 'So I'm off to Professor Dot's for a nightcap.'

Professor Dot, a tall, middle-aged astrologer, gave him a cheerful nod of greeting from across the bar.

'From *Henry IV*,' continued Bill. 'It's a classic!'

'Was that by Anthony Munday?' asked Lazare.

'No, you cod, it was by me!'

Fang did his best to ignore the argument. 'Another "fact-finding" mission, is it?' he asked Nell dryly.

'Maybe?' Nell replied. 'I think so? Dot's an astrology doctor, she says, so if anyone in town's going to have the answer to our whole "curse" issue, it's going to be her, right?'

'Also, she's tall and attractive,' noted Fang.

'There is that, yeah, but this is still purely for the quest, you understand. We might not have to bother Redthroat in her graciousness at all.'

'Mm. All for the quest, I'm sure.'

Nell patted his shoulder, unperturbed by his usual sarcasm. 'You going to be all right for the night, with kiddie here?'

'She's good as gold,' Fang told Nell, giving a soft glance down at Tem. 'Better than gold. She's good as...'

'Honey milk?' asked Tem.

'Yeah. She's good as honey milk,' said Fang.

'And you'll be all right with...' She raised her eyebrows and nodded at Lazare, still up on the table arguing with Bill, lit with dancing gold from a hundred candles. His big, silly peacock. Fang really wanted to go back to that kiss. Fang knew he couldn't go back to that kiss without breaking the Frenchman's heart.

'I can keep my hands off him for another night,' Fang told her quietly. 'Honestly, I still don't know why you choose to make him and I your business.'

'I'm not. OK, I did a little bit at first, but you two are grown-ups; you can make your own choices. I just know how good you are at hurting feelings.'

'I'm also adept at sparing feelings,' Fang told her, 'which is what I'm aiming for with regards to our noisy friend who thinks he's in love.'

'He said he's in love?' whispered Nell urgently.

'What are you talking about?' asked Tem.

'Nothing,' chorused Nell and Fang.

'Well, maybe if you'd cast me in the first place, I'd have learned the song,' Lazare told Bill, as Nell left the table.

'But I already have a Falstaff,' countered Bill, 'or... *had* a Falstaff; Marlowe poached him.'

'So why not cast me now?'

'Falstaff doesn't have wings, though.'

'Then why should I sing it?'

'Because it's a good song, Mr Quitbeef! I worked hard on that song! Oh... why do I bother?' Bill got up drunkenly. 'Why am I sitting around with people who can't even tell me from Anthony Bloody Munday? Why don't you write your own damnéd songs and plays, Mr Quitbeef, instead of constantly whining for others to cast your mediocre self? That's what I had to do, when "nobody wanted a romantic hero with

58

a yokel accent who's already half bald at twenty-five", but you don't hear me wailing about it!'

'Bill, sit down,' called Wulfric.

'Oh! You who sucks on blood in dead of night,' wailed Bill. 'Just as cruel London sucks the joy from life!'

'Great,' grumbled Wulfric, 'he's talking in iambic pentameter again. He always does this when he's drunk and emotional. Or when he's nervous. Not to mention all the puns.'

'I shall not sit! Like you, I do take flight,' continued Bill, 'and flutter to my children and my wife!'

'Bill, I'm your ride,' Wulfric reminded him, but Bill was too drunk and upset.

'I do not need the carriage of the damned!' Bill stormed off, accidentally knocking over a chair. 'I shall provide mine own way home to Anne!'

'That doesn't rhyme, Bill,' sighed Lazare

'It's a half rhyme,' screamed Bill. 'You all love it when Marlowe does them!' He left, slamming the door and taking with him the last of that night's celebratory atmosphere.

Wulfric got up and headed towards the door himself. 'Well, I'd better go and make sure he doesn't get mugged again. Mimi!' The vampire made a sort of squeaky kissy noise by sucking air between his fangs and the half-tailed cat trotted over and leaped onto his shoulder to a chorus of 'awwwww's.

Wulfric was not the only person who took Bill's departure as their own cue to leave. Soon, the only people left were a thin straggle of drinkers. Amber, her belly full and her chin utterly scritched, curled up in a happy little ball in front of the fire and promptly fell asleep, not before doing a colossal, toothy, smoky dragon yawn that set Tem off with yawns of her own.

'Hey,' said Lazare softly, sitting down at long last to eat some lukewarm stew. He still looked perturbed – being shouted at by Bill Shakespeare seemed to have really rattled the actor.

'Hi,' replied Fang, cradling Tem. 'Don't let that drunk get to you. You're a good… you know a lot of songs.'

Lazare nodded, with a small smile that didn't reach his eyes. 'I like picking them up. I'd love to add some Cathayan drinking songs to the mix, you should teach me a few.'

'We weren't big drinkers, where I grew up. My village was poor.' He faltered, not sure why he'd said that.

'I know,' Lazare replied lightly. 'About your village, I mean. The alchemist told us. No shame in peasantry – it's good, honest work… at least, that's what I've been told. And I did sort of notice that you're not a particularly hard drinker.'

Fang raised his eyebrows at him questioningly.

'You're a lightweight,' Lazare expanded.

'Hey.'

Lazare smiled, properly this time, at the memory. He still didn't look Fang directly in the eye, Fang noticed. 'Our first night together, you got *so* drunk.'

'I'd lost a lot of blood!'

'I bet that's still your first ale,' said Lazare, pointing at Fang's flagon.

'Well, pardon me for practising moderation when I'm in the middle of a quest, with a child.'

'And yet, you're still all pink,' noted Lazare, with a fond grin that he pointed up at the ceiling rather than at Fang.

'I am not.' Fang didn't want to draw attention to his cheeks by touching them, but he had to admit to himself, they did feel hot. Instead, Tem reached up and squidged his face.

'You're nice and warm like chocolate,' Tem informed him sleepily.

Lazare turned his smile to the child, and there was something about that smile and the softness of Lazare's dark eyes that made Fang afraid. They had no future, because any future would be at Tem's expense. That's why they were going to the dragon queen, to ensure they had no future, yet Lazare's warm smile was one that made a plaintive voice within Fang beg for a future they could not have... could they? No. No, they definitely couldn't. Pretending otherwise would only hurt Lazare, and he couldn't bear to hurt Lazare. He couldn't pretend it would be OK; he couldn't feel that tall, slim body pressing him to the wall again, or those strong, soft hands beneath his thighs. He couldn't. Could he? No.

Not, added another, sharper voice within him, that Lazare had shown any interest in pushing him against the wall again, in opening up his mouth with a desperate tongue, in grasping his thighs, ever since that one half of a kiss, ever since the alchemist had attacked. Come to think of it, since the alchemist had attacked them, Lazare had barely looked Fang in the eye.

Did he *want* Lazare to gaze at him, to lean towards him, to rest one hand against Fang's jaw and slide the other between his knees? No. Obviously, he would have to turn the poor

Frenchman down, and that would be cruel. So why was he still imagining it happening anyway…?

Fang got up. 'Better get this one to bed.'

'There's two rooms made up,' Jutte told him. 'One has a little bed for her, and you gentlemen can be just next door.'

Fang felt a familiar sinking feeling at the news he and Lazare were expected to share a room again.

'Our room,' he asked, 'is there only one bed?'

Jutte nodded. 'For warmth, yes.'

Fang risked a glance at Lazare. The Frenchman locked eyes with him for just a fragment of a second before hurriedly looking away with an unhappy, awkward expression that only made Fang's heart sink further. He nudged the sleeping dragon with his foot. 'Come on, dragon. We need you to heat up the kid's bed.'

Amber uncurled and gave him another impressively huge yawn before trotting up the stairs alongside him.

'And I'll, um, I'll warm up ours, shall I?' asked Lazare.

Fang pretended to ignore him. Pretended not to think about the heat of Lazare's own face, the sweet smells of sack and stew on his breath, the carefully oiled soft scratch of his beard against Fang's skin, the hot, hard urgency of their one and only kiss.

Lazare waited, warming up the bed. That was all he was doing, just warming it up. It was a cold night – wouldn't do to let any of their party get sick. Just because they couldn't die of a chill anymore didn't mean it wouldn't still be deeply unpleasant, and it wouldn't do to see any of the party suffer unnecessarily.

He closed his eyes, and again saw the vivid memory of Fang's drowned face, Tem screaming, Fang spluttering with agony as the life was shoved back in him, only for him to be drowned once more. Lazare opened his eyes.

He lay awake and continued to warm up the bed, alone, as he listened to Jutte closing up the inn for the night. Soon, even those sounds stopped, and he was left in a quiet that made every thought in his head far too loud. Bill's words came back to him, a spiral of sack-sodden cruelty. Lazare was sure the playwright had only called him whiny and mediocre out of drunken churlishness, but it still stung, just as, even though he knew Fang was safe from the alchemist now, the memories of his drowned face still slapped Lazare's soul afresh over and over again. Even with his eyes open, Lazare could see the pattern of it in the dark, like the green and grey after-images that remained immediately after looking at a bright light.

After a while, he got up, not because he was anxious about how long Fang was taking or anything, just to see if he needed help settling Tem. On cracking open the door to Tem's bedroom, he discovered the reason why Fang hadn't come in yet, and it was definitely not that he needed any help soothing the child. Tem was sleeping, cuddling both the toy dragon and its snoozing real-life counterpart. On the floor next to her lay Fang, pink-cheeked and asleep, his hand protectively over the child's shoulder. Fang falling asleep next to Tem was becoming a habit. As Lazare watched, Tem's face crumpled and her body twitched, troubled inside her dreams, the one place none of them could go to help her. But then, without waking, Fang's hand firmed its grip a little more on the child's shoulder, and her sleeping form relaxed. Lazare went to the other bedroom, picked up the bright green cloak he had gifted Fang the other day, and tucked Fang into it like a blanket. He watched Fang's sleeping face in the moonlight for longer than was probably courteous, but what was Fang going to do about it – he was asleep.

The man was a mess. He was always a mess. He was now wearing several borrowed items of Lazare's spare clothing, and managed to attract more filth, mud and blood to the clothes in a matter of hours than Lazare could over several weeks. Even the new cape was already grubby. Were Fang not asleep, one could be forgiven for thinking the mess was Fang's magical reverse glamour powers at work. It wasn't magic at all, but Lazare believed it was a carefully curated mess akin to a spell, telling others, without words, to stay away. Another wall, deliberately building a foreboding haunted house around the man.

Lazare was an actor. He knew a thing or two about the artful artifice of set dressing.

And look at Fang now, so many of those cobwebbed walls and creaking shutters wafted away like dissipating fog as he slept. He looked so peaceful, holding on to Tem's shoulder. Might Fang look as tranquil as that sleeping in a big, soft bed, in Lazare's arms? Lazare would never begrudge Tem the comfort she took from Fang's proximity, but he couldn't help but yearn a little for the weight of that hand on his own shoulder as he watched in the faint light. Fang's brow was smoothed in sleep, his nose flushed about the bridge from the single tankard of ale, his lips slackened to let out a gentle snore. Lazare wanted to kiss every part of him, enjoying Fang piece by piece as part of a lovely whole, like lines of a sonnet. Forehead, nose, mouth. Throat. Chest. And so on. He wanted to… his thoughts were interrupted by the memory of Fang's drowned face again, the violent image burning itself over the soft gentleness of Fang's sleeping form.

Lazare turned, and quietly left the trio in peaceful oblivion. He couldn't bear to seek that same oblivion for himself just yet, since doing so would involve an empty bed, a dark, quiet room and bright and noisy thoughts. The night was… not 'young', as such, but it was still before midnight. Back home in Upper London, the nightlife would just be getting started. Dancing, song, gambling, late-night performances by candlelight… it was too much to hope that a smaller town like this would have even a fraction of that late-night fun, no doubt. The students would be off sleeping before another day of study, or peering into their telescopes or hunched over textbooks at this time of night, right?

He took the inn's emergency key and let himself out for a brisk stroll, just to see for himself how pathetic the nightlife was here compared to his beloved big city.

It was, as he'd assumed, quiet. The inns were shut; no music drifted from the dorms, just the occasional light from a scribe's candle. Still that wretched silence that amplified the loudness of his thoughts. The vision of Fang's drowned face. He hadn't been able to help; he'd just had to stand there. What was he good for? Not heroics, certainly. Not loving, for he loved Fang, and yet he couldn't help the man, could bring him neither physical nor emotional succour. He loved Fang, who continued to seek an end to the curse, even though that meant death, rather than entertaining a future for the pair of them. He loved Fang, whose response to there only being one bed for them to share was always to sleep on the floor instead. He loved Fang, who, crucially, didn't even believe that Lazare truly loved him, but that the Frenchman was simply libidinous, frustrated and confused. Well, more fool Fang, because Lazare had spent most of his life libidinous, frustrated and confused, and it had never felt anything like this. Lazare loved Fang utterly, yet could not convince Fang of this truth.

And if he could not convince one man of an absolute truth, what hope had Lazare in convincing a whole audience of a fancy? Was he even good for acting? Had Bill been right? Was Lazare... mediocre? After all these years of trying, he still hadn't really got anywhere, despite ingratiating himself with as many playwrights as possible. He'd always watched as Burbage or Kempe, or some young and pretty lad, got all the accolades and the applause, and had told himself that his time would come, some day he would receive that outpouring of adoration, but now... Now, he was following Fang to probable death, and he really didn't feel that the world was about to be robbed of a great acting talent it never knew. He used to think that, when he finally fell in love, it would be a glorious, affirming event, a celebration of his own wonderfulness, to be completely seen and completely adored by another. But, now that it had happened, it just felt like a horrible epiphany that he was not enough. Perhaps he never had been. Bill's words kept coming back, like Fang's drowned face when Lazare had failed time again to save his love. Like the words Fang didn't need to say, Lazare knew they were there in the man's mind: vapid. Flimsy. Mediocre. Unworthy of attention, irritating that he craved said attention.

Why was he even out here in the dark, dead streets? What was he hoping to find? Peace? Or another insubstantial distraction? Lazare was about to turn tail and head back when he heard a voice echoing down a blackened alleyway. Not one filled with drunken argument or a mugger's menace, this voice had a lyrical meter to it. A recital! God's Bladder, had he had the good fortune to stumble upon Oxford's secret midnight theatre scene? Was there even such a thing? As insubstantial distractions went, a secret midnight play would drown out his loud and upsetting thoughts, at least. He followed the sound of the voice, swiftly but cautiously. It could also be a trap, of course, but if it were, oh what a succulent bait with which to set the snare!

He turned a corner, and discovered a gathering in a stable yard. An audience was watching one performer recite verse to a second man. Both performers stopped, and all eyes of the small crowd turned to him.

'Ah,' said one of the performers, 'you must be one of Marlowe's party, from London? He did say he had a vampire with him.'

'Not a vampire, and more of a loose acquaintance of Marlowe's than one of his party per se, but otherwise yes,' Lazare told them. 'Don't tell me he found the time to set up yet another theatre company in between astrologers.'

'He did try,' the performer told him, 'but we're not actors. We're poets. He spared five minutes to spit a verse…'

'A really dirty one,' added the other poet approvingly.

The first poet nodded, snorting a small laugh. 'Absolute filth about dryads and nymphs, before hoisting an astrologer over each shoulder and announcing he was off to witness a twin moon system cope with the scorpion in ascendance.'

'I don't think he really understands astrology,' said the second poet.

'But he did tell us there were more of you in town,' continued the first. 'Assured us more poets could join in with our evening of clandestine midnight sonnet battles.'

'Battles?' asked Lazare, concerned.

'Just a bit of fun,' the first poet assured him. 'Will you drop some iambic for us, sir?'

'Uh... no. Sorry. I'm an actor, you see. I bring words to life; I don't make them up...'

'You're making them up right now, good sir,' the first poet reminded him.

'I'll just watch, thank you,' replied Lazare.

'The actor dare not step upon the stage,' crowed the second poet,

'His knees do tremble and his cheeks flush warm
E'en though he is of much maturéd age
And clearly always desp'rate to perform.
Behold, his strutting, brightly coloured hose,
His doublet of attention-seeking hue!
His careful curls here, there and heaven knows
Where else he's coifféd, and indeed, for who.
We humble Oxford poets have no ken
Why Mister London Actor prowls at night
We ask him to perform for us but then
Oh no, he wails, for he is too polite!
What are you seeking out here, good *señor*?
If not the stage, then what is all this for?'

Lazare gazed at the poets, agape. 'That was really mean.'

'It's meant to be,' the first poet told him. 'And now, it's your turn to reply.'

'Er,' said Lazare. He drew in a breath, allowing his pride and innate urge to perform to take over his brain, and hoping they would come up with a decent counter-insult.

'I do dare, sir, the skills with which I'm blessed
I put to use in slaying tedium,
And here it seems that I've found boredom's nest.
What jaded envy I have chanced upon.
You note my beard is neat; my garb is bright –
I wear these things with pride. It is called "fashion".
As to the reason for my walk tonight,
I hoped the dullness would damp down my passion.
There is a man. A man so beautiful
That death and life fight over him in turn,
Yet his good heart, so kind and dutiful
Sets base desires aside – thus, I must yearn.
He loves so much, such is my compensation.
We are all kept alive by adoration.'

Lazare hoped that that would do. Honestly, he hadn't meant to segue into it being about Fang towards the end. It had just sort of happened. The poets and their audience gave him a smattering of applause. Small as it was, it felt nice.

'Not bad for your first try in your second language,' the first poet told him.

'"Tedium" doesn't really rhyme with "upon", though,' added the second poet.

'It's a half-rhyme,' Lazare told them weakly.

The first poet gave him a patronising little pat on the wing. 'If you find yourself back in Oxford, you'd be welcome to perform again.'

'You're inviting me back for an encore?' Lazare felt lifted. Perhaps Bill had been wrong, or falsely cruel in his inebriated anger. Those swirling thoughts of self-doubt weren't silenced, but they grew mumbling and hesitant in the face of this validation from strangers. Yes. He'd show them! 'I could perform *The Massacre At Paris*!'

'Not to recite someone else's words,' the second poet told him. 'Bring your own.'

'Write some more sonnets about that man you fancy,' advised the first poet. 'Might win him over – and even if it doesn't, I'd like to hear more about him. He sounds sexy. Maybe you can do a couplet about his bum.'

'Right,' said Lazare, bewildered. He left the poets and walked back to the inn. He'd just had his first appreciative audience for a monologue. His first encore. And it hadn't been for acting at all. They'd seen something deeper in him – his words, his thoughts. Even if those thoughts had mostly been over the general hotness of Fang.

The secret midnight poets continued with their night of rhyming insults after the strange not-quite-a-vampire had left. It was barely one in the morning, after all. It was just as they were getting into a really good argument about whether rhyming a word with its homonym was cheating that they were startled by a great terrible flapping of giant, feathered wings overhead. Even outside London, the students knew exactly what it was.

'Run,' they screamed, 'it's the feathers! Some bugger's called the guards!'

CHAPTER SIX
HONK HONK

'**M**orning,' said Professor Dot. 'I did eggs.'

'Thanks.' Nell searched around for her boots. 'D'you have coffee?'

Professor Dot laughed lightly. 'Of course not. I'm not rich.' She handed Nell the eggs and kissed the top of her head. 'I meant what I said last night, by the way. I'd love to do your charts, if you could bring yourself to stay another few hours…?'

'I'd love that too,' Nell told her, 'but if you really meant everything else you said last night, then I can't.'

'I have two doctorates in astrology, Miss Nell,' said Professor Dot, 'and I can tell you honestly that any answers for a fae curse as strong as yours won't be found through a telescope. Your best bet on the British island is—'

'The Lost City of Llanelli,' huffed Nell between forkfuls of egg. 'I know.'

'I'd love to see the Lost City,' Dot continued wistfully, 'and having family just a few miles away in Carmarthen should make things nice and easy for you, right? Free board while you get your application sorted?'

Nell grunted eggily.

'You're not at all excited to go home?' asked Dot, gazing out of the window at a minor commotion outside. 'Lording it over them all, the successful London businesswoman with the big, exciting curse?'

'Not really,' Nell admitted, 'specially since the curse is likely the only thing keeping me alive right now.' That wasn't the only reason Nell was extremely hesitant to go home to Carmarthen, but Dot certainly didn't need to hear any of that. 'But needs must, I suppose, when you've signed up on a quest to get a little fae kid home.' And, she thought to herself, when the only other option was getting taken prisoner by Elizabeth's swans. Big fans of the rack, those guys. Nell had never been keen on the idea of getting tortured in the first place, but having seen what happened when it was done to a fellow immortal really hammered home to her the importance of not getting dragged to the Tower by the Royal Guards.

'You never know,' replied Dot, frowning at the scene outside the window. 'Queen Redthroat is powerful and wise, is she not?'

'Oh, extremely so,' said Nell. 'Every other history lesson back home was a tale of her benevolence and grace. Protecting Wales from invaders with her miracles. We are forever in her debt.' She realised she'd sort of said this on autopilot. It was true, though; she really had been told a lot of tales of Queen Redthroat the Invincible's magically wondrous feats. And only a handful of them seemed particularly far-fetched.

'Well, then,' continued Dot, 'could it not be that a thousand-year-old mighty dragon queen might have better solutions than just "failure or death"? There must be a third option. A better option. And if there is, surely Redthroat would have it.'

'You think so?' Nell felt a flutter of hope even as she fruitlessly scanned the room to find her other boot.

'Jupiter's in the first house, babe,' Dot told her, still distracted by the scene outside the window. 'Auspicious for you. At least, in theory...' She trailed off.

'What's up?' asked Nell, going to the window.

'Bit of a fracas,' noted Dot. 'Something's spooked the students. I swear to the stars, they're always mouthing off, planning to change the world with no thought given to whether it's sedition or heresy or not. Giving it the Big I Am about their right to have a Catholic-themed party in the common room is all well and good until the feathers come pecking at the door.'

Nell glanced out of the window. Students were running. Flapping after them were giant ravens in the livery of the Royal Guard. She didn't need to see any more. She already knew that bloody swan would be out there as well.

'Must have come up here from London overnight,' noted Dot. 'Looks serious... where are you off to?'

Nell was already at the other end of Dot's flat, climbing out of a back window. This was starting to become a habit.

'Hey!' Dot started climbing out after her. 'That's rude!'

'Sorry,' called Nell.

'It's also a little bit exciting,' admitted Dot. 'Here. Found your other boot.'

She tossed it down just as Nell finished descending Dot's trellis.

'Good luck,' added Dot. 'Not that you'll need it, probably, what with Jupiter. It's your lucky star.'

'It's a planet, though,' Nell retorted, putting on her boot.

'Yes,' replied the astrology professor, 'I am aware. But it looks like a star from here. If Redthroat saves you, will you come back to me?'

Honestly, Nell had hoped to give the latest one-night lover a more romantic and hopeful farewell, but she was too preoccupied with how to get back to the others and get out of town before torture o'clock. She gazed up at the beautiful, clever doctor of the stars whose arms she'd found such bliss in only hours before

'Dunno,' she called, before hurrying away.

'Oh, Nell,' sighed Dot fondly, leaning against her balcony to watch her leave, 'wherefore art thou such a typical Sagittarius?'

Nell managed to avoid the guards as she rushed through the backstreets to Jutte's inn, where the others were anxiously waiting for her.

'Honkensby and her guards are searching the whole town for us,' Fang told her, trying to soothe a fretful Tem. 'They must have picked up a lead we were taking the Oxford road.'

Nell didn't even wait to get her puff back. 'Then let's grab Wulfric, get on the cart and go, while we still can.'

'Wulfric left town already,' Lazare told her. 'So did Bill, and heaven knows where Kit is. One of them took the cart, although in fairness if it was Wulfric, it was his cart.'

'So, your friends have stranded us,' said Fang.

'They're your friends too, Fang.'

A young man burst through the doors of the inn. 'I'm a friend,' he called.

'Student,' Jutte told them.

'A Secret Midnight Poet,' muttered Lazare.

'Sir,' replied the student to Lazare hotly, 'what part of "Secret" do you not understand?'

'Brian, calm down,' Jutte told the student. 'The guards aren't after your silly poetry club.'

'I know,' replied Brian. 'But could you all please stop talking about it? It's literally the first rule of the society. I am here with aid for Mr Quitbeef and party.'

Lazare clasped his hand to his chest. 'The Secret M... your society is helping us? After but one rave performance?'

'An anonymous benefactor has paid for you to have my carriage and pair,' Brian explained. 'Added ten shillings to my price, provided I ran to tell you immediately.'

'The carriage is stabled right here at the inn,' Jutte told the group. 'Come on.'

'To whom do we owe such a favour?' asked Nell.

'He was very particular not to be named,' explained Brian, 'as he considered it "more dashing" that way.'

'Marlowe,' chorused Lazare, Fang, Nell and Amber, as they hurried through to Jutte's stables.

'He just said, "Bravo, Lazzers, you don't know living til you've been chased cross country by the long neck of the law, we'll make a rapscallion of you yet"...'

'Marlowe,' they chorused again, throwing their things on board the carriage as Jutte readied the horses.

'And he had a message for Mr Fang, which was simply, um.' Brian awkwardly mimed squeezing air buttocks. '"Honk honk."'

'Marlowe,' they chorused, lifting Tem into the carriage as Nell clambered into the driving seat.

'Then he kissed me with tongues and was away,' concluded Brian. 'Truly, we will never know who that mystery man was.'

'It was Christopher Marlowe,' Lazare told him as Nell slapped the reins.

Brian sighed and waved them goodbye. 'I know. You lot are terrible at keeping secrets, you know that?'

'Marlowe is terrible at being incognito, to be fair,' Lazare told the occupants of the carriage as they sped away.

'Are we any better at it?' asked Amber, watching for swans.

'Maybe not, but Marlowe was technically supposed to be a spy for years before he died.' Lazare shook his head fondly. 'Stick to the poetry, Kit.' He looked thoughtful for a moment. 'Stick to the poetry.'

It was a good carriage, with excellent horses. Brian's family must have been very rich, but then, Nell supposed, that was students for you. They were out of Oxford quickly, and at least not immediately followed. Nell was a confident driver – fast, but nothing like Fang's deeply chaotic approach to wrangling a carriage. With these horses perhaps, against the odds, they'd make it to the Welsh border that day. Perhaps, against even greater odds, they'd be able to lose the guards' tail.

It would have been nice to have stopped to enjoy the rugged beauty of the Cotswolds, the pale-bricked wealth and glory of Cirencester, the… well, there wasn't much interesting about Stroud, but Nell was pretty sure she saw a shop there as they rattled past – so it would also have been nice to have stopped and enjoyed the shop of Stroud, but they couldn't spare the time. Indeed, just as they passed Stroud and its shop, Amber called that she could see a strange shape in the sky to the east. It was a giant swan in flight, and it was gaining on them.

Bugger it! Someone must have tipped the swan off, because it was proving impossible to shake her. They were far too visible on the open road, and there was no way out here to misdirect the bird. Fang did his best by casting awful illusions. The set of huge marauding dragons he cast at first did slow down the bird a little, but once she discovered they weren't real she quickly began catching up again, and just flew straight through his subsequent illusions. She wasn't even bothered by the pride of lions he created in the hope that a bird's hard-wired fear of cats could put her off the scent for a bit. Lazare and Amber's offers to fly over and fight her were swiftly rejected. Assaulting a Royal Guard in flight was a serious offence that would land them even more in trouble were they to lose said fight, which was likely even if they tried to tag-team her. Honkensby was a massive swan, for pity's sake. Those things were adept at breaking arms. So, that only left Nell. With regret over the horrible driving that was bound to follow, she passed the reins over to Fang and clambered onto the roof of the carriage.

Honkensby was so close now that Nell could see and hear her clearly.

'Pull over,' called Honkensby. 'In the name of the queen.'

'You're supposed to go "nee naw" if you want us to pull over,' shouted Nell.

Honkensby sighed. 'Nee naw, pull over! Her Majesty requests counsel with you, and when I say "requests", I mean "demands".'

'What was that?' shouted Nell. She needed the swan to get closer. Her potions wouldn't work at this distance. Just a little closer, and then Nell could introduce Honkensby to a wonderful soft world of chemically induced bliss. The swan would get to spend half an hour or so chilling out for a change in a large crumple of feathers and happy quacks, and Nell and her friends would be able to make it to Wales mercifully unarrested. Of course, there was the problem that drugging a Royal Guard very definitely counted as a form of assault, and if Nell ever tried to return to her beloved shop, she would be immediately hauled to the Tower for a terrible and eternal world of shackles and various torture implements, but she couldn't think of another way out of this right now.

At the front, Fang yanked the reins and the carriage swerved sharply to the left. Nell gripped on for her life, already rueing letting Fang drive.

Honkensby dipped her wing and performed a tight turn in the air, keeping up with them even as Fang slapped the horses on to a gallop.

'Pull over, I said,' shouted Honkensby. 'This is your last chance to come peacefully.'

'I'm sure this is all a big misunderstanding,' Nell called. 'Why don't you come over and we can talk it out?'

'I can't while you're running, can I?' Honkensby called, exasperated. 'Turn around, all of you. You're coming back to London.'

'We've got Deepside subjects on board,' attempted Nell.

'And while they're Upperside, they abide by our laws. You're coming in. All of you. The dragon. The girl. Especially the girl.'

Oh, now, that was going too far.

'The girl's nothing to do with you or your queen,' shouted Nell. 'You failed that poor mite once already, letting Upper London gangs kidnap her. She owes you nothing!'

'Her Majesty is aware of that.' Honkensby landed on the back of the carriage, and Nell raised her hand to the lace of her bodice. 'Unfortunately, Her Majesty is also aware of what you are, and what that means.'

Nell tugged at one of her laces. 'Oh, I'll *show* you what that means,' she breathed.

'There!' shouted Fang suddenly. 'Tough luck, Honkensby.'

'What?' asked Nell and Honkensby together.

Fang pulled at the reins, bringing the horses and carriage to a sudden, jolting halt. He pointed triumphantly behind the carriage, at a sign in the road a few feet back. One sign, pointing east, read *Upper England (Lloegr Uchaf)*. The other, pointing west, read *Cymru (Wales)*, and bore the likeness of Redthroat, the national emblem of Nell's homeland. The carriage, and all of its passengers, Honkensby included, were on the Welsh side of the signpost.

'Looks like you have no jurisdiction here, Captain,' Fang continued. 'Even if you did have any cause to arrest us – which you don't...'

'I do; I have the queen's seal.'

'Arresting us this side of the border,' continued Fang, 'would mean an awful lot of paperwork with the Welsh Crown.'

Honkensby narrowed her dark little eyes. 'You've threatened me with bureaucracy before, Mr Fang.'

'And it worked,' Fang reminded her, 'so I'm doing it again.'

'I'll...' There were flickers of doubt and internal wrangling on the swan's expression as she replied with just a smidge of hesitancy. 'I'll just say I arrested you before we got to the border.'

'And break the rules?' asked Fang, with a simpering sarcastic feigned innocence that didn't suit him one bit.

'Only by a few feet,' retorted Honkensby, increasingly bothered. 'It isn't as if there are independent witnesses who can corroborate...'

'*Croeso i Gymru*, officer,' rasped a voice. An elderly man with a big white beard and a copper false eye clopped past on horseback, seemingly from nowhere. 'A Queen's Guard, all the way here in Wales, that *is* exciting. Mind how y'go.'

Honkensby watched the elderly independent witness clop peacefully away. 'Not a problem,' she continued in a tone that betrayed that it absolutely was a problem. 'Llewellyn's embassy is expecting me, you know.'

'He's expecting you to kidnap a fae, a dragon and a Welshwoman in his territory without his say-so, is he? There'll be an awful fuss. Were you told you could cause a fuss? And what if he were to ask what your queen actually wants with us? What *does* she actually want with us, by the way?'

'I think you know,' said Honkensby.

'I have suspicions,' replied Fang, 'but I am a deeply suspicious man. Perhaps it's better I hear it from you – since you are merely upholding fair laws and keeping the peace, why don't you tell me how arresting us is going to be for the powers of good?'

'It *is* to keep the peace,' Honkensby hissed. 'To keep the peace in all of Europe! And beyond!'

'Well, that sounds admirable.' Fang folded his arms. 'Tell me how. Help a foreigner like me understand. Because if you arrest us here without permission and there's a fuss, you are going to have to help the Welsh king understand how Elizabeth Tudor intends to use us – including one of his subjects – in order to "keep the peace".'

Honkensby sighed wearily. 'Fine. Fine!'

'Fine, you'll tell us Elizabeth's plans?' asked Nell.

'No! Fine, I can write for permission from the outpost at Stroud,' replied Honkensby testily. 'Meanwhile, I do hope you enjoy doing paperwork as much as you love foisting it on others, Mr Fang, as magically uncategorisable foreigners such as yourself and Mr Quitbeef will need a considerable amount to so much as set foot inside the Lost City of Llanelli.'

'Better to have our hands occupied with their forms than your thumbscrews,' said Lazare.

Honkensby snorted. 'You haven't seen their forms yet.' She turned around and took off again, flapping east. 'Can't believe you're making me go to Stroud.'

'They have a nice-looking shop there,' Nell called helpfully. She looked at the sign again. It wasn't as if she'd promised herself she'd never be on this side of it ever again. Back home. It was just that, well. It didn't feel like home anymore. It didn't give her that nice cosy feeling she got on climbing the steps outside the fish shop on Griffin Alley, being hit by the warm smells of incense and coffee and badly masked haddock. It didn't make her exhale and smile the way she did around Fang's gruff huffs and soft eyes, or the way Lazare could manage to express himself with every one of his long limbs – even his wings would droop when he was sad. The image of Redthroat on her home nation's flag stood proud and snarling and magnificent, with none of Amber's stumpy, cheery dragon-y charm. And could any magical in Wales be as sweet as Tem? Would any wrap their arms around Nell's neck the way that little cutie did, or fuss over a tiny felt dragon? That was what 'home' felt like now, and this wasn't it. This was just a bilingual sign in the middle of a field. Raindrops began to fall on her – welcoming her 'home' with sparse, lazy drops that got down the back of her collar. She took the reins back from Fang and set them off towards Carmarthen.

'Hey,' Amber told Tem in the back, 'we're in Wales.'

'Oh,' replied the child politely.

'The flag is of a dragon,' added Amber with considerable pride.

'Ooh,' cooed Tem, suddenly impressed.

'Did it start raining almost as soon as we crossed the border?' asked Lazare.

'Yep,' grunted Nell. 'It'll do that. *Croeso i Gymru.*'

CHAPTER SEVEN
CROESO I GYMRU

The carriage was just about big enough for them all to sleep in overnight, with Lazare on one seat, and Nell on the other with Amber nestled on her skirts. Tem was offered a seat, but worried about 'nightmares pushing her off it' and instead slept on the floor, with Fang and his cloak wrapped around her. It wasn't as if they hadn't passed plenty of coaching houses before they bedded down for their uncomfortable night on the side of the road. It wasn't as if Lazare hadn't pointed out all of the warm, jolly-looking inns as they'd clattered past; it wasn't as if Lazare hadn't asked every time if they wouldn't prefer a nice hot meal and soft bed. It was more that, since neither Amber nor Tem minded where they slept, if Nell was also in no mood to make merry, then Lazare found himself rather outnumbered, and Wales had brought out a grouchiness in Nell that helped Lazare understand why she and Fang were such firm friends. Lazare slept fitfully on his seat. He blamed the nightmares on the discomfort of his makeshift bed – he woke multiple times with a start, the parade of horror forced upon him by his sleeping mind still immediate and disconcertingly real. At one point in the silent depths of the night he opened his eyes and was startled afresh to see Tem staring directly up at him from the floor.

'Bad dream,' she whispered, and Lazare wasn't sure whether she was telling him she'd had one, or asking if he had. He just nodded, and watched her until she closed her eyes again.

They continued west the following day and Wales passed by, all dark green rolling hills and dark grey skies and green and grey and green and grey and green and grey. Lazare did not mention Nell's continued mood at finally returning home, as dark and foreboding as the stunning landscape. As pleasant as his own upbringing had been, he wasn't sure how he'd feel about going back to Paris now, his bold dreams of becoming the greatest actor in London still tragically unfulfilled. And then there was the whole 'likely heading towards certain death' thing that came with trying to end the curse. As unfair as Lazare felt it was on himself to stop his magically extended existence, it seemed even worse for someone with as much joie de vivre as Nell. It wasn't fair, but it was the only way, for Tem's sake, right? Especially now that Queen Elizabeth wanted to drag that poor little kid to the Tower along with the rest of them. Yes, he thought as they clopped on through the gloomy damp towards the dragon's city and their certain deaths. This was the only way. It was just a really shit way.

As they rolled into Carmarthen that evening, Lazare noted with dismay that it was even smaller than Oxford.

Unlike Oxford, there were no palatial spires. Only the castle loomed over the houses and businesses of the riverside, a huge grey relic of the great Anglo-Cambrian war, built by King Dafydd III to keep the English from attempting an invasion upriver. Now used, Nell told them curtly, as a combination of artillery storage, prison, admin centre and logistics hub, not unlike the Tower of London. It was certainly not the seat of King Llewellyn V. The Welsh royal palace was Dolwyddelan, way up north, far from Redthroat's throne. A respectful distance from the dragon queen's seat of power, Nell assured him, and one that should buy them time as Honkensby's paperwork would take longer to arrive at the King's court at Dolwyddelan since it was, in her words, 'a bugger to get to'.

They clopped past houses, shops, warehouses, inns and, as Lazare had been warned, not a single theatre. Nell pointed out a poster promising an upcoming *Eisteddfod yn y Cyfnewid Yd (Eisteddfod at the Corn Exchange)*, but Lazare had no idea what an Eisteddfod was, or indeed what a corn exchange was. It all sounded horribly provincial to him.

'All the signs are in English as well as Welsh,' Amber noted.

'We get a lot of undead and magical refugees from England this close to the Lost City of Llanelli,' Nell explained. 'Folks who don't want to live Deep anymore, either making first steps settling in Llewellyn's friendly domain or seeking to apply for a new life in Redthroat's glorious capital. Carmarthen's been bilingual by default for centuries as a result. It won't be an issue that none of you can speak Welsh.'

'I should really learn to speak more Welsh,' sighed Amber. ''Tis the language of my people.'

'The language of your people?' Fang snorted. 'I thought you hatched under Chiswick.'

'Well, yeah, but spiritually speaking, 'tis the language of my people.'

'Dragon,' cried Tem happily, pointing at the full-body portrait of Redthroat the Invincible on a passing flag, just as she had done at all the many, many Welsh flags they had passed that day. Well, at least Tem was excited to be in Wales.

Nell, on the other hand, seemed more apprehensive with every street they turned down. Lazare briefly wondered where exactly she was taking them. Again, she hadn't given any local coaching houses even a second glance. Lazare was just about to try making a case that it wasn't fair on the horses to make them sleep outside for a second night when a stable came into view. The sign above it read: *Evan. Stabl. Ffariar. Prynu pedair pedol, mae pumed yn rhad ac am ddim. (Stable, Farrier, Buy four horseshoes, fifth is free).* She took a deep breath, and pulled the carriage into the stable. They were greeted by a young man, who did a double take at Nell.

'Hiya, Rees,' sighed Nell.

Rees didn't even reply to Nell, but turned and opened the door to the stable's adjoining house.

'Mam,' he bellowed. 'Da! You were right, she *did* come back eventually!'

'No but really, what happened?' fussed Nell's mother.

'Nothing, Mam,' lied Nell. 'I'm not in any trouble in London; I'm just helping out friends, and this kiddo.'

'Poor little dot,' murmured Nell's father, refilling Tem's cup with honey milk for a third time. 'No respect for the fae in that bloody country, nor dragons, that's what lost them the war, you know.'

'Da, please stop talking about the war like you were there; it was three hundred years ago.'

'I'm just saying,' her dad told her. He handed Amber yet another plate of offal.

'You're going to make those two sick, Da,' Nell sighed.

'I'm fine,' Amber told her, her mouth full of sheep intestine.

'*We* treat our magical community with grace,' her father said pointedly. 'It's how we won the war, Redthroat-be-praised, and the great dragon queen has bestowed a thousand blessings upon us ever since, so you eat up, *boneddiges ddraig*.'

'Shall do,' Amber replied happily.

'And your little shop definitely isn't in difficulty again or anything?' Nell's mother asked.

'No, Mam! It's thriving! I'll pick up more stock while I'm here, in fact! Do all the local craftsmen a favour by selling their stuff in my fancy London boutique!'

'What's a booteek when it's at home, then?' asked Rees, fully in Annoying Little Brother flow even at his big, grown-up age.

'It's French for "lovely shop",' Nell seethed. 'Lazare taught it me.'

'That your vampire fancy man, is it?' Rees grinned. 'Thought you'd be more into Cheekbones by here.'

'He is not a vampire and nobody's my "fancy man", and don't call Fang "Cheekbones",' snapped Nell.

'Well, it's lovely to have you home, fancy man or not,' Nell's father told her. 'But whatever your business is, it'll have to wait til tomorrow – it's late. Obviously, you all have free board with us for as long as you need. Rees, you're sleeping downstairs.'

'Aw, Da,' whined Rees.

'Nell needs her room back, and since neither of these fellows is her fancy man, they can share your old room.' Nell's dad smiled at Lazare and Fang. 'Hope you don't mind getting cosy, gentlemen – there's only one bed.'

Lazare couldn't sleep, again. And it wasn't just because he was hyper-aware of the man in the room with him. Fang had immediately, infuriatingly, offered to sleep on the floor instead of sharing the bed, and Lazare had been too tired from the road to complain or offer to swap, or just to generally be freshly offended at Fang's ongoing refusal to share a bed with him, as if Lazare wouldn't be able to keep his hands off him otherwise. But now, tired as he was, those bright, noisy worries yet again filled the dark quiet of night by dancing and caterwauling around his head, chasing sleep away.

'Are we doing the right thing?' he asked out loud.

'What choice do we have?' mumbled Fang from the floor. 'If we don't stop the curse, Elizabeth's guards'll never stop chasing us. That swan wanted to take Tem. We can't let that happen.'

'And now we're getting Nell's whole family involved,' worried Lazare. 'Even if we can break the spell, would people stop chasing Tem? And won't we all just... die? Who would protect Tem then?'

'We just need to get her home to the fae,' insisted Fang wearily. 'Then she'll be safe. She won't need us.'

'Won't she?' Lazare asked the dark. 'The fae didn't want her, Fang. We took her home and they refused her.'

'Because of us.'

'No. Because they're dicks.'

'Shut up,' sighed Fang.

'They were dicks to her before we got tangled up in this,' Lazare reminded him. 'They don't like half-human kids. Have you even asked Tem whether she wants to go back? She loves you. Loves all of us, adores Amber, but you... you're the one she goes to when she gets nightmares. You're the one she holds her arms up to, every time. She calls you "Dad".'

'Shut *up*. Don't try to guilt me into keeping the curse on all of us, just so we don't die.'

'Don't make out that not wanting us all to die is some sort of disgustingly selfish opinion! It's true, I don't particularly want to die alone in my twenties – how unreasonable of me. Nell doesn't want to die, either. Not all of us seek constant self-destruction, Fang. Some of us have dreams. Dreams that we can't pursue dead, or in Wales.'

'Is this still because there's no theatres in Carmarthen?' asked Fang. 'You do recall that the guards pecked down the door of Nell's shop? We had to get out of town – *so* sorry that keeping you from arrest and torture wrecked your dreams of being a famous actor.'

'You think that's where my dreams begin and end?' Lazare huffed. 'Fame and fortune? More fool me if it were; I haven't exactly succeeded on that front, have I?'

Fang sighed, and spoke again in a softer voice. 'I'm being harsh on you. Apologies.'

'It's fine, I'm used to it. Like I'm used to you sleeping on the floor instead of with me.' Lazare bit the inside of his lip, annoyed at himself for saying that second part. At least he didn't add out loud the further thought that jangled in his mind – *and you would rather be dead than spend forever in my arms.*

'I am genuinely sorry that this situation has messed up your dreams,' said Fang, and for a moment Lazare wondered if somehow the other man knew about the nightmares he'd been having. 'Nell's dreams too,' added Fang ruefully. 'Her poor shop. Honestly, I find it admirable that the pair of you have so much you want to do with your lives. But there's a bigger picture to worry about right now. There's a little girl who was hurt and tormented until she could make people immortal, and the dying old Queen of Upper England knows about her powers. She has to, right? That's why she wants to take her to the Tower. Wants to force Tem to create an even bigger army... The alchemist was bad enough; can you imagine what would happen if a human monarch got their hands on her? We *have* to undo the spell as soon as possible. Undo her powers entirely, if we can, and then...'

'Then send her back to a hole in the ground with people who don't love her.'

There was a pause. 'If there was another way...?' Fang trailed off, his tone almost hopeful, as if Lazare might have some other solution to hand, or that if only he could get to the end of the sentence, some brilliant new plan where they could all live happily ever after would spring fully formed from it.

Lazare could think of no other solution. No brilliant plan crawled from either of their heads, birthed like Athena. The silence stretched, becoming heavier between them with every second.

'We should t—' said Lazare at the same moment that Fang blurted, 'Listen, I—'

They both fell into another awkward silence, waiting for the other man to finish his thought. Neither did. Lazare raised one hand a little, contemplating lowering it down the side of the bed to brush Fang's side on the floor. He didn't. Fang had chosen the floor, and Lazare should respect that, not cajole the other man to join him. Bigger picture and all that. Instead, Lazare turned over to face him. Just to say goodnight. As he did, he was sure he caught Fang's outstretched hand darting back.

'Fang?' he asked.

'Try to sleep,' muttered Fang.

'You said you were sorry for my dreams, and Nell's,' continued Lazare. 'But what about you? Do you have any dreams?'

For half a second, Fang's dark eyes met Lazare's in the gloom, then Fang looked away. 'I always dream about a peach tree,' said Fang.

'I didn't mean literally,' sighed Lazare.

'I know,' mumbled Fang. 'Just... literal dreams are the only ones I'm ready to talk about right now. What about you?'

Lazare rolled onto his back again. 'Mostly, these nights, they've been about you.'

'Are you flirting with me again?'

Lazare risked a glance. Fang was turned towards him once more. Maybe it was the gloom, but that darkness in his eyes reminded Lazare of the way Fang had looked just before they had kissed. Two inky dark pools of want, begging him to dive in. And then, Lazare blinked, and saw burned into the back of his eyelids the image of Fang's face hanging slack, wet, gaping, drowned, those dark eyes lifeless hollows.

Lazare fully rolled over, curling into a ball, his back to Fang. 'No.'

CHAPTER EIGHT
THE WIDOWER AND THE EX

'Sleep all right, fellas?'

Nell's polite question was met only with a nod from Lazare and a noncommittal grunt from Fang as he gathered a freshly breakfasted Tem up in his arms. None of the travellers asked Amber how she had slept. If they had, she would reply that it was still taking her a while getting used to sleeping with a small child hugging her, but that this was now becoming a bit of a norm with Tem, who regularly insisted on cuddling the dragon as well as her dollie counterpart in the night, and it was pleasant enough, not to mention softer and warmer than curling up in a nest. Usually, Amber was used to nobody asking how she'd slept, or whether she wanted any more breakfast, but Nell's mother, father and brother had all asked after her already this morning. She'd been given a bowl of giblets, three eggs and a whole pan of bacon fat to lick clean. They'd called her '*boneddiges ddraig*'. She could get used to this sort of deference. It was just sad that Nell clearly hadn't inherited the rest of her family's manners. Indeed, the apothecary remained in a much grumpier mood than Amber was used to. And the two men clearly still hadn't sorted out whatever had been causing a weird, uncomfortable tension between them ever since the unpleasantness with Fang's repeated drownings. The things Amber put up with, honestly.

The rain had stopped, and early morning sunlight shone down on Carmarthen in rays through gaps in the cloud. Amber trotted alongside the others down the street as Nell talked about 'special dispensation to visit the Lost City of Llanelli' this and 'application through Redthroat's emissary for a royal audience' that. None of them even mentioned that they wouldn't need to do any special paperwork for Amber. As a dragon, she could just waddle straight into the Lost City of Llanelli any time she wanted. Probably they didn't want Amber to go ahead of them because they'd miss her too much, Amber decided. And she felt that she didn't need to proudly point out to them just how many of Carmarthen's citizens stopped to greet her politely with a bow, a curtsey, a tip of the hat or a '*bore da, boneddiges ddraig*'. Honestly, all that, for her? It was embarrassing, really; they were meant to be avoiding attention. It wasn't Amber's fault that round these parts, Tem wasn't the only person with a dragon fixation. She didn't want Fang or Lazare to get even more irritable than they already were, and she certainly didn't want Nell to feel bad that on her big homecoming trip, it was Amber who was getting all the attention.

'Oh! Excuse me!'

Amber puffed herself up a bit to greet yet another new admirer, and then deflated again when she saw that it hadn't been directed at her at all; Nell had accidentally bumped into a large man, causing him to drop a ridiculous quantity of chair legs, which immediately started trying to wriggle away. Nell stooped to help him pick them up.

'Sorry,' exclaimed the stranger, grabbing at writhing, enchanted wood. 'Wasn't looking where I went. I was startled by a goose.' The stranger looked over at Nell, and squinted, curious recognition in his eyes.

'Nell?' he asked. 'Nell ver'Evan?'

Nell sighed a little, warily. 'Yes?'

'It's me – Jenkin. From the enchanted carpenter's over the road from your shop... or, you know. Where your shop used to be. We were so sorry to see you close down. I always meant to go in, but you know how it is – money, time. And with Rowland being as sick as he was, we didn't... well, the doctor said that if he took any medicines it could affect the efficiency of the charms and healing spells...' He trailed off, and added quietly, 'For all the good that did.' With all the uncooperative chair legs collected now, Jenkin stood, clutching all the wriggling furniture parts to his broad chest. 'Still. Word is, you set up a new business in That London; is that...' He flicked a worried glance over Nell and the others. 'How's that going...?'

'Absolutely brilliantly,' replied Nell quickly. 'Just here on... business. London business. With some of my London colleagues.'

Jenkin bowed at Amber and, with a little gasp of realisation over what she was, bowed even deeper at Tem, allowing two chair legs to kick free from him again.

Nell picked up the squirming chair legs for him once more. 'And we're in a bit of a rush, so...'

'I'd love to hear about it,' added Jenkin, flustered. 'London, that is. If you have time, we could get dinner? I could catch you up on all the news from Carmarthen, although I suppose it'll all sound horribly parochial to a London businesswoman such as yourself.'

Nell softened a little. 'I'll see. Nice meeting you again, Jenkin. Give my love to your husband.'

'Oh!' replied Jenkin. Amber could tell Nell's faux pas even before her expression betrayed that she'd worked out what she'd said wrong too. 'Um, I'm afraid Rowland didn't... the doctors couldn't...'

'I am *so* sorry,' blurted Nell. 'Let's, yeah, let's grab a drink really soon, OK?'

'OK,' replied Jenkin, still clutching chair legs and watching her go as she scurried past, mortified, with the rest of the group in her wake.

Only once Jenkin was out of earshot did Nell acknowledge the sardonic smirk Fang had been giving her throughout. 'What?'

'You were mean to a widow. That's the sort of thing you'd tell me off for.'

'I didn't realise he was a widow.'

'And then,' added Lazare with a grin, 'you arranged a hot date with a widow. That's the sort of thing you'd tell *me* off for.'

'Not a date! Just a catch-up. A catch-up with a very attractive man who's good with his hands and is, due to a tragic illness that wasn't properly medicated, single now. And seemed kind of into me.' Nell blinked. 'God's Thumb, I think I'm accidentally dating a widow.'

'A window?' asked Tem.

'No,' replied Fang. 'Maybe we should discuss that after we've arranged passage to the Lost City of Llanelli, since

96

clearly the longer we're out on the streets of Nell's home town, the more she's going to accidentally agree to dates with her former neighbours.'

'One,' argued Nell. 'One accidental date, it's not like I'm going to keep—'

A woman in full bard garb ran straight into Nell, scattering pages of folio, her dropped lute bouncing across the cobbles, magically playing an arpeggio of distress as it went.

'Nellie?' asked the bard, picking herself up. 'Didn't you leave to set up shop in That London?'

Nell picked up the lute grumpily, holding it out at arm's length as it twanged miserably that the person currently clutching it was not its rightful owner.

'Yes, Sioned,' she told the bard, 'very successful, business trip, terrible hurry.'

'I'm so glad it worked out for you in the end,' Sioned the bard told her, taking back and soothing the lute. 'Your shop always looked so interesting; I'd have loved to have bought some of your stuff, but, you know. The Eisteddfod was coming up; I couldn't confuse this one's magic.' She petted the lute some more. 'Did you get my letters? I made Star Bard last year! So, both our dreams came true.'

'Yes,' replied Nell begrudgingly. 'And I'm happy for you, and… Gunhild, was it?'

'Oh! That relationship didn't work out,' replied Sioned. 'It wasn't that she was a vampire…' Here, she glanced awkwardly at Lazare. 'It was the Viking aspect; she was always trying to get me to write poems about Norse things – you try getting "Svaðilfari" into a sonnet.' She turned her attention back to Nell. 'One must be true to oneself in one's writing, like you were true to yourself with your little shop; even after it failed in Carmarthen, you made it work in London. Inspirational, is what you are. I should write a sonnet about that, really.'

'Well,' replied Nell, 'I'm glad I can still inspire you.'

'So am I. You were always so cool, Nellie.'

Sioned smiled at Nell for a moment longer than Amber felt should really be necessary.

'We know lots of pome writers,' squeaked Tem anxiously, as if to fill the heavy pause. 'One gave me this flower.' She showed Sioned the wilted flower Marlowe had handed her, still plaited into her dark hair. 'He wants something called a "magnifersent arse", and says my daddy has it.'

Fang and Lazare both coughed awkwardly, derailing the child.

'Well,' continued Sioned hurriedly, 'next Eisteddfod's coming up really soon...'

'Pardon, *mademoiselle*, but at this point I must ask,' interjected Lazare, 'what *is* an Eisteddfod?'

'Cultural festival,' Sioned told him proudly.

'So... food stalls, dances, that sort of thing?' Lazare asked.

Amber noticed the excitement of Tem's face at the suggestion of food stalls and dances.

'Kind of,' Sioned replied, 'but also it includes a highly tense and stressful poetry tournament to rank who's the best at poetry, the winner becoming the Star Bard.'

'You can't rank poetry from worst to best,' mumbled Fang. 'It's subjective.'

'Yes we can, and I'm the best,' Sioned informed him. 'If you wanted to challenge that, well, it's open entry. Come and have a go if you think you're bard enough.'

Fang glanced hurriedly around the group. 'We're actually on an important quest, and in a rush, so. We don't have time for poetry contests, or this little chat.'

Sioned scoffed a bit, and smiled at Nell. 'London folk are all hurry hurry hurry, aren't they? I'll let you get on. Mind the goose.'

'What goose?' Amber asked.

'Don't know, *boneddiges ddraig*,' admitted Sioned. 'There's just a goose about. We get much bigger magicals round here than geese, mind. That's Wales for you.'

Indeed, at that point, two large dragons loped past. Sioned clutched her hand over her heart as well as she could with her arms full and gave them a long, deep bow. Amber tried to give the dragons a friendly nod, but they barely paid any attention to her. Instead, they looked at the rest of Amber's group. Amber didn't much care for the other dragons' expressions.

'Whatever has become of manners?' the grey dragon asked Amber's companions. 'Have the humans of Wales forgotten to whom they owe their freedom? To which race they owe an eternal debt for Redthroat's many benevolent miracles?'

Nell's eyes widened with the realisation she had forgotten to bow to the dragons, and did so immediately, hand on heart. The grey dragon watched Fang and Lazare, with a sneer. 'Well?' he asked.

'They're not humans,' said the grey dragon's companion – a slightly larger dragon with iridescent blue scales. 'Can't you smell it on them?' The blue dragon nodded at Tem. 'That one's a fae... no. Half-fae. Yuck. Didn't know the fae-folk were still pumping those out.'

Fang, Lazare and Nell all bristled, almost as one. Nell straightened suddenly from her bow, dropping her hands to her sides with clenched fists. Amber's snout crinkled with disgust at the smell of the thin slime emanating from Nell's right wrist. She recognised the stench as dragonsbane, a dragon-deterrent potion Upper Londoners sometimes left on fresh graves during lean months. Lazare gripped Fang's arm and half-opened his wings, as if he were seconds away from flying both Fang and Tem away from the situation. Fang just glowered. A few feet away, underground sewage appeared to burble up from a nearby drain.

'They'll let all sorts into Carmarthen, I see,' huffed the grey dragon, sneering at the scene, and turning his own nose up at the growing dragonsbane stink, and the rising sewage. 'First that silly goose flapping all over town this morning, now whatever this mess is. I suppose that's Welsh hospitality for you – they may be literally ankle deep in turds, but they'll welcome anyone, even a half-breed.'

'Even,' added the blue dragon pointedly, 'if some of them *still* forget to bow.'

'We're not all Welsh,' Fang told the dragons frostily. A second drain began to seep sewage.

'A subject of the Ming,' noted the grey dragon in a particularly nasty tone. 'Well, *you* should mind your manners around us even more than others. Didn't we used to own you people?'

Amber really didn't like the way this was going. Tiny as she was compared to the other two dragons, she was still their peer, was she not? She took a couple of waddling steps forward, in what she hoped was an assertive fashion.

'That was centuries ago and half a world away', she reminded the bigger dragons. 'And technically it was the eastern loong who kept all the Cathayan humans in servitude, not us European dragons, so, y'know…' Any confidence she had quickly crumbled away under the twin glares of the other dragons. She cringed as they looked down their snouts at her, their nostrils faintly glowing with the casual reminders that they could incinerate a runt like her in a single puff. 'So, y'know,' she attempted, her voice cracking nervously, 'pack it in? A bit? Please?'

The blue dragon tried to create some particularly imposing nostril-embers, but gagged on the inhale. 'These wretches stink. All chemicals and half-breed magic. And look at the state of their drains. Disgusting. Let's just go and laugh at that goose again.'

They continued to lollop past the group, with the grey dragon flicking his tail at Fang and Lazare's ankles as he passed, knocking both men off their feet and onto their knees. Tem squeaked with shock and Fang had to scrabble not to drop her as he fell.

The grey dragon rolled a laugh like distant thunder. 'Good to see you smelly knaves kneeling after all. Remember that for next time.'

Amber said nothing, but glared angrily at them… after they had their backs to her, of course.

Sioned straightened from her bow and looked at Nell once more. 'Nellie,' she breathed, 'is that dragonsbane coming from you? Are you… not human anymore?'

'Yes on the potion,' replied Nell. 'And "not quite" on the human thing. It's a long story.'

Sioned beamed. 'That's even cooler!'

Nell gave Sioned a polite smile as the men got to their feet. As they set off towards the castle again, a man with a drain rod hurried over to the 'overspilling' drains, and was surprised to find they were completely fine.

'The dragons,' said Tem as they walked, her voice quiet with shocked distress. 'They were... *horrid*.'

'Yeah,' sighed Amber. 'Some of the bigger ones can get like that. Specially in Wales. They're always telling me, "Little runt, if you want respect you should go to Wales; the humans have manners over there." Dragons here must get used to being treated a certain way.'

'They *were* horrid, weren't they?' added Nell, troubled. 'I never noticed it before I moved to London, but Welsh dragons are awful. No offence, Amber.'

'None taken, pal,' Amber told them. 'It's not even as if those guys were royalty. Now, dragon *royalty*, you can understand *them* getting all high and mighty.'

'Oh, Redthroat would *never* behave like that,' said Nell, as if automatically. 'Everyone knows she's full of the grace eternal that comes from true power and majesty.' She looked around at the others awkwardly. 'At least, that's what I was always taught. My nan's neighbour's cousin met Redthroat once, and said she was magnificent. And, y'know. She did save Wales amongst her thousand years of magical miracles. She's great.' Nell gave Tem an encouraging little smile. 'She'll help us, just you wait and see. Dragon royalty have magical wisdom and power that even the fae could never dream of. Legend has it, it was the dragon kings and queens that made the fae-folk in the first place.'

'Ooh yeah,' chimed in Amber, 'I heard that one too.'

'A dragon made me?' asked Tem, her eyes wide with delight, her horror at the two mean bigger dragons' unpleasant behaviour chased away.

'Your ancestors, at least,' said Amber happily, pleased to have cheered up the child.

'It's only a story,' added Lazare cautiously.

'Maybe,' Amber conceded, 'but it's a nice story, right?'

Tem nodded enthusiastically, clutching her dragon doll and beaming. 'A dragon that can make fae.'

Amber noticed that Fang was sporting a rare smile as well. He elbowed Nell as they walked. 'You never told me you used to date the Star Bard of Carmarthen.'

'She wasn't Star Bard back the—' Nell broke off, realising what she was admitting to. 'You don't know Sioned's my ex!'

'Oh come off it, it's painfully obvious.' Fang smirked. 'She's still very into you, too. At least you didn't accidentally agree to a date with her like you did that widow.'

'Nellie,' called Sioned after them, 'if you're still around for the Eisteddfod, you could maybe come along? As my VIP?'

'Sounds great,' Nell called back hurriedly, before turning back to notice Fang's mocking grin. 'What?'

'You just did it again.'

Honkensby had only been in Carmarthen for about an hour, but she had already learned the hard way to avoid dragons and not to flap at humans. Back in Upper London, flapping at people was a wonderful means of establishing a good healthy sense of intimidation. Humans and undead alike would answer her questions quickly and courteously, while keeping wary eyes on her wings, and worrying about broken arms. In Wales, it just made the population – unused as they were to a properly disciplined Royal Guard of magical birds – run away in a panic. Honkensby *really* missed Upper London. She missed dragons knowing their place and having a bit of respect. Here, they just laughed at her. She had a nagging feeling they may have smelled through her disguise as well, and were only mocking when they continued to refer to her as a silly English goose, but even if it was meant in cruelty, at least her cover hadn't yet been officially blown. She really didn't enjoy going undercover disguised as a giant goose. The fake beak was uncomfortable, and she was generally concerned that dressing as a goose might be a bit racist. Honestly, she wasn't; many of her friends were geese. Or, at least, some of her associates were geese. She was sure she'd have goose friends if she had any friends.

She waddled up to a carpenter, who was struggling to carry armfuls of enchanted wriggling chair legs.

'Er, honk honk?' she said, cringing inwardly at her goose accent.

The carpenter jumped a little, clutching the chair legs tighter to himself. 'You, again! Don't flap at me; haven't you caused enough trouble already?'

Oh, no. She'd already run into this fellow this morning, hadn't she? She'd startled him so badly that he'd run off down an alleyway. She awkwardly looked around herself. An old woman with a wooden eye was watching the scene with suspicious interest.

'Apologies, mister. I am...' She sighed a little to herself. '... but a silly goose.'

The carpenter softened his tone and stance. Honkensby really didn't care for a human suddenly looking quite so relaxed and unwary around her. She wasn't used to that. 'Magical refugees from England like yourself often do take a while to settle down. You'll get used to it here. No more need to scrap over resources, no more need to hide underground. Just...

keep your beak down, yeah? Don't go throwing your weight around; the dragons won't like it. And if the dragons round here don't like your attitude, well. They might prefer you as an entrée, if you catch my drift. If you don't watch it, you'll be roast dinner. If you *really* don't watch it, you'll be pâté.'

Honkensby wasn't sure to make of any of that. Kindly intentioned as it was, it was still wasting her time. She decided to just come straight out with her questioning.

'Have you seen a group of foreigners with weird qi?'

The carpenter pulled a face at her. 'Weird cheese?'

'Qi, it's a Cathayan thing. One's from Cathay, one's got wings and a silly accent, there's a kid and a Welshwoman...'

'A Welshwoman wouldn't exactly be a foreigner, would she, Miss Goose? You've got to stop thinking like an English; you're with us now. Embrace it.'

'Yes, but have you seen them?' asked Honkensby. 'I had a tip-off that they were here. They seem undead but also not. They can do weird magic, and that's probably illegal here too, right? Unregulated magic? Disgusting stuff. One of the gong farmers said there was a weird problem with the drains today. Was that them? Think! It's important!'

'Why? Do they owe you money or something, Miss Goose? Let it go!'

'It's not that, it's just...'

One of the chair legs wriggled out of the carpenter's arms, and in his attempt to catch it, he dropped the rest of them. 'Bugger. One mo.'

'Ask a lot of questions for such a silly goose, don't you?' called the old woman with the wooden eye. 'What sort of goose be you, anyway? Your beak looks weird.'

Honkensby hurried away before the old woman could say any more and before the uncooperative carpenter could retrieve his chair leg and get a proper look at her. This guy definitely knew something. Her quarry had been in Carmarthen recently – maybe they were still here. She wished she could question the carpenter further. If she could get some evidence they'd broken a Welsh law, no matter how minor, maybe performed their strange magics without licence, then perhaps she could arrest them on that pretence – make out she was doing the Welsh king a favour, since none of Llewellyn's Royal Guards seemed to be operating in this town so far south. First, she needed to get eyes on the fugitives. Actually, no – first, she needed permission from the attaché, because technically until she had that, she wasn't supposed to be here – hence the disguise. She just couldn't sit around in Stroud and let the subjects of her pursuit get further and further away from her. She tried not to think about how she – *she* – was kind of sort of breaki – no – *bending* the law, at this moment. She *was* the law. Elizabeth's law. Not King Llewellyn's law, or Queen Redthroat's law. It was Queen Elizabeth's word that mattered. Being a good Royal Guard meant putting personal squeamishness aside for one's monarch, did it not? She just wished she could explain this logic to the pit of her stomach, which felt sick for every moment she was here, every law she kind of sort of bent.

The immortal fugitives were here. It was a small town. She would find them, no matter what, and bring them and the child back to her queen, and then it would all be OK; it would all be worth it. She began waddling as goose-ishly as she could, towards the castle.

CHAPTER NINE
THE CASTLE

Nell and the group walked through the castle. It was a bit of a warren, as repurposed old buildings so often are. Signs in Welsh and English pointed in different directions to the gaol, the tax office, town planning, the Mayor's office, the dragon reception lobby, Eisteddfod planning committee room, emergency housing department and the cafeteria, with an additional sign beneath the latter announcing that they couldn't cater for dragons or vampires until the next executions, which would be Thursday. Ignoring Amber's protestations that the dragon reception lobby might be nice, and could have a welcome pack for a little dragon or something, Nell found a sign for *Licences & Llanelli Consulate*, which took them through a long and winding corridor. She nudged Fang as they passed the Eisteddfod planning room.

'Sure you don't want to take up Sioned's challenge and apply?' she teased.

'Of course not,' replied Fang. 'Nobody can be the "best poet".'

'I could,' suggested Lazare. 'Apply, that is,' he added quickly, when they all looked at him.

'It's not an acting contest,' Fang reminded him.

'How sweet of you to believe I would fare well in an acting contest,' replied Lazare, 'but in fact I can also put quill to parchment, at a push. *Some* people think I'm pretty good at it.'

'Oh, well,' said Fang with a vaguely fond roll of his eyes, 'that *definitely* means you could beat Carmarthen's best bard in a poetry competition, in the middle of a quest.'

'You just said there was no such thing as a "best bard",' Nell reminded Fang. 'You should go for it, Lazare. Might wipe the smug satisfaction off Sioned's face.'

'Is this just a human mating thing?' asked Amber. 'Showing sexual interest by being mean to each other?'

Fang covered Tem's ears at the mention of sexual interest. 'What have I done wrong this time?' he asked the dragon.

'Not you,' Amber told him. 'Nell.'

'What?' asked Nell.

'You still like your ex,' Amber said matter-of-factly. 'And you like that carpenter. I could smell the pheromones on you when you talked to them; you reeked of potential sex.'

Fang, having wrongly assumed it was safe for Tem to hear the rest of the conversation, covered the child's ears again quickly, and glared poison down at Amber.

'But you're so huffy with them both, like how Fang is when he's pumping out sex pheromones.'

'Confucius's Liver, little dragon, if you keep talking, I swear—'

'They never came to my first shop,' said Nell quietly. 'None of these buggers did. They don't get to pretend they always supported me now I'm successful. So yeah, you go ahead and apply, Lazare. See if *my* cool London actor friend can teach them a thing or two. Carmarthen's not all that.'

'You think I'm cool?' Lazare beamed. He held up a dramatic hand. *'Mesdames et monsieur,* let us make haste to the application forms! I'm going to become a bard!'

'How comes he's got time to become a bard, but I don't have time to go to the dragon reception lounge and get a welcome pack?' Amber whined.

'We don't know there's a welcome pack,' Nell told the dragon for the fourth time.

'We are on,' Fang reminded them all urgently, 'a quest!'

And, thought Nell, yes, Fang had a good point. The Eisteddfod office was two twisty corridors and a staircase in the other direction now, and they were practically at the entryway to licences, with the Llanelli consulate just next door to that.

'Quest paperwork first,' she told them, 'poetry and revenge paperwork after.'

This seemed to satisfy everyone involved. Amber was even more satisfied when the woman arranging their passes for the Lost City of Llanelli informed the dragon that she was entitled to a welcome pack, after all. They didn't even need to go down to the dragon reception lobby; the bureaucrat just opened up a drawer in her desk and pulled out a bag of dried newts, pigskins and coupons for local butchers and coroners for the dragon.

The bureaucrat's attentions weren't on Amber, though, but Tem. She apologised profusely that she had no fae welcome pack to hand, called in a panic for the kitchen to roast Tem some acorns, panicked further when the child asked for chocolate and none was available, and was eventually persuaded by Fang that some honey milk and things for the child to draw with would be sufficient.

There was far more politeness in general than Nell was used to experiencing in Carmarthen. It left her with the same uncomfortable feeling that Jenkin and Sioned had given her that morning. Sioned had been fun and all, but Nell had definitely always come second to the poetry, which was why she hadn't felt guilty about letting the shop come before Sioned, until they had both been at a point where it was just the poetry and the shop, two lives and focuses sitting parallel, and they both stopped pretending it was anything but. As for Jenkin, in the old days, he'd offered her the same pleasantries he had to all his neighbours, but that had been it. She supposed that was understandable, with the weight his husband's sickness had pressed upon his soul, but something had changed now. And she wasn't sure it was just poor Rowland's passing.

She'd often dreamed of rolling back into town, her head held high, really sticking it to every sod who'd stood idly by watching her dream slowly die. She'd fantasised about the awe in their eyes, but now that she saw it, it felt... unearned, unpleasant, even. They didn't know how hard she'd worked; all they knew was that she was rocking up from London with a dragon and a half-fae child in tow – *that* was what impressed them. She was already regretting telling Lazare to apply for the Eisteddfod. So she had a handsome fancy flamboyant London friend – so what? If they were impressed by him, then that wasn't down to anything she'd actually done, was it? And, come on, he was no professional poet; he wasn't exactly a hot favourite to storm the contest. By that point, though, Lazare was too excited for her to bear even trying to talk him down with a 'Lazare, I changed my mind, I'm worried either you'll be good and steal my thunder or you'll lose spectacularly'.

Anyway, chances were it was all moot. In another couple of days, they'd have their passes to visit the Lost City of Llanelli and speak with Queen Redthroat, entreat the wise and mighty dragon queen to break their shared spell with one of her many gracious magical miracles. Nell would go back to being dead, and there would be no Eisteddfod for any of them. She had to keep reminding herself that her quest was a march towards her death. Stopping at Carmarthen was merely Nell's chance to say goodbye, to her family, her old neighbours, her ex. Maybe she should go on those dates with Sioned and Jenkin, while she could. She sniffed her right armpit, troubled.

'What on earth?' Fang asked, catching her at it.

'What Amber said about sex pheromones touched a nerve,' Nell admitted. 'My curse makes me leak my old aphrodisiac potion – right armpit. I'm just checking I'm not accidentally drugging people.' She offered him her armpit. 'This smell sexy to you?'

Fang recoiled. 'No. A lonely widower and your stuck-up ex asked you on dates; it doesn't mean you're chemically irresistible.'

And then, Fang did something Nell wasn't expecting.

'Which d'you think you'll choose?' he asked.

Nell decided not to reiterate out loud that if their quest went to plan, there would be no dating for any of them – no nothing for any of them at all. Instead, she flashed him a grin.

'I have to choose one?'

'You're impossible,' growled Fang, before snapping his head over to a fretful cry of 'Something happened!' from Tem, and hurrying over to mop up the ink that the little girl had spilled all over the flagstones.

Nell rushed to get blotting paper and help. She noticed the picture that Tem was holding up, out of the way of the spilled ink. It was of a girl and a little dragon protecting three stick people from two bigger, mean-looking dragons. Nell could already tell from the scratched-out details that the two stick people holding hands were meant to be Fang and Lazare, and the stick person in the big dress was meant to be her. Stick Nell had a big, wide smile.

It wasn't just Nell's old friends and family she had to say goodbye to in Carmarthen – it was this new family as well. The thought made Nell horribly sad. She would take this time to enjoy what she had, she resolved. At least they weren't all being chased anymore.

'A goose?'

'That's what all the reports state, Majesty,' Lady Angharad told the Welsh king. 'Waddling around Carmarthen, making a scene.'

In Dolwyddelan Castle, King Llewellyn frowned down at the sheaves of paper in front of him. '*Could* it just be a silly English goose seeking refuge from those wretched Deep English enclaves?'

'It *could*,' replied Lady Angharad. 'But it's asking a lot more questions than one would expect a silly English goose to ask.'

'What sort of questions would we expect a silly English goose to ask?'

Lady Angharad shrugged. As a winged cyhyraeth, her shrugs were always impressive and unsettling to witness. '"Honk honk, which way to Swindon?"' Lady Angharad suggested. 'It's all rather suspicious, Majesty, what with the missive from Elizabeth and the request that came in from the Stroud outpost this morning, for one of the English Crown's Royal Guards to conduct an investigation in your territory.'

'We didn't grant it, did we?'

'We're still telling the English it takes five days for messages just to get to you, Majesty.'

King Llewellyn snorted a little laugh. It was adorable that that potty old bag Elizabeth Tudor thought she was the only human monarch on this island with her own airborne fleet of magicals.

'And now, there's this,' added Lady Angharad. She passed the King a duplicate of a document fresh from Carmarthen's consulate to Redthroat. 'One of your subjects, asking for passage to the Lost City of Llanelli, along with a Frenchman, a Cathayan, a dragon and a fae.'

'That matches the descriptions our spies in the Deep London Embassy sent us,' noted the King. 'Chatter amongst the púca is, these travellers might have stumbled upon the secret to eternal life. But they vanished from Deep London days ago…'

'And it seems they have reappeared, on *your* soil, sire. Although, not for long. Doubtless, as soon as Redthroat realises who and what they are, she'll expedite their passage to Llanelli, and then they'll be out of your reach before you can say "special diplomatic relationship". And if that "goose" is working for Elizabeth, well. I wouldn't put it past the English Crown to pull a fast one, would you?'

King Llewellyn nodded. The secret of eternal life. Not undeath – something new. Something *better*. The actual prize that mankind's emperors had been searching for all those centuries ago, when they'd stumbled upon zombiism. Eternal life – the one thing that could raise humanity above all magickind, above even the dragons. With the prospect of James of Scotland taking over Upper England, and the war that would surely follow – the secret of eternal life. With the empires of Europe and the New World pushing at his little nation on all sides, the secret of eternal life.

With Redthroat forever breathing down his bloody neck from her golden nest in the city *she* took from *his* ancestors, demanding more concessions, more resources, more power, more special immunity for the magicals that just kept pouring into Wales, all in return for support in a conflict that had been over three hundred years before he was even born. He was sick of her telling him he should be grateful Wales hadn't been colonised while her subjects trampled all over the place throwing their weight around in a manner that often seemed rather colonial to him. Not that he would ever be rude enough to say so to his great ally Redthroat, of course. The Welsh Crown had always taken pride in respecting magicals even before the war; he had his court full of magical beings, did he not? It was his pleasure to make his land a haven to magical refugees from the purges and inequities of the rest of the British island, of course, but the practicalities of grace and gratitude were getting harder. Because of course the Welsh Crown appreciated the needs of magicals. And, because if he did not ensure there were livestock and cadavers aplenty for dragonkind, then how long before Redthroat requested the further concession to make limited human killings legal for magicals in his territory? How long before Redthroat requested that anyway? How confident was Llewellyn that he would be able to refuse it to a being who could immolate his fragile, mortal, human body in one snort?

The secret of eternal life.

He imagined such a secret in the claws of Redthroat, or that mad old crone Elizabeth, or, God forbid, James Stuart.

'Fetch Gruff,' he told Lady Angharad. 'You have done well, My Lady. Go and treat yourself to a really good screech off the ramparts.'

Lady Angharad curtseyed low, her tangled black hair cascading over the floor like ink spilled by a nervous child.

'There,' said Fang, mopping up the last of the ink. 'Good as new.'

It wasn't 'good as new' at all – that particular flagstone would have a dark stain on it for some time to come.

'I lost the ink,' sighed Tem. 'Lazare needed it to write his pome.'

Lazare gave her a smile. 'I'll write it in my head.'

Tem nodded seriously. This idea made sense to her.

Fang looked Lazare in the eye and drew his breath, and Lazare silently braced himself for some mocking barb, or a lecture on the futility of signing himself up for a poetry competition none of them may live to attend.

'So, what's it about?' asked Fang.

'*Quoi?*'

'Your poem, what's it going to be about? Upper London, I bet. Or French cooking, you're always banging on about that.'

'Or dragons,' squeaked Tem.

Lazare gazed at Fang. Fang's tone hadn't been in the slightest bit sarcastic. His expression was uncommonly candid. It was unsettling.

'Are you feeling all right?' Lazare asked him.

'I'm just asking about your poem.'

'Write it about dragons,' repeated Tem. 'That's what I'd write a pome about, if we had ink left and I could write.' She blinked. 'I'll write one in *my* head.' She scampered away towards Amber and Nell. 'Amber! What pomes with "dragon"?'

'Flagon?' called Amber helpfully. 'Wagon? Braggin'?'

Lazare continued to look askance at Fang. 'What happened?' he asked. 'You're exhibiting positivity. Were you hit on the head?'

'I've been hit on the head more times than you've had hot baguettes,' Fang told him, 'but that's not it today.' He lowered his voice, and Lazare saw a little glint of something he hadn't seen before in Fang's eyes. It looked like hope. A frantic sort of hope. 'What Amber said earlier, about dragons creating the fae...'

Lazare frowned. That was a folk tale! Fang didn't believe in that nonsense, surely? Fang didn't believe in anything.

'I've heard that story before,' continued Fang, with a quiet intensity. 'In my homeland, they said huli jing and other minor magicals were made by the king of the loong. And then, in the Mughal Empire, the Ottoman Empire, Egypt, Europe... different versions of that story kept coming up. The highest-ranking dragons, creating magicals.' Fang searched Lazare's expression. 'I mean, it makes sense, right? Old Emperor Qin Shi Huang made the undead races. The alchemist made... whatever it is we are. Or he made Tem, and forced her to make us, so it's possible...'

'Where are you going with this?' Lazare asked, still troubled by the unfamiliar glint in Fang's eyes. There was something desperate about it, like the desperation of their one kiss, like Fang was grabbing on to something – anything – for dear life.

'What if Redthroat can make fae?' Fang's expression was almost pleading now, begging Lazare to follow his logic and tell him it was sound. 'What if Redthroat can make *us* fae? Then we wouldn't be these strange new immortal things anymore; we'd just be fae. Pointy ears, long but not eternal lives, glamour magic – you and Nell would probably enjoy having glamour magic more than I do. That's a concession we could all live with, right? If we were just normal fae, we'd be no prize for Queen Elizabeth, her guard would stop chasing us around, and... well. If we were fae, then we wouldn't be polluting Tem's magic with our humanness anymore. And, we could go with her to the fae enclave. We could stay in her old home, at the edges, away from the other fae, and we could look after her. Together. The four of us, and Amber could visit. You'd be a proper Deepsider; you could join the Deepside Players, or write poetry, write plays! Give that lecherous zombie Christopher Marlowe a run for his money.' Panic started to set in to Fang's expression as he continued to search Lazare's bewildered face. Fang reached out a couple of fingers and rested them against the chest of Lazare's doublet, silently imploring him, seemingly without realising he was doing it. 'We wouldn't have to die, not yet. Isn't that what you all want? Isn't that what *you* want, Lazare? Another way? Uncrushed dreams? A future?'

It was the most far-fetched plan Lazare had heard yet, in several days' worth of deeply far-fetched plans. But it was, at least, a plan. No. It was more than that. His blinks of surprise were not merely due to Fang's straw-clutching coming from something as insubstantial as a folk tale. Fang wasn't choosing death anymore. His hope lay in finding a way to keep them all together now, instead of splintering them apart in oblivion.

It wasn't exactly a declaration of love, or even an acceptance of Lazare's love, but it was, for once, a reversal of rejection. A shunning of despair. This was big. Fang wanted to live! He wanted to live together with Lazare. And with Tem, Nell and Amber, obviously, who were all very important too, Lazare reminded himself hurriedly. Yes. Lazare wanted a future, desperately, and one with Fang by his side in some gorgeously carved fae abode sounded infinitely better than dying – but he needed Fang to have everything he wanted too. He needed Fang to have the peace he'd been chasing all his life. Would a lengthy fae existence bring that? Fang had already been hurt and humiliated so much in his life, and not just by that *connard* alchemist.

'Is that what *you* want?' Lazare asked him.

'I want another way, too. I want...' Fang glanced over at Tem. 'I want to be sure she's OK.' He paused. 'No. I want to be sure you're *all* OK.'

And would Fang be OK?

Fang's drowned face, frozen in agony, his hair pooling in the water. The alchemist's disgusting smirk on revealing he'd gone back in time to seduce Fang at his lowest ebb. The desperation of Fang's kiss, the desperation of the fingers now against Lazare's chest. Lazare tried to chase the thoughts away, and focus only on that spark of hope in Fang's eyes when he'd mentioned this ridiculous, thoughtful, lovely plan. Lazare attempted a genuine smile.

'It's certainly worth a try,' he told Fang. 'The fae are stuck-up assholes, but I could bear living amongst them, with you.'

Fang looked down, and seemed to realise for the first time that he was touching Lazare's doublet. He pulled his fingers away. 'I wanted to say...'

'With *all* of you,' added Lazare hurriedly, accidentally talking over him. He stopped himself quickly. 'I'm sorry, you wanted to say...?'

Fang hesitated.

'Lads,' called Amber, 'come and listen to Tem's poem! It's called "Amber is a Brilliant Dragon"!'

'It's not called that,' added Tem quietly.

Amber huffed a little. 'Well, the title's a work in progress.'

CHAPTER TEN
IT'S A LOVELY DAY IN CARMARTHEN, AND YOU ARE A HORRIBLE GOOSE

'Travel visas to the Lost City of Llanelli usually take a few days even though we're just around the bay,' Nell told them as they made their way back to her parents' house. 'They've got to get paperwork sealed in crystallised dragon spit and whatnot. We should get comfy here til tomorrow at least.'

'Time enough for you to go on both dates?' Fang teased.

'See, "accidentally ending up dating two different people in my hometown" is exactly the sort of circumstance for which I wish I'd packed more underpants,' Nell teased back, 'but you said no.'

Fang snorted a little laugh. He felt lighter than usual. He was used to feeling a sense of relief whenever he fled west, but in the past, it had come with an ache of loneliness and despair, that he was just escaping again, and that it was impossible to run away forever. For once, he felt as if there was something he could run towards. He wasn't naïve; he knew the chances of getting Redthroat to allow them to stay in the fae enclave were slim, but... their chances were always slim, and they'd muddled through on those slim chances so far. This plan was something to at least try to grasp, and for once he wanted to grasp. Tem clung to him, and 'walked' the toy dragon over his head, making up a story about telling 'mean' Welsh dragons to behave in a voice so tiny that only Fang could hear it, soft up against his ear. Lazare walked ahead, and Fang couldn't help but allow his gaze to settle on the other man's gait – that silly, rolling strut that he'd initially assumed Lazare was putting on for show. Lazare's huge wings, folded over his back like a warm, buff leather cape, obscured most of him from behind, but the strut remained. He looked ridiculous, like some exotic bird embarking on a mating dance.

'You're smiling,' noted Tem.

'Just thinking of something funny,' Fang lied.

Tem nodded, and laughed a little, as if joining in with his imaginary funny thought. 'Like the goose?'

'Mm?'

'They say there's a big goose in town, being all silly.'

'So they do,' replied Fang.

Tem's smile twisted into a sudden expression of worry. 'Was it a goose chasing us, before?'

'No,' Fang told her, 'that was a—'

'Nell,' cried Jenkin, running into the group. The carpenter was carrying a small end table that wriggled in his arms like a cat that didn't want to be picked up. 'I was looking for you!'

'Er, yeah,' managed Nell, 'listen, earlier, did I agree to a date?'

'Yes, but that's not... it's the goose, Nell.' Jenkin tried to pull a serious face, which was very difficult to pull off while wrangling with a small table. 'She was asking all these questions.'

'Why do we keep hearing about this goose?' Lazare asked. 'We haven't even seen a goose; are you *sure* it was a goose?'

'That's the thing,' Jenkin admitted. 'I'm don't know. Its beak was weird. It could be two gnomes in a goose suit. Or a dragon wearing feathers. Anything!' He rested a hand on Nell's shoulder – again, not easy while trying to placate a wriggly table. 'I think it would be best if all of you came to hide out in my workshop til the goose is gone. Perhaps I could make dinner—'

He was interrupted by the twanging of a magical lute. 'Nell,' cried Sioned, hurrying to the side of Nell that was not currently occupied with a widowed enchanted carpenter. 'Thank goodness I found you. You guys need to hide.'

'From the goose?' Fang asked. 'Jenkin was just saying—'

'Not from the goose,' interrupted Sioned. 'Although, yeah, that goose isn't right; have you seen it? It's bloody English; I don't trust it. No, this is something else, er...' She looked around herself frantically. The street was full of passers-by, giving the group understandably odd looks. 'Why don't we go back to mine and talk it through?'

'They were coming back to my workshop, thank you,' Jenkin told her.

'What,' replied Sioned, 'your very open carpentry workshop that everyone knows about?'

'The goose doesn't know about it,' argued Jenkin.

'We are not talking about the goose,' hissed Sioned in reply. 'We're talking… look, can we all just take as read that a Star Bard is party to certain information that a carpenter isn't, and go back to my place with its lovely, *quiet and private* thinking spot where we can talk further?'

'Why should we?' Fang asked. 'Why should we all go back to either of your places? It's Nell you both want; I'm sure you can all settle on a means to share her…'

Nell tutted at him.

'Trust me,' Sioned told them, 'you'll want to come back to mine. Hasn't one of you signed up to the Eisteddfod? You'll need peace and quiet to write your poem.'

'Wait, how did you know that?' asked Lazare. 'I only just signed up, minutes ago.'

'I *know* stuff, OK?' asked Sioned. Unplucked, the lute on her back played an ominous tune. 'Come with me and hide.'

'How are you going to hide them from a goose with that thing playing incidental music all the time?' Jenkin asked, nodding at the lute.

'We are not hiding from a goose!' Sioned had to raise her voice over her lute's background music. She tugged at Nell's shoulder a little. Jenkin tugged back, jolting Nell in the other direction.

'Stop it, the pair of you,' Nell told them. 'I didn't come home to be fought over by a hot carpenter and my hot ex. I came here to help my friends.'

'That's what I'm trying to do,' chorused Jenkin and Sioned.

'Come on, Nell,' shouted Sioned. 'Look, I was warned by a crone, OK?'

'What crone?' Nell demanded.

'Just a crone, with a wooden eye. You can always trust a crone in Carmarthen.'

Jenkin pulled at Nell. 'Oh, and this mysterious "crone" told you Nell *had* to go to yours?'

'Just trust me, Nell,' argued Sioned. 'I can even help your French friend write a poem...'

Sioned pulled Nell so hard that she caused Nell to stumble. Lazare darted over and pulled both would-be suitors off the apothecary.

'I don't need your help,' he shouted over the increasingly bombastic lute music. 'I already *have* a poem! My lover's smile is not a beaming sun...'

Wait, thought Fang. *What?*

'We don't have time for you to start reciting poetry,' argued Sioned, but Lazare was already in full flow, shouting angrily above the music.

'It does not warm the world, bring day to night,' continued Lazare.

'It does not shine for free on everyone,

It is a small and precious candlelight...'

All the warm lightness in Fang was eroding away at Lazare shouting out those words for everyone to hear. He felt a heaviness on his chest, a panic, with a hefty added weight of self-admonishment. He'd encouraged Lazare to write a poem! He'd even dangled the prospect of a future for him and Lazare in front of the man! He should have known! But Lazare should have known too, right? If he truly understood Fang as much as he claimed, he should have known he would never want something like this. 'What?'

'Once hidden, now revealed to just we few,' cried Lazare.

'This firelight dances sometimes just for me

And I rejoice in its sweet glow anew

Each time he shares...'

'What the *Hell*, Lazare?' Fang shouted, cutting him off.

'What?' asked Lazare. 'Don't you like it? I didn't put in any half-rhymes this time.'

'Is that supposed to be me?' shouted Fang over the increasingly frantic and angry lute music.

'Well, yes,' Lazare yelled. 'I have made my feelings plain enough, have I not? You said to write a poem; what else did you think I would write it about?'

Fang shook his head, agog. How... *dare* he. Lazare had barely spoken to him of romance for days – had barely been able to hold eye contact – and now he was coming out with this? Their small moments, his private vulnerabilities, his confusion and pain, just out there for everyone, commodified and mangled into a sodding meter, made all *nice*.

'How *dare* you!'

'We don't have time for this,' shouted both Sioned and Jenkin.

Tem, still terrified of raised voices, trembled in Fang's arms. He held her tighter, even as Lazare threw his hands up into the air in a pantomime of frustrated despair.

'What now?' Lazare cried. 'Do you still tell me how I feel? Do you still deny that I love you, that you have somehow seen into my soul and found no feeling there of substance? Do you still claim to hold all rights to love, that there can only be one love and it must be nothing but pain?'

The swirling anger reminded Fang of every awkward, sad silence since their one dreadful, desperate, wonderful, aborted kiss. Every time since then that Lazare had refused to meet his gaze. The few times that Fang – *Fang!* – had tried to start a conversation about the way that their relationship had been left, only to be shut down. Fang hated talking about feelings! So Lazare couldn't talk to Fang about it in privacy but he could blurt a sonnet out in front of everyone? This wasn't fair.

'That's not fair. I don't do that!'

'Yes, you do! And now apparently I can't even write a poem about it?'

'Well, certainly not right now,' argued Sioned. 'Come *on*!'

'You have your rights to whatever ridiculous denials you choose to hold,' argued Lazare, 'but *my* feelings are my own!'

'Stop shouting?' squeaked Tem.

'Then why display your private illusion of me for everyone to see?' Fang railed. 'Shouting it in the street. Were you going to perform that on stage in front of hundreds?'

'Thousands,' corrected Nell.

'Yes, I was,' argued Lazare. 'I thought it was good.'

Sioned twisted a quick 'not really' expression. 'You did know that for Eisteddfod, it's meant to be in Welsh, right?'

'*Merde*. Would French do?'

'Obviously not. Let's discuss this at mine,' Sioned said, tugging at Nell again. 'You need to lay low. Right now.'

The panic in Fang was still rising, and not just because of the tussle between Nell's would-be suitors, neither of whom

Nell seemed to trust an inch. He tried to tell himself that it was simply anger at Lazare's poem, that it was dishonest... no – too honest... no – dishonest. Looming up behind the helixing spirals of conflicting rage at Lazare was a further thought that he kept trying to ignore. The rage at Lazare was a lie. Lazare was not the dishonest one here. Lazare was not the illusionist amongst them. Fang was. Fang had filled himself with so many ugly lies that they had started magically spilling from him. Inside and out, the ugly lies were his defence; he *needed* them! The thought of someone seeing through them, wafting them away like mist, terrified him. So why, the looming thought asked him, to his shame, did he keep courting it? With Lazare, and with Tem, Nell and Amber as well? He didn't want to be seen, but he did. The idea of it comforted as much as it terrified. The looming thought slapped him with a horrible truth.

You're angry, it told him with a sting, *because a part of you thought his terrible poem was lovely.*

The slap of the thought hit through to older wounds, an old bruise on his soul that had never healed. Memories of the last time someone had seen him, had made grand, public gestures of their feelings, spun a beautiful image of him that he'd wanted to believe in. Memories of screams and blood and dashed fox fur.

You're doing it again, said the thought, and Fang couldn't stand it anymore, forced himself to ignore the thought again.

'It wasn't even really me,' Fang cried at Lazare. 'It's a made-up, nicer me because everything's a performance for you!'

'Stop shouting,' repeated Tem.

'Ha!' cried Lazare. 'Says you! Mr Shamble-Pants. I've seen behind the grouchy mask. I've seen your little smiles.'

'No! No, you just imagined it for your stupid poem...'

'You have hope, *monsieur*! Admit it! You have hope and joy and love!'

For a moment, the swirling anger dispersed, and the great, dark, looming thought stepped back, and yes. He could admit to himself that there was hope within him – hope that had not been there before Lazare and Tem had fallen into his life. It was a small and fragile thing – a new butterfly, stretching out its translucent, shimmering wings as it emerged. It needed to be protected, kept nestled amongst leaves, because to get too close to it right now would be to kill it. Within the core of that butterfly of hope, he knew, was another spiralling paradox. It was created from the very hope that he was worthy of that same hope. Created from the hope that maybe this time, the hope wasn't a horrible trap, to lull him and one he loved to doze in one another's arms as hatred and danger and pain crept closer. The dark and looming thought rushed back, with the shrieks of a dying vixen. Screams and blood and dashed fox fur, and... tears running from Lazare's warm brown eyes, a perfectly coiffed beard stretched in a scream, mangled, mighty, tawny wings, and...

'No!'

'Stop *shouting*!' Tem wriggled right out of Fang's arms and ran from him. She only fled as far as Amber, hugging the dragon for comfort, but it hit Fang like an icicle to the stomach. Fang found himself meeting eyes with Jenkin, looking oddly smug that he was still successfully holding his own wriggly ward of an enchanted table. He moved his gaze away, only to catch Lazare's eye. Lazare looked away quickly, his expression a second stab of ice to the gut. He tried looking at Nell, but she had her eyes on the sky, with a deeply worried expression.

'You guys?' she said. 'I think the hot local dickheads were right.'

'Yeah,' said Jenkin, looking up.

'I did say,' added Sioned, doing the same.

There were two large shapes in the sky, both coming towards them – one from the north, the other from the direction of town. One was a giant bird.

'The goose,' sighed Jenkin.

'That's no goose,' breathed Amber.

'It's not the goose I'm worried about,' Sioned told them.

'It's not a goose…'

'It's *that*,' continued Sioned, pointing at the other shape.

It was further away, but at least twice the size of the giant bird. It wasn't a dragon, either. It was too furry.

'The adar llwch gwin,' Sioned told them, pulling Nell away. 'We need to hide from him.'

'The what?' asked Lazare.

'King Llewellyn's right-hand monster,' Sioned told them. 'Body of a lion, head and wings of an eagle.'

'So,' said Fang, 'a griffin, then.'

'No,' snapped Sioned, 'an adar llwch gwin. And he's here to abduct you and take you to the King, so come on.'

'Well, that's a coincidence,' called Lazare as they all finally followed Sioned's lead in earnest.

'Why?' asked Jenkin.

A giant white bird that was very obviously Captain Honkensby in a ridiculous fake beak, flapped down and landed aggressively, blocking their path. 'Come with me,' she said, 'if you want to live.'

Fang stepped defensively between Honkensby and the others. 'We're going to live, whether any of us like it or not.'

'Then,' Honkensby replied, 'come with me if you don't want your eternity to involve having your eyes and livers pecked out.'

'Is that a threat?' asked Fang.

'No,' snarled Honkensby through the terrible wooden beak, 'it's a warning. Come! Right now!'

'Geese can't peck out livers,' sneered Sioned, pulling Nell towards a side street.

'I am no goose.' Honkensby shook her head, and the wooden beak fell with a sad little *donk* to the cobbles.

'God's Thighs,' Jenkin gasped, dropping his table, which scampered over to kick the little wooden beak. 'There's a swan under there!'

'Swans can't peck out livers either,' Fang reminded Honkensby.

'I'm not talking about me,' Honkensby snapped. 'I'm trying to help you, you eggs! The Welsh king's sent his griffin after you!'

'I,' boomed a voice above them, 'am an adar llwch gwin.' There was the deepest flap Fang had ever heard, and a great shadow fell over them all. Fang and all the others looked up. Tem whimpered and clung even tighter to Amber's neck, choking the dragon a little. The beast descending upon them was the size of an Asian elephant. The black hooked beak alone was bigger than Fang's head. Brown feathers covered its head, neck and twenty-foot wings, fluffing into fur over its lion-like body. As it landed with a scrape of claws and a heavy *floomph* of feathers, blocking their alternative path of escape, Fang was certain of two things – they were in big trouble, and, come on, that was definitely a griffin.

'You may call me,' added the adar llwch gwin, 'Gruff.'

'Griff?' repeated Lazare

'*Gruff*,' Nell corrected him, although honestly, it sounded exactly like 'Griff' to Fang, and did it really matter? Every one of his friends had been pronouncing *his* name slightly wrong since he'd met them; he just couldn't be bothered to put them right at this point.

'If I didn't want people to think I was a griffin, I certainly wouldn't go around being called "Griff",' huffed Honkensby, drawing herself up and spreading her wings a little to make up for the fact Gruff was thrice her size and looked ten times more ferocious.

'And if *I* were one of Elizabeth Tudor's little serving-birds, I wouldn't encroach on King Llewellyn's territory and try to sneak one of his subjects and assorted magicals out of his country without any of the correct paperwork,' Gruff replied. 'You don't even have permission to set a flipper past Hereford yet, do you?'

Honkensby stretched her neck out even longer. 'I was never going to receive said permission, was I?'

Gruff rumbled a laugh. 'When did you work that out?'

'Soon enough,' replied Honkensby. 'I simply applied logic and the Welsh king's stubborn inability to co-operate with—'

'It was when you saw me flying in a few minutes back, wasn't it?'

Honkensby's eye twitched ever so slightly. 'What's important is these people are fugitives from the Upper English Law, so they're under arrest.'

'Not if they've been keeping their noses clean in Wales, they're not,' snapped Gruff, circling Honkensby and Fang's group with the heavy, easy pace of a large cat around a trapped nest of mice. 'King Llewellyn believes in second chances – in fact, he sent me to extend a royal invitation to all of you – not you, Honkensby. Miss ver'Evan's party.' He loped towards Tem, and softened his voice when he saw that the child still shrank back from him in fear. 'It has been so long since we have heard of a half-fae being born; His Majesty would love to meet you, young miss. The Welsh king knows how to show magicals respect, and perhaps if any of you had any magical problems, he could help?'

Tem blinked, and gazed up at Fang hopefully. Fang trusted Gruff about as far as he could throw him, and he really wouldn't be able to throw a creature of that size very far at all.

'Ah,' interjected Honkensby with a slightly manic air of triumph, 'but they haven't been keeping their noses clean!' She nodded at Fang. 'That one's been performing forbidden new magic. Multiple witnesses saw him make a drain overflow and then go back to normal again.'

'Hardly a crime worthy of an international operation,' replied Gruff, still far too close to Fang and Tem for comfort. 'And if said magical crimes did take place here in Carmarthen, then I am afraid it is I who must arrest them, in the name of the King.'

Yep, there it was. Gruff's intervention was definitely not one of warm diplomacy, as if there had ever been any doubt. Fang took a couple of steps towards Amber and Tem, meeting eyes meaningfully again with Nell. Perhaps the swan and the adar llwch gwin fighting between themselves was just the distraction they needed to make an escape. It was a big risk, especially now they had to ensure Sioned and Jenkin's safety, thanks to Nell's ridiculous sex appeal round here, but right now, it was preferable to being taken prisoner by either monarch. Lazare was right by Fang's shoulder, as if reading his mind.

'These fugitives have caused chaos in both Upper and Deep England these past few days,' continued Honkensby hotly. 'I'm sure you don't want to hamper an investigation into those who have menaced your peaceful neighbour Elizabeth *and* Redthroat's throne...'

Gruff narrowed his yellow eagle eyes. 'What have you heard from Redthroat?'

With both of their would-be captors distracted by the intricacies of geopolitical rivalry, Fang decided to leg it. He darted towards a gap behind Gruff, yanking Jenkin along by the collar. He reached down to scoop up Tem, but Amber had already taken off at his cue with the child, remaining in no mood to be picked up by Fang, on the little dragon's back. Nell grabbed Sioned's elbow and followed at speed.

'No you don't,' chorused Honkensby and Gruff. Honkensby flapped towards them as Gruff began the arduous task of turning his massive body. This was probably a bad idea after all, thought Fang. It wasn't enough of a distraction for them to all get away safely. Perhaps if Lazare carried Jenkin, then…

But Lazare was already airborne. He soared over Fang's head in a single flap and landed between the group and the two creatures chasing them, his wings fully spread. Before Fang could double back, grab him and tell him not to be a fool, Lazare flapped again – not to lift himself off the ground this time, but with his wings tilted to gust dusty air at the swan and the adar llwch gwin, causing them to shrink back, guarding their eyes.

'Go,' cried Lazare.

Fang shoved Jenkin at Nell and grabbed the back of Lazare's doublet. 'Not without you, clown.'

Lazare flapped again. 'So I'm now not to write poems or even save your bacon?'

'Not now, Lazare!' Fang tried pulling Lazare backwards as he flapped, but the Frenchman stood firm. A quick glance over his shoulder showed that the others were almost at a narrow alley where Gruff at least wouldn't be able to follow. He was loath to admit it, but Lazare's ridiculous, dangerous gallantry was actually sort of working. Perhaps if he and Lazare stood and fought together, Fang could also get that silly brave parakeet of a man out of danger. Fang concentrated, and the wind that Lazare blew at the pursuers became thick and black with flies.

'Get *out* of here,' cried Lazare.

'Nope.'

'I'm still mad at you.'

'I'm still mad at *you*.'

'It was just a poem!'

'It wasn't just the poem, it was what's beneath the poem. You still won't even—'

Gruff's giant, murder-beaked face loomed out of the cloud of dust, wind and flies towards them. 'Interesting,' he boomed. 'These two are tupping, swan.'

'We are not,' chorused Fang and Lazare.

'How can you see through this?' called Honkensby from within the maelstrom.

'Nictitating membrane,' Gruff told her proudly. 'And now if you don't mind, let's have you two lovers away to the King. Or should I hurt one of you, and make the other one watch?'

Fang could only see the side of Lazare's face, but the panic on his expression was clear. He stopped flapping his wings immediately, and held up his hands.

'I surrender,' called the Frenchman. 'Don't hurt him.'

'Lazare.' Fang tried thickening the fly illusion. Maybe Gruff had eye protection from wind and dust, but what good would that do if blocked by an illusion he couldn't see through? 'Come on! What are you doing? I've been hurt before; I'm always fine.'

'No.' Lazare's breaths were fast and shallow. 'I can't watch it happen again, Fang, I can't...'

'Quacking Hell,' came Honkensby's voice, 'you *are* tupping. That's interesting indeed.'

'We are not "tupping",' called Fang. 'Lazare. You're just panicking. Come with me.'

'Lads,' called Nell, running back into danger, both hands dripping noxious potions, 'come with me.'

Honkensby flapped desperately to try to rise above the fly cloud. 'You're coming with *me*.'

'No,' growled Gruff, pounding forth with his great paws and standing right in front of them, his head still covered in flies, 'they're coming with *me*.'

There was a huge plume of flame, many times bigger than anything Amber could have mustered up. It arced towards Honkensby and Gruff. Both dodged it just in time, and Fang learned a new Welsh curse word in the process. Fang turned to see where the fire had come from, and saw a depressingly familiar set of faces. Sioned and Jenkin both lingered in the mouth of the alley, gazing back at Nell in concern. Amber and Tem had also not got far. They were on the roof of a nearby building, flanked on both sides by two large dragons – one grey, and one blue. The dickhead dragons from earlier. Had they just been saved by a pair of dickhead bully dragons? As little as Fang wanted to owe a debt of thanks to two such awful blaggards, he'd still take it if it meant everyone's safety was assured, although from Amber's hunched, worried body language, their safety likely was *not* yet assured.

Fang relaxed his focus on the illusion, and the flies vanished. Gruff stared up at the two dragons, cocking his head a little, birdlike. A magical apex predator sizing up two rivals.

'Greetings from King Llewellyn V,' Gruff called to them, in an assertion of royal authority.

'Well met,' called down the blue dragon, 'and greetings in return from the court of Her Ancient Majesty Queen Redthroat the Invincible.'

Fang heard Gruff emit a faint, frustrated growl. Behind him, Honkensby began backing away, it now plainly clear that the swan was entirely out of her depth here.

'Miss ver'Evan, Messrs Quitbeef and Fang,' called down the blue dragon grumpily, 'your request for passage to the Lost City of Llanelli and an audience with Queen Redthroat has been granted by royal decree.'

'How?' Honkensby called incredulously. 'They've only just got here; isn't the paperwork meant to take weeks? How quick can your bureaucrats possibly be?'

'Well, they're púca, so pretty bloody fast,' called down the grey dragon, his voice dripping with the same sneering aggression as before. He spat a crystal down at Fang's group. It smashed in half in front of their feet, spattering their shins with crystal flakes and globs of its wet, sulphurous coating. Nell reached down and pulled a damp scroll from the shattered crystal.

'Seal's legit,' muttered Nell cautiously.

'Bugger,' breathed Gruff.

'Quack,' huffed Honkensby.

Lazare's panic was abating – actually, no, thought Fang, it wasn't exactly that, it was more that Lazare was... swallowing it, somehow. Gulping down the foul, rising fear and replacing its outwards appearance with his usual paint-thin mask of smiling charm, like a colourful mural daubed over a rotting wall.

'We thank you for informing us so swiftly, good dragons,' Lazare called up, 'indeed, your system is so fast that it has rather caught us unawares, as you can see. We would be thrilled to journey to the great dragon city tomorrow, after taking tonight to settle our affairs here – thank our hosts, feed and calm the child; one of us promised to go on two separate dates...'

'You can send letters of thanks to your hosts,' grumped the blue dragon, 'and we have plenty of dates in Llanelli, couriered fresh from Damascus by an azhdaha, everything you could wish for in our magical land. And the child will have every whim catered to – she will be fed; she will be calm.'

That last bit had definitely sounded more like a demand than a gentle assurance.

Still, Tem clung to Amber.

'This runt...' The grey dragon corrected himself. 'This little one can be your personal dragon chaperone if you wish, young faelet. There will be milk and honey. In a teeny tiny porcelain saucer.'

Tem hesitated, then whispered something into Amber's ear.

'She says "And chocolate?"' called Amber to the larger dragons.

'I can get you chocolate,' blurted Honkensby desperately.

'Bribing children?' Gruff sighed down at her. 'Isn't that beneath you, swan?'

'Not a bribe,' panicked Honkensby, 'just a sweetener, a display of Elizabeth's generosity! We've got loads of freshly confiscated chocolate back at the Tower; it'd just be... putting it to good use.'

'Wait,' added Nell, 'you mean *my* chocolate? From *my* shop? You'll put that back where you found it, thank you.'

'And now you've been stealing from a Welsh business-woman?' Gruff added. 'Honkensby, I thought you were by the book.'

Honkensby took a second, clearly thinking of a witty and watertight reply. 'Shut up,' she hissed, flustered.

'Chocolate,' announced the blue dragon after a moment of conferring with his grey companion, 'can be arranged. What say you?'

Tem shot a glance to Fang, as if seeking his assent.

It was a leap of faith, but what choice did they have? There was no way he was letting Honkensby or Gruff arrest them. Redthroat's messenger dragons were kind of arseholes, but that did nothing to change the fact she was their best chance of a happy future, for Tem, for Nell. For Lazare and him. For… for Lazare and also for him, separately.

He risked another glance at Lazare. The fear that the Frenchman had swallowed down looked like it was in danger of being vomited back up, along with impossible stomachfuls of bitterness and rage. Fang turned his attention back to Tem and nodded her an encouragement. Going with a couple of dickhead dragons might not be ideal, but Llanelli was still their best chance. And they deserved a chance, didn't they?

CHAPTER ELEVEN
THE HIGH LIFE, WHERE EVERYTHING'S SWELL

The blue dragon, it transpired, was named Bluejohn, and his grey companion was called Haearn. The best way into the Lost City of Llanelli was by air, the big dragons insisted; they could easily split the load of the flightless members of the group on their backs, especially since neither Sioned nor Jenkin were invited – a fact that elicited in Nell a visible exhalation of relief. Tem still wanted to sit with Amber and Nell for the journey rather than Fang.

Fang conceded that his outburst in Lazare's direction had been too much, if only in the regard that he shouldn't have exhibited such anger in front of a child, especially one who had known such violence and mistreatment in her little life. He agreed to journey on Haearn's back, letting Nell ride with Tem on the back of Bluejohn. He had never ridden on dragonback before – when he'd stopped off for a week in Qom on his long journey west, a merchant azhdaha had offered him passage to Augsburg, but the cost had proved prohibitively expensive. The only time Fang had ever been airborne had been the handful of times Lazare had carried him, all of which he'd complained bitterly about, even though the experience had been far more secure than grasping desperately to Haearn's neck scales as he took off from the streets of Carmarthen.

Haearn's size made for awkward seating – he was far too big to straddle him like a horse, but not large enough to give adequate room if Fang were to tumble or slide sideways. All Fang could do was cling tightly, hope that Nell and Tem could do the same, and refuse to ever admit that flying dragonback made him miss being hoisted aloft by Lazare.

As well as being a precarious mount, Haearn was much faster than anything Fang was used to, and ahead of them, the slightly larger Bluejohn soared even faster. It was quickly clear that Amber would have no chance of keeping up with the party on her stubby little wings. With a grunt of effort she managed to catch up with Bluejohn enough to land on his tail, and clambered over to sit with Tem and Nell. Lazare valiantly flapped away in an attempt to keep up with Haearn's speed, but after only five minutes or so, Fang could tell that the Frenchman was running out of breath. He began to lag, falling further and further behind. After a short while, Haearn let out an audible sneer and slowed his flight, so that Lazare could catch up.

'You can get on, you know,' called Haearn. 'I know you're used to runts, but a proper dragon like me can carry you both.'

'I'm fine,' puffed Lazare.

'It's annoying for me to fly at weakling speed just to keep up with your puny wings,' retorted Haearn. 'Just get on. Or you could surrender yourself to the swan or the griffin?'

'adar llwch gwin,' corrected Fang.

'Oh, come on, it's just a bloody griffin with a high opinion of himself,' grumbled Haearn.

Lazare landed on Haearn's back, gulping for air, his usually perfect hairdo rumpled and sticky with sweat. 'Fine,' he gasped, 'I will accept a lift, but only so as not to split the group.' He gave Fang a meaningful glance as a guilt-laden reminder that the last time the group had split up, Fang had, for reasons that were perfectly rational at the time, thrown himself off a cliff. Lazare had the same difficulty as Fang in remaining seated and stable on Haearn's back, and after sitting down the tail end of the dragon and almost falling off, the Frenchman finally crawled along to kneel right next to Fang, clutching the grey dragon's raised ruff of neck scales with him.

There was a moment's stony silence, followed by another sneer from Haearn. 'Well, you two are either love rivals or you're tupping,' noted the dragon. 'And given that the woman already had two potential mates with her, I'm guessing it's the latter.'

'We are *not*,' argued Lazare.

'Where do people even keep getting that idea?' added Fang, as innocently as possible.

'Quarrelling mates it is,' replied Haearn. 'Humans are so predictable; you may as well be doing a courtship dance at each other. No funny business on my back, please and thank you.'

'We're not...' Lazare sighed, and tried again. 'We're quarrelling because he didn't like my poem and he was rude about it.'

'That's not what that was about,' snapped Fang. 'It... it wasn't a bad poem; it rhymed and everything. Even Marlowe can't make his stuff fully rhyme and he keeps telling me he's a genius, so on a purely technical level, yours was... acceptable.'

'Then there was hardly reason for you to shout at me, was there?'

'You weren't listening!' Fang was aware that he was raising his voice again, but honestly, it was only to be heard above the whipping wind and flapping dragon wings. 'You're still not! I'm not your muse any more than I'm your swooning prize to pluck into the air and rescue.'

'I never saw you as a "prize", Fang! God's Tonsils, man, the only reason I keep having to rescue you is because you are a magnet for peril and pain—'

Fang carried on, over Lazare. 'It's because you always need to perform! Scooping me up, reciting sonnets with all these romanticised ideals—'

It was Lazare's turn to interrupt. 'And you are a patronising ass, trying to own *my* feelings and rejecting every single means I have of expressing them! All "Bleh bleh bleh, I'm Fang, I know it all but won't actually voice anything except insults"…'

'Oh, that's me, is it? Very mature.' Fang seethed. 'Well, this is you – "hon hee hon, *je suis* a suffering arteest in lerve, and the grubby leetle peasant man is not grateful enough to be my object and it makes me all huffy. Big word, big word, French curse, rhyming couplet, something about fashion".'

'This is you,' shouted Lazare. '"Grump grumpy grump grump, I'm mad at everyone for something that wasn't their fault, nobody mention how sweet and kind I really am, it'll hurt my precious false illusion of untouchable muck; even though I'm surrounded by people who love me, I'm going to mope around claiming otherwise, because I'm scared"…'

Fang risked releasing Haearn's scales for a moment, to point angrily at Lazare. 'That's not true.'

'Oh, please.'

'Well, maybe once, but it's not anymore. I appreciate how Tem and Nell and Amber feel. And you. I care about you. A lot.'

Lazare softened a little. 'That's... thank you, Fang. And, for what it's worth, I appreciate that you're trying to find a way to keep us all alive together.'

Beneath them, Haearn rumbled a sigh. 'Dragons court by puffing up our flame sacs at each other. So much simpler than whatever the Hell this nonsense is; you should try it.'

Fang nodded. 'The first time in years, I'm not running in fear, but in hope. For Tem. For all of you. Because... I... care about you.'

'This is painful,' added Haearn. 'Seriously. I can lend you both prosthetic flame sacs.'

'I thought you'd be happy about the new plan,' Fang continued. 'But something's still wrong, isn't it? It's like, these days the only me you care to see is the me you've built up in your head, this object floating in the ether having wistful poems written about it.'

'Stop,' warned Lazare.

'The actual me only seems to upset you,' continued Fang. 'You barely look at me, and when you do it's like you've seen a ghost.'

'I said, *stop*.'

'Me?' asked Haearn.

'No, not...' Lazare took a frustrated breath. 'Look, Haearn, I know we're having this quarrel on your back, but would you mind zoning out of our conversation for a bit? Maybe humming to yourself?'

Haearn sighed again. 'I preferred you people when you were knee-deep in Welsh mud and not esteemed guests of Her Majesty.'

'I love you,' Lazare told Fang. 'I love the real you, the pompous dick who keeps telling me how he thinks I feel. The danger magnet, who gets hurt over and over again, who throws himself off cliffs.'

'That was one time...'

'You didn't get drowned one time, though, did you?' snapped Lazare. Fang noticed that there were tears in the Frenchman's eyes. Possibly due to the wind, but probably not. 'The things that alchemist did to you. The things we all had to bear witness to, even the kid. And, I can't... it's not you, it's that alchemist, Fang. I just can't get over it; it's like I'm still there in the river every time I close my eyes...'

'This is about the alchemist?' Now that Fang thought about it, yes, Lazare had been distancing himself and avoiding Fang's gaze ever since their altercation with the alchemist. Ever since the alchemist had gone back in time to seduce Fang in the past. Initially, Fang had assumed it had been to humiliate and punish Fang alone. But, if Lazare was into this whole courtly love thing with him, well then. Goodness knows neither of them were anywhere even close to blushing virgins, but did sleeping with the enemy way back in Kashgar make him 'tainted' now to Lazare?

'Of course it's about the alchemist! I can't stop picturing it; the nightmares haunt me; I can barely sleep. It's like... it was you he was doing that stuff to, but somehow I'm the one who broke, and I... I...'

'Oh.' Fang felt a horrible, leaden sensation deep in his core. 'You should know, it was nothing to me, truly...'

'How?' Lazare blurted. 'How can you be so OK with it all? How can you be carrying on as usual?'

'I just... can.' Fang tried to speak softly, despite the whipping wind. 'What happened in the past is in the past, and there's no changing that. I mean, *we're* not time travellers, right?'

Lazare's expression made it very clear that this was not the right occasion to try to crack a joke.

'I should know as well as anyone,' continued Fang, 'that no amount of wallowing in unfortunate events of the past can change them. But we can make decisions that hope for a better future.'

'Oh, *now* you've decided it's indulgent to wallow?' asked Lazare. 'And how can you possibly call what that *connard* did to you merely "an unfortunate incident"?'

'Well, that's all it was to me!' Fang faltered, regarding Lazare's incredulous face. 'You know, in the grand scheme of things... maybe I compartmentalise, maybe I bury acts of hurt, maybe I have to, to survive, maybe I've always had to, ever since I watched my mother smash my fiancée's head in with a rock—'

He stopped himself suddenly. He'd never said those words out loud before. His eyes had started watering, too. The wind, no doubt.

Lazare's expression became more sorrowful. 'Perhaps that's what I've been doing, too. Compartmentalising, trying to pack away the mess that alchemist left behind. My mind making you a romanticised muse, an untouchable idea of you. A version of you that can't be...'

He trailed off, and whether that sentence was going to end with 'seduced by the enemy' or 'needlessly hurtful' or 'a thoughtless disappointment', Fang was not to know. Perhaps it was better left unsaid; Fang knew his failings only too well without hearing them from the man he... cared about. Both men were still gripping tightly to Haearn's scales, their hands close. In a small gesture of contrition, Fang shifted his little finger across to brush the side of Lazare's hand.

'I know we can't undo what happened with the alchemist,' Fang told him. 'But you should know, before he intervened, when you got angry, and you kissed me, it was like all those compartments, all the masks faded away, and I finally saw you. And you saw me. And then, the alchemist interrupted us, and all the masks went on again. You won't kiss me anymore. You won't try. You won't even truly see me; you turn your eyes away and picture a better me, and that...' He blinked at the realisation, blinking away the silly watery eyes that the silly wind was giving him. 'That hurts. It hurts that that – what did you call him, an *connard*? – was able to do that to us.'

Lazare's little finger moved to rest on top of Fang's. 'What are you saying?'

The wind was whipping his hair about and it stung his eyes, and one hand was white and cold clenched around the dragon's scales, but he paid all of that little heed compared to the fixation of the sensation of Lazare's finger as it hooked around his own. He wasn't sure *what* he was saying, or whether it was wise to say it.

'I miss you. I miss the you that I saw in the embassy, the you that saw me.' He realised that he was leaning in towards

Lazare as the wind caught locks of his long hair and slapped Lazare around the cheeks with them. 'I miss the you that held my thighs and called me a shambling fool. I miss the you that kisses me like I'm dinner.'

He leaned in further, and brushed a tentative kiss upon Lazare's lips. His heart leaped as Lazare caught the kiss and engulfed it with a harder, hungrier, needier kiss of his own, a kiss that rang with the loud echoes of their first kiss, that aching moment in the embassy against the wallpaper, and for that one moment, Fang could have thrown what little decency he retained to the wind. He could have let go of the dragon's scales to clasp Lazare with both hands. He could have fallen onto the dragon's back beneath this man, both the starving beggar and the hot meal, consuming and being consumed. He could have pushed his hands up beneath Lazare's bright doublet to feel the warm soft skin of the actor's chest, could have welcomed Lazare's hands roaming under his windswept shirt, over his breeches, over the thin leather strap that laced them at the front. Fang could undo a codpiece in seconds – he'd done so atop a camel once; he could definitely do the same on an irritable dragon in flight. He could have done so, happily, if that was what Lazare wanted from this starving kiss. But, after the briefest moment, Lazare stopped and pulled away, his expression twisted with an inner distress, or disgust, or a combination of the two, Fang couldn't tell. Fang moved his hand away and looked down, wiping his eyes. Stupid wind.

'I'm sorry,' attempted Lazare.

'I should think so too,' rumbled Haearn. 'I specifically said, "no funny business on my back"!'

Lazare felt wretched, and not due to any minor embarrassment the barely-a-kiss might have caused Haearn. Lazare knew Fang was trying so hard, and honestly, that just made things worse. This was the man whose initial plan had been to find some way to slip as swiftly and gently into death as possible, now willing to beg a powerful dragon for the strange and lengthy life of a fae, just to give Lazare and the others some sort of future, no matter how hard those long lives would be. Fang was trying, but he only seemed to be setting himself up for yet more hurt. The thought of Fang hurting again, who had been hurt so much already, who had run half the world away to flee pain... it made Lazare's heart hammer and his breath choke halfway up his throat. It flashed the image in his mind of meeting those beautiful dark eyes glazed and unseeing as the alchemist pulled Fang's drowned face out of the water. Mind you, Lazare saw that image over and over again no matter what. When he'd been torturing Fang, the alchemist had at one point threatened to drown him ten thousand times. Lazare believed that he may have now seen Fang drown that many times, unbidden in his mind's eye. When Fang had kissed him, he'd felt that same exquisite lurch in his stomach he had felt the first time they'd kissed, that sensation of catching hold of something solid and real after a lifetime of grasping at intangible shadows, and Lazare had kissed back, and then his mind had flashed the horror of the alchemist interrupting their first kiss, hurting and humiliating them all, and then Fang's staring, drowned face and... and, he couldn't. It hurt too much.

Maybe Fang had been right all along. Maybe love *was* pain. Lazare had never felt another man's pain before. For all his character studies and attempts to inhabit the emotional spheres of Mephistopheles or Oberon or what have you, he had never before felt someone else's anguish in his bones and his belly and his dreams. He could feel Fang drowning, every time. He could feel the man getting shot and stabbed and staked and beaten, and what if Fang got hurt again? Even worse this time? This was a mess. *He* was a mess. And he hadn't been able to go through with the kiss. The visions, the second-hand pain that his memories flashed at him like new – it had been too much. And he still hadn't got used to the expression of hurt disappointment on Fang whenever Lazare rejected a kiss – even though by now, Lazare had rejected Fang's kisses a *lot*. But before the alchemist, he'd pulled back from the kisses because Fang had looked so bloody miserable about it. Now, Fang looked hopeful. And that made it worse. Lazare was too used to being the happy-go-lucky one, coasting through life on a wink and a song and a particularly fashionable set of hose. He had always wanted to fall in love, but he'd expected it to involve more posy-picking, moonlit serenades and fireside lovemaking, and fewer painful silences, hurt glares and horrific nightmares. He'd definitely expected falling in love to involve less shooting, stabbing, falling and drowning, and he didn't feel that that had been a particularly unreasonable expectation. Yet, here he was, on the back of an unpleasant dragon, and in love, and in the middle of a massive mess. Why couldn't it be like a sonnet, he wondered. It would be so much easier if love were like the love in a sonnet. Everything would make sense. Everything would rhyme. Or at least half-rhyme.

CHAPTER TWELVE
THE LOST CITY OF LLANELLI

Lazare and Fang sat in a shared unhappy silence for the rest of the journey as wings flapped and wind rushed past them, until they approached a huge, stone wall, with immense, rearing dragons carved into the masonry – giant heads with mouths eternally open, roaring out silent warnings to any would-be invaders. All of the stone dragons looked very samey, and Lazare didn't think it was due to any particular lack of creativity on the part of the sculptor. He had a feeling that these were all supposed to be Redthroat the Invincible. A couple of dragon guards resting atop one of the carved stone dragon heads nodded Bluejohn and Haearn through, and Lazare's party were flown over the top of the imposing walls. What opened up ahead of them actually took Lazare's breath away.

Lazare had grown up in Paris, he had lived a decade in Upper London and had recently visited the vast, firelit magical underground city of Deep London, but he had never seen anything like this. The theme of huge dragon statues continued within the walls, pocked with holes in place of the stone dragons' eyes, nostrils or missing scales, and only when he saw a dragon emerge from an eyehole did Lazare realise that these statues must be hollowed-out apartment blocks of sorts, like the high-density 'corescrapers' of Deep London. Other buildings glimmered away as well, some in pale stone, some in filigreed metalwork; some buildings actually appeared to be made out of glazed painted porcelain. Grand houses balanced impossibly in the boughs of huge oak trees. All had large, dragon-sized doorways placed at a height one would need wings to access, Lazare noticed. It took him a little while longer to see any ground-level dwellings with openings suited to non-dragon magicals. Those buildings were rather drabber, stone and slate affairs much like the houses of Deep London, often more crowded around one another like the poorer areas of a human city. Lazare could make out a lot of European and Asian dragons, as well as ogres, griffins, goblins, fauns, púca, even djinn, and what looked like they could possibly be unicorns in the immaculate streets below. The cleanliness was a real surprise; he'd never seen a city look so well kept before. He noticed that quite a few of the more human-shaped magicals had brooms and bins strapped to their backs. Over to the southwest of the city was a wetland area splashing with merfolk, with rocks riddled with dwelling-caves and an honest to goodness rainbow hanging over it, and in front of it all lay the glittering sea, surrounding the largest, most intricately carved palace that Lazare had ever seen. It rose out of the water, shimmering with decorations in mother-of-pearl and precious stones, and tipped with gold. Lazare darted a glance at Fang – Fang, who had seen the glories of Athens, Alexandria, Qom, Constantinople and so much more, and had maintained a dogmatic attitude of world-weariness with every wonder witnessed. Even Fang's expression was agog at Llanelli. His jaw was slack, until somebody poked a grimy, feathery finger into his open mouth. Fang gagged, and Lazare glared daggers at the two harpies who exploded into laughter as they flew past the dragon convoy.

'Gutter-dwellers,' rumbled Haearn. 'Ignore them.'

'Close that pretty mouth, sweetie-cakes,' shouted the finger-poking harpy at Fang. 'You'll catch flies.'

'You're terrible, Megara,' giggled the other harpy.

'He's nice though, isn't he, Xanthippe.' Megara the harpy nudged her companion as they wheeled around to pester Fang some more. 'Oi, angel-pants!'

'Leave him alone,' called Lazare hotly. 'We're on a quest!'

'OoooOOOOoooh,' teased the harpies, as one.

'That your *erastes* there, Mr Chiselled-Chops?' added Megara.

'Did we interrupt a great big snog?' Xanthippe called merrily.

Fang scowled at that, bitterness on his expression and, Lazare believed, a touch of embarrassment.

'Xanthippe,' crowed Megara to her companion, 'have you done a big shit all over your tail feathers?'

'I have not,' Xanthippe exclaimed. 'You're the one with the mucky old feathers.'

'I preened this morning! How dare you!'

'Maybe it's some sort of *skatá*-spell,' said Xanthippe. 'I feel a kind of a weird wiggly fae magic in my wing tips.'

Both harpies turned their attention back to Fang, who swiftly turned away from them and tried to hide the fact he'd been casting one of his grotesque illusions.

'Are you doing fae magics on us, sexy hair?' Megara cawed. 'How'd you learn to do that? You rub your pretty bits all over some poor lonely fae-folk til they give you magic? Or did you steal it?'

'What are you doing here, anyways,' added Xanthippe, 'lowly zombie like you? Come to be a servant? Or a prostitute?'

'Oh, you'd both make brilliant prostitutes,' continued Megara. 'Sign me up for a double whammy.'

'Begone, harpies,' called a familiar voice. Amber was perched on the tip of Bluejohn's tail, directly in front of Haearn. 'We're guests of the queen, so. Leave 'em be. Dragon's orders.'

'Pffft, *Malaka*.' The harpies retained a defiant tone, but Lazare noticed them pull back at Amber's demand.

'We were only joking,' claimed Xanthippe. 'They'd probably make terrible prostitutes actually, 'cause of the smell.'

'What was that?' called Amber.

'Sorry,' called both harpies, in a chorus of sullen sarcasm.

'Thought so,' Amber told them, clambering back along Bluejohn to Tem and Nell.

'Since when did Redthroat invite smelly old vampires and zombies as special guests?' added Megara, continuing to pull back away from them. 'Used to be standards around here. Bye then, smelly sexy zombie! Make sure your big stringbean vampire boyfriend doesn't burn up in the sunshine!'

'Wretched, flea-bitten things,' muttered Haearn as the harpies flew off. 'They shouldn't be allowed. The mighty

Redthroat is *far* too gracious in welcoming feathered foreign wretches like them, if you ask me. If it weren't for the wisdom of her residential zoning laws, their kind would be befouling our grand dragon dwellings before you could say "taramasalata".'

Lazare pulled a disgusted face at Haearn's comments and looked to Fang in hopes of a shared moment of unspoken disapproval, but Fang was looking down at the streets with a frown.

'I don't see any undead in the city,' noted Fang.

'Besides a few servants and whores for the perverts, there aren't any – which makes you all the more honoured that Her Majesty has made an exception for your group.' Haearn sped up a little to fly alongside Bluejohn as they approached a particularly fine treehouse, not far from the shimmering palace.

The harpies weren't the only residents of Llanelli flying up to gawp at the newcomers. A few more dragons flapped past, as well as a griffin and a roc, and then a creature that made Tem shriek at a pitch Lazare had not heard the tiny child issue ever before. An alicorn flapped past, her coat and horn glimmering like a million seashells, her mane, tail and wings the iridescent teal of a kingfisher's plumes. She whinnied disapprovingly as she passed, legs pedalling against the air as if in a ponderous canter. From the expression of rapt wonder on Tem's face, her cry had definitely been one of delight and excitement rather than alarm. Perhaps Tem was coming out of her dragon-loving phase and going into a unicorn-loving phase, although from the alicorn's haughty huff, Lazare doubted that they would prove any more positive a fascination for the child than most dragons were.

'Not delighted by how much attention we're drawing to ourselves,' worried Fang quietly.

'Is it me,' muttered Lazare as quietly as the whipping wind would allow, 'or are they a bit caste-obsessed here? They seem annoyed we're being given the big diplomatic welcome as "lowly undead". As far as they're all concerned, we're supposed to serve steak and suck kinky dragon shaft.'

Fang mouthed, 'Well, we're not undead, are we?' at Lazare.

Lazare mouthed, 'Well, they don't know that, do they?' back.

And, Lazare thought, these 'lowly undead' had been given expedited permission to see the queen, with full dragon escort, right in the nick of time, and it wasn't yet clear why. It was fishy. It was fishier than a mermaid eating bouillabaisse at a fish market.

He sighed as the dragons landed in the giant oak boughs supporting the treehouse. Only as he flapped off Haearn's back did he realise the one detail of what the harpies had said that really bothered him – the weather in Llanelli was beautiful; gorgeous golden afternoon sunlight beamed down from an azure sky. If Haearn and Bluejohn truly assumed that Lazare was a vampire, why had neither of them expressed concern even once that Lazare could catch on fire?

Fang refused Lazare's help off the dragon's back, and climbed down the scales himself, onto oak boughs as wide as a street. Tem allowed Amber to fly her down to the tree branch. The child kept her eyes on the sky, possibly looking around for any more alicorns. At least, that was what Fang hoped the girl's reasons were for still not making eye contact with him.

'High up here, isn't it?' noted Nell. 'Hard for us to get down, if we wanted to leave.'

'It's a guest house,' grumbled Bluejohn. 'Our finest one – when esteemed visitors come to a hidden magical city, they generally enjoy board in an enchanted treehouse or the like. They find it whimsical.'

'Can most of said visitors fly to the ground if they want to?' countered Nell. 'I mean, what if there's a fire or something?'

'There won't be a fire,' snapped Haearn, his flame sac glowing with irritation even as he perched on the incredibly flammable structure. 'God's Scales, we're trying to be nice here.'

'You weren't nice earlier,' said Tem quietly, and Fang realised that she wasn't looking at either of the dragons, but was addressing Fang's knees. 'You were... um...'

'You were mean,' Amber told the dragons.

Tem nodded at Fang's knees. 'Mean,' she echoed quietly.

Haearn just growled with frustration.

'We... regret if what was intended as light-hearted fun made you feel that way,' mumbled Bluejohn reluctantly.

'Yeah,' muttered Haearn, 'sorry if physically flying you out of danger and to where you said you wanted to go wasn't enough for you bloody people.'

'We *are* guests here, aren't we?' Lazare asked the dragons. 'Not prisoners? You'll forgive us for having trust issues, especially with—'

'Big meanies,' interjected Tem, still in a quiet voice.

Bluejohn and Haearn both glared down at Amber, who, to her credit, did not flinch back, in spite of the colossal size difference between the dragons.

'Her Majesty was informed by her ambassadors of your altercation with the alchemist,' sighed Bluejohn. 'Your wariness has been noted. As has the urgent nature of your problem.'

Bluejohn gave them all meaningful glares, and the speed and dragon escort all now made sense to Lazare. Grubble or some other púca ambassador had briefed the dragon queen already. She knew what they were. That she wanted to see them straight away was probably a good sign, right?

'Queen Redthroat is engaged in court business until dusk,' continued Bluejohn, 'after which you may seek her counsel, provided you are escorted by a dragon – any dragon will do. Even an urban runt, if you're unbothered by making a good impression.'

'*I* can be the official royal escort?' gasped Amber, her icy tone over the other dragons' 'meanness' suddenly melting away at her delight at this news.

'If that's what you want,' replied Bluejohn. 'Our only task was to bring you to the city, and you may leave whenever you wish – if, that is, you're truly stupid enough to go straight back to Elizabeth's swan and Llewellyn's griffin – you know they'll both be waiting for you as soon as you step foot outside the city walls. And I really doubt either the King of Wales or the Queen of Upper England just wants a friendly chat to see how they can help.'

'But Redthroat does?' mumbled Lazare, more to the group than the dragons.

Nell nodded at him seriously. 'Her benevolence knows no bounds. I could rattle out a hundred histories of it. The slaying of Sir George, ridding Wales of the three plagues—'

'Which is why,' interrupted Haearn, '*you* people begged to see *her*! Because she's just better! We're just better.'

'Haearn,' warned Bluejohn.

'Well, we are,' grumbled Haearn. 'Stay, leave, we don't care. Enjoy your magical treehouse filled with wonders, you stinky little ingrates.'

And with that, Haearn took off and flapped sullenly away. Bluejohn cast an almost sympathetic gaze across the group.

'I'd like to apologise for him,' he said, 'but I can't, because he's right.'

And Bluejohn too took flight, leaving the group on giant branches thirty feet up in the air, next to an impossible, immaculate guesthouse of woven branches, vines and blossoms. Fang noted the concerned expressions of Nell and Lazare with a silent apology. Was there a chance this was a trap? A trap they'd asked to enter, and were free to leave? Perhaps. So many other things had been a trap that at this point it would be a nice change if it wasn't. But he couldn't stop now. He didn't know where else they could go, what else they could do. Meeting Redthroat at least gave them a chance of a future. It was the slimmest of chances, but he felt duty bound to grasp at that chance tightly. For the sake of the kid – the kid who still wouldn't look into his eyes right now.

'Me,' said Amber merrily, as they entered through the gorgeously intricate doors to the guest house, 'little Amber of Deep Chiswick! The official royal escort for Redthroat herself! I wonder if she's gracious. She'll be gracious, right?'

'*Ever* so gracious,' Nell told her. 'My mam's friend's auntie's hairdresser saw her open a mermaid hospital in Fishguard. She only saw her spine scales through the crowd but she said they were magnificent. Regal, you know. A real sense of care and community spirit.'

'Wow,' breathed Amber and Tem in enthralled unison.

'Amber,' added Tem, 'did I show you my curtsey?'

'Yes,' replied Amber. 'Needs more twirls.'

'Amber's party,' called a horsey voice as they passed into the lobby. Fang looked over in its direction, and saw another alicorn, gazing expectantly at them by the stunningly carved oaken grand staircase. This alicorn's mane, tail and wings were a shimmering rainbow, with a golden coat and horn. Tem managed to not emit a full shriek this time, but Fang bit down a fond smile when she let out a little whimper of joy. 'I'm Raynebow Sprynkles; looks like it's down to me to be the host for yourselves,' the alicorn told them in an irritable tone. 'Suites are upstairs. There are two bedrooms – share as yourselves see fit.'

Fang hoped that this didn't mean the only bed available to him would be one he'd be expected to share with Lazare, although at this point he was resigned to that in fact being the case, as it had done with every bed he'd encountered since the first day he'd met the frustrating Frenchman. It was fine – he was used to sleeping on the floor. He tried to take

Tem's hand as she climbed the stairs, but she ignored his offer and scurried up to the alicorn.

'Mummy told me about unicorns,' she said shyly. 'She said you're egg-sink where I live.'

'Alicorn, not unicorn.' Raynebow Sprynkles shook her wings. 'Learn the difference, mule. And we're hardly "extinct", we just don't want to live in a hole in the ground with the wretched Deep English. No offence. I'm sure the fae enclave is the loveliest part of that damp dark little burrow swarming with undead humans.'

'Er, Deep London is a thrumming metropolis, actually,' called Amber. 'And don't call her a "mule" please, you make it sound like hate talk.'

Raynebow Sprynkles gave Amber a distasteful glance. 'Apologies, mistress dragon.' She looked down at Tem. 'What term do *your* people give to a half-breed, half-breed?'

'Just "half-breed",' admitted Tem with a sad expression, 'or "that dirty one".'

'Call her Tem,' said Fang hurriedly. He tried again to take Tem's hand, and again she pulled away.

'Come on, poppet,' he said to her gently. 'I'm sorry I shouted, before. It wasn't at you.'

'Don't care.' Tem's voice quavered, and she rubbed at her nose with the back of her sleeve.

The alicorn stopped and turned to them. 'Oh, what Deep English nonsense is this now? Can one of you undead not control your half-breed?'

'Don't *call* her that!' Amber's little flame sac began to glow.

Raynebow Sprynkles's horsey expression flashed with concern at the luminous fire brewing in Amber's throat. 'Mistress dragon? Might I remind you, this is a wooden house, up a tree, with no fire escapes, and—'

'"Mistress dragon", that's right,' growled little Amber. 'I am a *dragon*, and you will obey me, you trumped-up cone-pony! Now apologise to my friend!'

'I—' began the alicorn.

She was cut off by Tem's sudden, miserable, angry howl. The child threw her dragon dollie overarm, straight at Amber. The felt doll bounced harmlessly off the real-life little dragon's head and tumbled down several steps.

'Tem, what—?' managed Fang.

'No,' Tem screamed, and ran up the staircase away from them.

'Stay there,' cried Fang to the others, bounding up the stairs after her, and of course, none of his group listened to him. Nell and Amber chased after the dropped doll, while Lazare flapped to follow Fang. Thankfully, Tem didn't get far on her tiny legs. She reached the upper mezzanine and slid herself into a nook between two intertwining spirals of a decorative wooden pillar, curled up small, covered her face and began to weep.

'Tem,' soothed Lazare, hurrying over to her with Fang, 'what's wrong?'

Tem shook her head as much as the tight nook would allow.

'You can't just hide away and sulk and not say what's wrong,' continued Lazare gently. 'That's what Fang does; what's he supposed to do if you steal his whole thing?'

If that had been meant to lighten the mood, it hadn't worked. Tem wailed again. 'Everyone's being so mean! I thought unicorns would be nice, I thought dragons were nice, they're mean!'

'The alicorn shouldn't have called you those names,' Fang sighed. 'And those big dragons… well, you get big bullies everywhere, I suppose, but Amber—'

'Amber was being like them,' cried Tem. 'She was talking like those big mean ones; I didn't like it.'

'Ah.' She had a point.

'Power can go to people's heads,' Lazare told the child, with a small shrug. 'You see it happen all the time. In one day, Amber went from being at the bottom of the pile, living in a hole, eating scraps, to being treated like she's better than everyone. Those big dragons act the way they do because they've come to expect that sort of treatment, but Amber'd never let herself get like that, I'm sure. Just, when you're not used to something, it can be overwhelming.'

'*I'm* not used to *this*,' sobbed Tem. 'You're *all* being mean and shouting.'

'Well.' Fang sat cross-legged in front of Tem, and ran his knuckles soothingly over the one part of the girl he could actually reach – the shin of her boot. 'Maybe we're all a bit overwhelmed.'

''Cause of me?'

'Of course not.'

Lazare spoke up again. 'Returning to your hometown and all the people who ignored or abandoned you suddenly wanting a slice of you now you're a big successful businesswoman? That's a lot for Nell to unpack.'

'We didn't get to unpack,' sighed Tem. 'All the bags are still at Nell's daddy's house.'

'That's not...' Lazare started again. 'After all my years trying to act, I finally found an appreciative audience, but it was for a love poem instead of acting, and I let the applause go to my head. I didn't think about whether the subject – the *object* – of the poem ever wanted to be that.' Lazare shot an apologetic glance at Fang. 'We're not being mean, Tem, we just... mess up. Grown-ups do that all the time, I'm afraid. Even grown-up dragons, although I have no idea whether Amber's fully grown or not, she's so tiny.'

'But your pome was nice,' said Tem, her tears calming down. 'It rhymed. It was about Fang, wasn't it? 'Cause his smile *is* like a little candle, all secret and special.'

'Tem,' sighed Fang, still stroking the front of her boot, 'poppet, I—'

'And then you were *so mean* about it,' cried Tem.

'To Lazare, you mean?' It was Fang's turn to shoot Lazare an apologetic glance, even as the memory of the other man flinching away from his kiss kicked at his stomach. 'Tem, Lazare and I, we have... grown-up issues to get through, and sometimes—'

'Sometimes grown-ups mess up, like Lazare said?' Tem asked.

'Well', conceded Fang, 'yes, but—'

'Is it the bad dreams, too?'

'What?' Fang asked.

'I get such bad dreams,' whimpered Tem. 'About... him. The man who wanted to take us all away.'

Fang leaned his forehead against the wooden pillar Tem remained wedged inside. 'I know you do. I wish I could help with those. I wish I could go with you into them and protect you.'

'No,' replied Tem miserably.

'All I can do,' Fang continued, 'is be here when you wake up, and remind you you're safe now, those dreams are just your brain healing, and sometimes things hurt while they heal, like a bruise. You have a lot to heal from. You had to go through so much, poppet. But nobody's going to hurt you again while I'm here.'

Tem started to cry yet again. 'But that's what the dreams are.'

'I don't understand.'

'He hurted you. And he hurted and hurted and hurted you and he made me keep bringing you back and so *I* hurted you, and you're in the dreams and still getting hurted—' Tem broke off into loud sobs once more.

Oh, no. Tem had been forced by that disgusting alchemist to witness Fang's torture – forced to partake in it, in fact. Memories of Fang's past flashed unbidden – his older brothers holding him back, the rock in his mother's hands, the vixen screams of the huli jing mixing with his own. Blood and fox fur on the grass. Having to see the torture of someone you care for, having to be a part of it – he knew from experience just how steadfastly and vividly that lodged in your nightmares, shaking you from sleep, haunting your waking hours. He'd dealt with his treatment at the alchemist's hands the way he'd dealt with all hurt and humiliation since fleeing his home village – by ignoring it, mentally packing it away as an unpleasantness that was now over. It had been his own hurt. But the alchemist had changed that. He'd made the others share Fang's hurt, and it turned out, a burden shared was a burden multiplied many times over, and now Lazare saw him as tainted and Tem was left traumatised, and it was all the fault of his hurt, spilling over to harm them too. Maybe, for all his desperate hopes, he was still destined to spread pain and fear no matter where he went.

'Oh, Tem. I had no idea.' And he *still* had no idea how to fix it. He so desperately wanted to fix everything about Tem that hurt, immediately. He wanted to be able to hand her something easy and instant that would make everything OK. He wanted to kiss the pain away like a boo-boo and watch her play happily, forever. Fixing the curse was enough of a pipe dream; how could he go about pulling the pain he'd created out of her nightmares?

'I miss Mummy,' sniffled Tem. She had seen her mother get mortally wounded before being forced to see Fang get repeatedly killed. It was too much for such a little thing; how could she be expected to bear it?

'I know,' he sighed.

'*She* wouldn't get cross about a bad dream,' continued Tem.

'I would never be cross at you for your dreams.'

Tem's little arm snaked out of the hiding nook. '*His* bad dreams.' She was pointing at Lazare.

'Wait, what?' Fang frowned at Lazare. The Frenchman's expression was a strange combination of shame and distress.

'He gets them too, and you shout at him,' continued Tem. 'You're cross now!'

Fang tried to stop frowning. 'Lazare doesn't get your dreams.'

'He does,' said Tem. 'I seen him. At night, when the dream wakes him up. I seen him look around for you, like I do.'

Fang continued to look at Lazare. Lazare gave him a nod of confirmation. 'It's as I said to you when we were on the dragon's back... what that *connard* did to you, I just can't stop thinking about it; it goes around and around in my head, sleeping and waking. Seeing you hurt like that.' He dropped his voice to a whisper. 'Drowned. And there was nothing I could do. And now, every time I try to kiss you, if I so much as look at you, that's what I see.'

Fang's mouth felt dry. 'It's the drowning that upset you? Not the fact I...' He gave an anxious little glance at Tem, who was taking it all in. 'Gave him a cuddle, in the past?'

'Fang, why would that fact upset me? I've... "cuddled" half of Upper London. I've "cuddled" Marlowe.'

'Mr Marlowe doesn't seem very cuddly,' noted Tem seriously.

'You think I am so shallow?' continued Lazare.

'I'm sorry.' Fang felt wretched.

'No,' sighed Lazare, '*I'm* sorry. It was your pain, I'm not trying to blame you for my nightmares, but God's Teeth, man, did you simply not understand what that terror did to the rest of us?'

No. Clearly he hadn't understood, at all.

'It was scary in the river,' Tem told Fang. 'We was all scared. Weren't you?'

'Maybe not as scared as I should have been,' Fang admitted. He took the child's hand. Tem gazed into Fang's eyes, then looked meaningfully at Lazare. Fang held out his free hand towards Lazare. Lazare took his hand, still with that unhappy expression.

'I'm sorry I got cross, and I'm sorry I gave you nightmares,' he told them both.

'It's not your fault,' mumbled Lazare.

Tem nodded seriously at Fang. 'OK, Daddy.' She started pulling herself out of the nook, and both Fang and Lazare pretended they hadn't heard her use that word again. 'I think I still like dragons best out of them and allycorns,' she said conversationally, as if the tearful discussion of trauma and nightmares hadn't happened, 'but Amber should still be nicer to them.'

Fang picked Tem up, relieved to have her happily in his arms again. 'Well, you were very good at getting me to see sense and apologise; maybe you should talk to Amber as well.'

He smiled as encouragingly as he could at Tem, then tried turning the smile across to Lazare. Lazare still looked wretched. Apologising hadn't helped the Frenchman one bit. Even if it hadn't been by sleeping with Fang, the alchemist had still reached through time again from beyond the grave, hurting his family, tearing him from Lazare. Lazare still wanted to kiss him. This news should have elated him, but it did no such thing. It wasn't lack of desire stopping Lazare, but pain and guilt. This knowledge made Fang feel every bit as bad as Lazare looked.

CHAPTER THIRTEEN
WATERY FOWLS

Raynebow Sprynkles watched aloof from her spot on the grand staircase as the two strange undead men chased the half-breed child up it, and the woman and the runt dragon chased the doll down it.

'I really upset her, didn't I?' puffed Amber guiltily as she hurried down the stairs. 'I went too far. It's being in dragon country; it's gone to my head.'

Yes, thought Raynebow Sprynkles, the dragon *had* gone too far, and the needlessly high status bestowed on dragons round these parts *had* gone to her silly little lizard head, and it *had* ruffled the alicorn's feathers – although Raynebow Sprynkles supposed that the dragon felt bad about upsetting the little half-fae, and not a majestic alicorn.

'Hey. Psst hey, rainbow-mane.'

A couple of harpies perched in the open windows of the alcove halfway up the staircase. Well, that was all Raynebow Sprynkles needed. She'd had run-ins with Megara and Xanthippe before. She left the Welshwoman and the dragon to their conversation as they dusted off the retrieved doll, and clopped over to the alcove to shoo the feathery pests away.

'Hello, my clippy-cloppy lovely.' Megara grinned. 'How's the fancy hoteliering?'

'None of your business,' Raynebow Sprynkles told them. 'Haven't you two been banned from the premises?'

'We didn't do anything wrong' replied Xanthippe innocently. 'It was an all-you-can-eat breakfast buffet; it was practically in the rules for us to eat all we could eat.'

'You were told at the time, that buffet was for paying guests only, and under no circumstance was anybody supposed to pick up the entire patisserie table and fly it out of the window!'

'Well you should have made your silly sniffy rules clearer, then, shouldn't you?' interjected Megara. 'Not our fault we're not used to snooty-person etiquettes at fancy hotels... not that you're much of a fancy hotel anymore, mind you.'

'What's *that* supposed to mean?' huffed Raynebow Sprynkles.

'Putting up zombies, a vampire and a half-breed?' cooed Megara in an infuriatingly musical tone of mockery. 'Bit downmarket for Llanelli, isn't it, my lovely?'

'Her Majesty doesn't think so,' grumbled Raynebow Sprynkles. 'She sent royal escorts after all—'

'Why do you think that was?' Xanthippe interrupted. 'She'd never roll out the sparkly carpet for undead usually. Unless... do you think maybe there's something strange about them? Something "off"?'

'Off?' Now that Raynebow Sprynkles thought about it, her new guests did seem a bit 'off'.

'The pretty one can cast fae glamours, you know,' Megara told the alicorn, lowering her voice in faux confidentiality. 'Weird ones. Very *skatá*-centric ones.'

'Which one's "the pretty one"?' asked Raynebow Sprynkles. She cast a quick glance out of the alcove and down the grand staircase again, where the Welshwoman had taken off a boot and seemed to be trying to get a stain out of the doll by rubbing the arch of her left foot on it. Odd.

'Lots of lovely natural light in here too, isn't there?' added Xanthippe. 'Great big skylight in the middle of the hall and everything, practically glows on a nice afternoon like this.'

'Thank you?' replied Raynebow Sprynkles.

'And yet I take it that "vampire" hasn't turned into a big ashen fire hazard in all the sunlight,' continued Xanthippe. 'Bet you haven't even seen him smouldering a smidge.'

'Except figuratively,' added Megara appreciatively.

Now, that was a point. Raynebow Sprynkles glanced up the stairs this time. The 'vampire' was on the mezzanine, in uncomfortable conversation with the Cathayan and a pillar. Late afternoon sunshine beamed directly at him through a large side window. He seemed to not even notice it. Nary a wisp of smoke emanated from his skin.

'Do you know what,' said Megara, poorly pretending that this was the first she'd considered it, 'I think maybe they're not proper undead. I think they might be something new. Something weird.'

'Redthroat would want to monitor a new breed of undead,' muttered Raynebow Sprynkles.

'Just "monitor"?' asked Xanthippe. 'Or destroy? Or even control?'

'Her Majesty would do no such thing in her good grace,' huffed Raynebow Sprynkles automatically.

'Oh, please,' replied Megara. 'Drop the whole "Ooh, Redthroat's a big kindly scaly miracle angel" thing. That's what we tell those stupid human Welsh peasants. That's what we tell *tourists*. We've been here long enough to know that's a great big pile of nonsense.'

'Well,' said Raynebow Sprynkles quietly, 'whichever way Her Majesty uses, if they're a new breed, they should be secured.'

'*Are* they secure, in your hotel?' Megara asked. '*We* got in here, and we're technically banned.'

This only proved to remind Raynebow Sprynkles that she'd meant to shoo away the nuisance harpies in the first place. 'Right. That's it – out.'

The harpies fluttered a little. 'Don't sprain a wing protecting these weirdos for the queen, will you?' hissed Xanthippe. 'Didn't realise majestic alicorns enjoyed being bossed around by dragons so much.'

Raynebow Sprynkles huffed at that.

'That runt dragon they're with's got a mouth on her, hasn't she?' added Megara. 'She was really rude to us; she didn't gob off at you too, did she?'

'What are you getting at?' asked the alicorn.

Xanthippe shrugged, scattering feathers. 'When we moved here from Rhodes—'

''Cause of the bloody Byzantines,' interrupted Megara.

''Cause of the bloody Byzantines, but that's beside the point,' continued Xanthippe. 'When we moved to Llanelli it was under the assumption that it was a wonderful hidden magical utopia for all, and what do we get? Bossed around by the dragons instead of the Byzantines. Better than being in Deep England in some hole in the ground, but still. Sometimes it feels like there's not much difference. Do you alicorns never get annoyed by that?' Xanthippe cocked her head at Raynebow Sprynkles, bird like. 'Just 'cause, when all the harpies started leaving the Byzantine Empire, it was high sign that the pecking order there was all lopsided. You act all high and mighty but here you are, reduced to running a hotel for the latecomers the palace can't fit into their guest suites, making beds and breakfasts with your poor hooves. Ever seen an alicorn around here with a properly good job, a dragon-level job?'

'How many unicorns and alicorns have left the British island since the war again, my lovely?' Megara added. 'Eighty, ninety per cent?

Raynebow Sprynkles just stared at her.

Xanthippe lowered her voice some more. 'Say the security in your nice hotel wasn't so good, and these strange "guests" of Redthroat's were to accidentally go missing, perhaps ending up in the wings of some different, noble, majestic magicals. Would that not give an interesting leverage over a certain fire-breathing race that has possibly got a little bit big for its scales? If these undead weirdos had some sort of incredible power that could be utilised – I'm not saying that would be abused by any potential... I don't want to say "abductors", it's a horrible word – "temporary hosts", let's say... I'm just talking about levelling out the perch a bit, which would be better for everyone, wouldn't it?'

Raynebow Sprynkles watched from the edge of the alcove as both parties of her strange new guests met up again in the middle of the staircase. The half-breed kid had stopped crying now at least, and clung to the Cathayan in a manner that suggested she was his offspring. The runt dragon flapped up with the child's doll in her jaw and passed it gently to the half-fae, who accepted it happily, in spite of all the petrol-stinking dragon spit.

'Sorry I upset you,' said the dragon.

The child nodded. 'You should say sorry to Raynebow.'

'That's fair.' The dragon turned mid-air to look around. Raynebow Sprynkles shrank back into the alcove, out of view. 'Where'd she go? Some host.'

Raynebow Sprynkles darted a sideways glance at the harpies. 'You people can hypnotise, right?' she whispered.

'A couple of thousand smashed-up sailors in the Aegean Sea can attest to that,' Megara whispered back. 'Or they could if they weren't dead.'

Raynebow Sprynkles nodded. 'Stay out of sight; follow my lead.'

Lazare and the others looked around. Extraordinary that a full-sized, shimmering gold and rainbow alicorn had managed to completely hide herself on a large flight of stairs, but apparently that was what had happened.

'Should we just take ourselves up to our rooms?' he wondered aloud.

'Amber still has to say sorry, though,' Tem told them urgently. 'And then everything will be happier because she's a nice dragon really.'

'Thank you, Tem,' said Amber.

'And you just got to show all the other dragons how to be nice like you,' added Tem.

'I—' Amber did a double take, which Lazare had never seen a dragon do before. 'Wait, what?'

'I'm sure she'll have a chance, after we've found our rooms,' Fang told Tem. He handed the child over to Nell. 'Could you give us a bit?' he asked the Welshwoman quietly.

Nell darted a glance from Fang to Lazare and back again, and nodded.

'How am I supposed to convince all the dragons in Llanelli to stop acting all dragon-y?' whined Amber, following Nell as she took Tem up the rest of the stairs.

Lazare was about to follow close by, but Fang held out a hand to stop him. The hand on Lazare's chest jolted a sharp physical reminder of their first, interrupted kiss through Lazare's heart, lungs and belly. The thrill of the kiss and the horror of the alchemist's violence were still all horribly mashed up together for Lazare. And now, Fang knew. Fang knew that Lazare was weak, that he couldn't cope. Lazare was supposed to be the emotionally stable one, the cheerful popinjay only ever thrown into temporary dismay by the loss of a role or a bad review – someone who could chase Fang's ghosts away with sunshine. And here he was, falling apart after a fraction of what Fang had endured throughout his terrible life. What use was he to Fang? What use was he to any of them? What use had he ever been? Just some washed-up failed actor who didn't have the wherewithal to give up.

Fang took his hand, and began leading him up the stairs, a few feet behind the others.

'I'm sorry about the dreams,' said Fang quietly.

'Don't talk like it's your fault,' Lazare sighed. 'It's your pain; it belongs to you – my brain just decided to appropriate it.'

'Her name was Flower,' Fang told him suddenly. 'Well – to me, her name was Hua, but she told me her name was also Phool, and Kkoch, and Tsetseg, and Çiçek and two dozen names more, so you may as well know her as Flower, or Fleur.'

'The huli jing,' murmured Lazare. 'Your, um, ex.'

'I have watched her die, over and over, a thousand times, unbidden,' Fang told him. 'In sleeping, in waking, in the terrible paralysed place in between. I know what it's like to be locked in your dreams with another person's torture. I know what it does to a man.' He indicated to his own beautiful but dishevelled face. 'I wouldn't wish it on my worst enemy, let alone someone I... care for a lot.'

Lazare stopped Fang. Fang turned to him still hand in hand, a step higher than Lazare so that they stood at even eye level for a change. Lazare linked fingers with him.

'That alchemist – typical time traveller, right?' continued Fang with a sad smile. 'Still hurting us after he's dead. Still pulling us apart. He's nothing but hollowed-out bones now, yet he's still poisoned me for you.'

'Pois— what?' Lazare could feel his face crumpling, could sense his horror at that sad statement causing whole new ugly wrinkles. 'You think I see you as...? Why would you...?' He realised he was going to have to finish a sentence sooner or later. 'I have very much never wanted anyone more, Fang of Cathay,' he replied, dropping his voice to little more than a whisper. 'I want you like life. Like sunlight. Like food. Like coffee. I crave you. I think about that kiss and I say goodbye to my stomach; it goes on a little trip all over my insides. I do not see you as poisoned or tainted. He is the poison. But we can disperse that poison, together.'

'You think so? Even though you can't kiss me?' Fang started walking up the stairs again after the others, pulling Lazare along. 'Even though you can barely look at me? Have I just handed you the same suffering I could barely cope with, and announced my new plan is for you to have to bear that for a fae's long years?'

'Fang, in all honesty your plan may well not work, but it's still the loveliest plan. I want us to have a future. I see you fighting for it; I just can't see you get hurt anymore.' Lazare tugged at Fang's hand, stopping his ascent, turning the other man around to face him once more. Fang's words scratched and jangled in his brain – that Fang believed Lazare couldn't kiss him – couldn't kiss this man whom he so desperately wanted to kiss, and who craved his kisses so, this man who he wanted like a parched man wanted water. That Fang believed the alchemist had poisoned him for Lazare, tainted him. Fang was still hurting. Lazare grabbed Fang's face with his free hand and kissed him hard, trying to concentrate on the deliciousness of the firm, begging kiss in return, the light scruff of Fang's stubble and the fluff where he'd shaved badly, the softness of his hair, the promise of Fang's eagerly opening mouth. The images of Fang's drowned face flashed again as they always did, but Lazare fought through it. It was over. The alchemist was dead. Lazare would learn to package the horror away, if only to stop the alchemist from reaching through time to hurt and humiliate Fang, snatching a final cruel victory even after death. Lazare told the images of Fang's drowned face that the danger they screamed of had passed, that they had no power anymore. The images didn't vanish, but they changed. They became images of Fang being captured and held prisoner in some human monarch's dungeon. Of Fang living miserably as a magically transformed fae. Of Fang in a mighty throne room between a huge red dragon's jaws... great. He'd packaged away the hurt of the past, and just gone straight to worrying about potential hurt in the future.

It was Fang who pulled away from the kiss this time, his brow furrowed, watching Lazare's expression with concern, as if he had been able to read Lazare's worries on his tongue. Well – trying to hide his fears from Fang had just made matters worse; Lazare decided he should be honest with a man straight after kissing him.

'Fang, I adore your hope. I adore that your plan has a future. I adore you. Can you accept that, at least?'

Fang ran the tip of his tongue over his own lower lip, as if taking in the aftertaste of the kiss. His expression was serious, but open. He nodded, and Lazare surprised himself by exhaling a breath he didn't realise he'd been holding.

'Yes,' murmured Fang, also sounding softly surprised. 'I should have believed you before; I just... didn't understand. I think I do, now.'

He knew he was worthy of love, just as he knew he was worthy of a future – of hope. Lazare wished his tumbling anxieties would give him the thoughtspace to rejoice in that, but they did not. He brushed fingers lightly up Fang's arm.

'But I'm so worried, Fang. This plan... I'm worried that asking Redthroat to turn us fae is only going to hurt you again.'

Fang turned that now familiar haunted-house expression of chilling hostility back at Lazare, pulling his arm away. 'Then why are you going along with it, if my plan's so bad?'

'I'm not saying it's bad, just that... maybe it's... not that good?'

'Do you have a better plan?'

Fang's words were spat out as an accusation, because of course Lazare didn't have one. He'd never had a plan. He just followed the others around, and back before the alchemist attacked, at least there had been a point to him doing so – he'd spread cheer, and helped out with his wings. But now? Now, he just moped, and hitched rides on other people's carts, and other flying beings' backs, and he wrote poems in the wrong language that the love of his life hated, and chased hollow applause. He was useless, he had no plan and Fang was never going to stop throwing himself in danger and even voicing his concerns made Fang angry, and even kissing him like he wanted seemed to make things worse, even Fang accepting he was loved hadn't fixed a damned thing, and so Lazare just chased pointless distraction after pointless distraction, and—

He was distracted by a flash of gold and rainbow, flying up from some shadowy alcove. Raynebow Sprynkles was back, seemingly from nowhere.

'Oh, *there* you are,' called Nell from the mezzanine. 'We thought we'd check ourselves in, but so far, that's involved opening a lot of wrong doors up here.'

'Have you been to the seaside yet?' asked the alicorn suddenly. 'It's number one on the to-do guides.'

'Number one on *our* to-do guide is to speak with Queen Redthroat,' Fang told her. 'Perhaps afterwards, if it goes well—'

'Lots of mermaids at the seaside, little girl,' added the alicorn. 'You might even see an afanc; it's like a sort of a crocodile-beaver chimaera; kids like those, right?' Raynebow Sprynkles darted a glance up at the skylight. 'You'll like it! Lots of interesting rocks and sea-caves.'

'No,' cried Lazare hotly. 'No more waterlogged caves, not ever.'

'Plenty of secluded grottos,' continued the alicorn to Lazare and Fang. 'Good for mating; I take it you two are...?'

Fang opened his mouth to reply testily, but was cut off by the sound of singing, from above. The artist in Lazare understood that the voices were harsh, amateurish, singing a song that was simplistic to the point of being rather banal. Every other part of him, however, was flooded with a single thought that drowned out all reason – this was, somehow, the most beautiful song he had ever heard. Indeed, as he looked around himself, Fang and Nell too stood, utterly transfixed by the scintillating song.

'Oh, you do like to be beside the seaside,' sang the enchanters, 'oh, you do like to be beside the sea.'

So, thought Amber, the harpies were back. And they were singing – yikes. They sang like a cross between a gaggle of drunk grannies in the front row of a bawdy play and two seagulls fighting over a dropped sausage. How on earth this was supposed to lure sailors to their doom was beyond Amber – maybe sailors had particularly low standards.

'Yes, that's right,' cooed Raynebow Sprynkles, ushering the group with her wings, 'come and see the caves.'

Amber wasn't sure what was more offensive – that yet another faction was trying to abduct them; that even a hotelier wasn't a safe ally; or that said hotelier thought this could possibly work. She glanced up at Fang to say as such, and found him gazing up towards the high window slack-jawed. Lazare and Nell were the same. Uh-oh.

Tiny hands grabbed the nape of Amber's neck. Tem looked terrified. 'What's wrong with them?'

'Nothing's wrong,' soothed the alicorn. 'Come on, let's see the sea!'

'Oh, you do like to stroll around the rocks, and go where the harpies sing "hey nonny nonny no",' continued the harpies from the window.

'I don't like this,' panicked Tem. 'It's like before, with him, the bad man.' She gazed at Raynebow Sprynkes, her eyes bright with disappointed tears. 'You're a bad unicorn!'

'Alicorn,' snapped Raynebow Sprynkles. 'Now, do as you're told and come see our glorious award-winning coastline!'

Amber tried drawing herself up. 'As a dragon, I must insist that you cease and desist in this egregious endeavour—'

'Shut up, runt,' chorused the alicorn and both harpies, before the song started up again.

The others, hypnotised, began to walk back towards the staircase. Amber scooped up Tem, and flew her up to Nell's eyeline. 'Can you sing, kiddo?'

'Not well,' worried the little girl.

'Perfect, me neither,' Amber told her, getting them both right up in Nell's glazed face. 'Sing anything,' she instructed Tem. 'Loud as you can. Drown out the other song.'

'Er,' fretted Tem.

'Anything,' repeated Amber. Fang and Lazare, ahead, were already descending the stairs as Raynebow Sprynkles ushered them.

'Stop being difficult,' the alicorn ordered Amber and Tem. 'Things are about to change round here, then you'll be sorry.'

'Theeeeeee,' sang Tem suddenly, in a loud and rather tone-deaf voice, 'wings on the dragon go flap flap flap, flap flap flap, flap flap flap.'

Amber joined in, at the top of her gravelly voice. 'The wings on the dragon go flap flap flap, with a hey nonny nonny and a folderol-derol. The Frenchman on the dragon goes "not the hair, not the hair, not the hair"—'

Nell blinked out of her stupor and focused on Amber. 'What...?'

'Keep singing, kid,' Amber called to Tem, and shouted at Nell as the child broke into a third verse, about the apothecary on the dragon going 'I like dockers'.

'Harpy magic,' yelled Amber. 'Only affects you if you're into women, so you three are in big trouble.'

Raynebow Sprynkles turned to them – a difficult feat for an alicorn on the stairs. 'Hey, you! Stop that!'

'Us?' called one of the harpies from the window.

'Obviously not you,' shouted the alicorn. 'You know what? Fine, I'll just take the men.'

'So – plan?' shouted Nell. 'We all sing?'

'Uh,' panicked Tem, still singing, 'the Tems on the dragon say "I don't know".'

She was clearly running out of things to sing about being on the dragon.

'Wait.' Nell hitched up her skirts to the thigh. 'The Nells on the, er, stairs, say "scrape off what's behind my knee".'

Amber flew Tem down, and the child did as requested. 'It's very icky,' sang the girl.

'Yeah, sorry 'bout that,' sang Nell. 'It can plug up ears so give it to me, with a hey nonny nonny and a folderol-derol.'

Nell bunged her own ears with some of the waxy paste Tem had scraped off her.

'No,' warned Raynebow Sprynkles.

'The daddies on the dragon go "I love you, I love you, I love you",' shout-sang Tem, as Nell and Amber rushed towards Fang and Lazare, darting and dodging past the alicorn's dangerously lunging horn. 'The daddies on the dragon go "I love you", with a hey nonny nonny and a folderol-derol...'

Tem reached out to bung Fang's ears, as Nell did the same for Lazare. The child struggled a bit with Fang's long hair.

'Er... derol-derol-derol-derol,' she improvised, finishing off the job.

Lazare and Fang blinked, looked at one another, then at Nell, Amber and Tem, then at the furious alicorn.

'What—?' asked Fang.

'Nothing, we're off to the beach,' shouted Raynebow Sprynkles.

'Harpy attack,' shouted Amber at them.

'What?' called Lazare.

'Come on,' shouted Nell, leading the way at a run down the stairs. 'We're escaping!'

'What?' shouted Fang.

'You will do no such thing,' whinnied Raynebow Sprynkles, in hot pursuit.

'What?' shouted Nell.

'*C'était quoi ça?*' shouted Lazare, which at least broke up all the cries of 'What?'

Amber snuck a glance behind her and saw that Raynebow Sprynkles was less than a foot away from them, charging, wings unfurling and horn lowered at an angle to do maximum damage to a little dragon that might find herself in said horn's way.

Lazare grabbed Amber and Tem, and with a single flap of his wings, he flew them all straight down the staircase. Over Lazare's shoulder, she saw Fang shoot a glare of concentration behind him, and the three stairs between them and Raynebow Sprynkles swiftly rotted away.

Raynebow Sprynkles reared up, horrified. 'My lovely stairs!'

'It's pretty-boy magic,' called Megara the harpy, flying down towards them from the high window. Nell flicked something at the harpy from her left thumb, and the harpy descended into a fit of sneezes.

Lazare barrelled out of the guesthouse, Amber and Tem still in his arms, and stopped suddenly on the huge branch outside.

'*Zut.* Forgot we were still up a tree.'

Amber turned and saw Bluejohn, perched on a higher branch, watching the unfolding scene with concern.

'What's going on in there?' demanded Bluejohn as Nell and Fang came crashing out of the doors. Lazare let go of Amber and whipped out a hand to grab Fang's shirt and stop him overshooting the branch. Raynebow Sprynkles followed close behind, fluttering to a stop at the sight of Bluejohn.

'Nothing, good sir dragon,' called Raynebow Sprynkles. 'They wanted to go to the seaside.'

'What?' asked Nell, cleaning out her ears.

'Did I hear harpy song in there?' added Bluejohn.

'No you didn't,' cried Xanthippe, flying away from the guest house window, dragging a sneezing Megara along with her. 'It was just some great big sneezes. Treehouses – terrible for allergies.'

Fang pulled out his own ear stoppers. 'We'll probably pass on the guest house,' he told Bluejohn. 'We'll just go to the castle now; we can wait for the queen in the lobby or something.'

'If you insist,' rumbled Bluejohn, 'but refreshment facilities are deeply limited.'

Tem was set down on the branch, and immediately reached out to give Amber a hug. 'You don't need to say sorry to that unicorn.'

'Fair dos,' replied Amber. 'I liked your song, by the way. Who taught you it?'

Tem glanced very briefly at Fang, who looked away, pink around the nose.

'Secret,' she told the dragon solemnly.

Fang was aware it would have been faster for all involved if he'd just waited for Lazare to fly him down to the ground after flying down Nell. Fang decided he'd just climb down the tree himself anyway. He could do with a moment to himself when he wasn't being hypnotised or chased or harassed. Even if it did mean getting scratches and splinters as he clambered down two dozen feet of branches. They weren't even safe here, in the supposed magical sanctuary of Llanelli. They couldn't even trust an alicorn guest-house manager to so much as check them in. People would keep finding out about the curse – or at least, that they were something new and strange – and would keep trying to use that to their advantage, to create immortal bodyguards, or worse. Fang didn't know for sure what exactly Elizabeth of England or Llewellyn of Wales actually intended to do with them to wring eternal political power from their curse. Had that alicorn even had a plan beyond 'lure them out to a cave'? Maybe these kings and queens and assorted others were relying on a plan presenting itself once they had him and his little family in chains. Maybe it involved centuries of enslavement; maybe it involved taking them apart. He was determined not to let any of it happen, and yet it was getting harder and harder to do so. They had barely won out against a single power-crazed alchemist – by waiting around for him to fatally self-sabotage – and even so, it had left two of his dearest companions horribly traumatised. Now, they were up against agents from at least two different monarchs, *and* random passing magicals. How were they supposed to evade all that when they could barely stop one man? How were they supposed to trust anyone?

No. No, he was going to stay positive, wasn't he? He was going to hang on to a new, hopeful outlook, for the sake of Tem and Lazare and the others. There were still good folk in the world that he could trust. His little group, that went without saying – and Nell's family seemed fine. And there was Wulfric, wasn't there, and those playwrights. Fang didn't really like to admit even to himself that he counted amongst his currently most trusted allies the lascivious zombie of Christopher bloody Marlowe, but the man did make himself useful, even if it was to try to get into either Fang's or Lazare's hose or, most likely, both at the same time. If he could trust Kit Marlowe, a man who had almost certainly got himself killed and reanimated to slither out of multiple criminal charges, then maybe he could trust an ancient and mighty dragon queen. Maybe.

He dropped down the last couple of feet to the ground and wiped sap, lichen and general tree detritus off his hands and onto his cape. After only a couple of days, the bright parakeet green of the gifted cape was already sporting multiple grubby smears. Camouflage, Fang told himself. He tried giving Lazare an encouraging little smile, as a peace offering. He wasn't sure how well he pulled it off – up until this week, he hadn't attempted any encouraging little smiles in almost a decade, so he was out of practice. Lazare still had that awful, worried expression that punched at Fang's gut. Well, Fang supposed, immediately after Lazare had opened up about his trauma over the danger they were always getting in, they'd gone and very nearly got abducted again. That wasn't exactly going to help matters, was it? He found himself missing the Frenchman's annoying grin, the shifting soft brown curls of his moustache as his mouth widened, the way those curls felt against Fang's lips…

Fang picked up Tem. 'You all right?' he asked. 'Did the harpies scare you?'

'Yes,' said Lazare quietly.

'Not really,' Tem replied, over the Frenchman.

'She saved us, back there,' Nell said, ruffling Tem's hair. 'Little hero.'

'No...' Tem flushed slightly, pink around the cheeks like a human, but with a faint glimmer of a fae aura around her head. 'It was Amber's plan.'

'Nah, Nell's right, you *were* a little hero,' Amber told the child proudly. 'One of the gang, aren't you?'

'Just don't go round trying to be *too* heroic,' Lazare added seriously. 'Don't want to end up like your daddy, always getting in scrapes.'

The sparkling flush left Tem. 'I do get in scrapes,' she said.

'Like daddy, like daughter,' added Fang before he could stop himself. Letting a distressed young orphan call him 'daddy' as she sought some form of stability in her life was one thing. Going along with it was another. It was utterly unethical, and selfish, and... and Tem gave him a tight hug, and he knew he should be sorry he had said it, but he wasn't. He would fix this. He had to, for all of them, living and unliving, and dead. He'd fix this, and earn the title of 'daddy', and honour Tem's mother – Confucius's Knees, he still didn't know the dead fae's name. He'd give the nightmares plaguing Tem and Lazare the time and space they needed to fade. Maybe even his own nightmares would have a chance to do the same. He just needed this plan to work, against all the odds, and then everything would be fine.

He made the decision to ignore the horrible boiling in his stomach telling him that it almost certainly wouldn't all be fine, and followed Amber towards the palace.

He was choosing hope.

Just as he had done before they'd murdered Flower.

CHAPTER FOURTEEN
VOLUMES OF FORGOTTEN LORE

Lady Anne Boleyn – Queen Mother, victim, survivor, cephalophore – found her elderly daughter poring over documents when she entered the royal study. With a now very familiar heft, she held her severed head in place upon her ragged, chopped neck so that she could speak.

'How goes it, Bessie?'

Elizabeth checked briefly that there was nobody else in the room before removing her huge, heavy auburn wig and scratching at her fuzz of close-cropped silver hair in frustration.

'I'm getting old, Mummy. What I learned of Cathayan script in my youth I've since half forgotten, and that's when I can see.'

She tried holding a piece of parchment out at arm's length and squinting at it. Anne walked to her side and held her head towards the manuscript. Her own vision was stuck forever as that of a thirty-five-year-old woman whose only blindness in life had been for the eventual dangers of a tempestuous king's flattering flirting, and her afterlife as a diplomat had involved considerable on-the-job schooling in reading multiple different world languages.

'Documents about Qin Shi Huang's search for the elixir of life,' noted Anne. She sighed. 'Dear heart. That man went mad with power, and the search for eternal life drove him madder still.' Anne chose not to add which other ageing, powerful, monstrous man that sounded like, or that the more her dear Bessie focused on this matter with the fugitives and their 'weird qi', the more Anne recognised the unsettling glint in her daughter's old eyes.

'Your concern is noted, Mother.' Elizabeth squinted at the manuscript again. 'Just... perhaps a detail was missed. Perhaps the elixir was there in Cathay all along; what if the Wanli Emperor is building an army of them and this fugitive of ours escaped? What if he was made?'

'By the loong, you mean?' Anne frowned softly at her daughter. 'I did hear rumour that the loong kings can make magicals, but surely it's just that – rumour.'

'I don't know,' sighed Elizabeth. 'And then there's the Frenchman and the Welshwoman, and this half-fae in the middle of it. When's the last time we heard of a half-fae being born? Interbreeding's been taboo for centuries. Unless...' She spread multiple documents over her desk, some in Cathayan, others in French and Welsh and English, even the runic written language of the European dragons. 'Unless they're up to something.'

'The fae?'

'Maybe!' And there was that horrible glint in Bessie's eye again. The glint *he'd* got when he'd started convincing himself that Anne had birthed a daughter instead of a son on purpose, to undermine him. 'Maybe Redthroat has given new orders. My ancestors gave that dragon a whole city right beneath our feet to keep the peace, but what if she's decided to start using that against us? Undermining us? Literally!'

'Bessie?' asked Anne, troubled. 'When's the last time you slept? Rest, my love. And do remember, you merely wish to speak with these fugitives, to gently persuade them to help you keep James from the throne. You are the one getting the upper hand here. You're not fighting a conspiracy by the Wanli Emperor or Redthroat or...'

There was a rapping at the chamber door. Elizabeth hurriedly put on her wig. 'Enter.'

A raven did as bidden. 'Message from Captain Honkensby, ma'am,' croaked the bird nervously.

Elizabeth snatched it from the raven, squinted angrily at it from an arm's length and huffed an irritable sigh. 'Anything else?'

The raven glanced nervously from Elizabeth to Anne and back to Elizabeth again in a manner that screamed 'yes there is something else but I was told it's a secret'.

'I keep no secrets from my mother, Constable,' Elizabeth reminded the raven.

The raven nodded, with a manic nervousness. 'There was also this, ma'am. Sent most urgently from an anonymous well-wisher in Carmarthen.' She passed over another note, which Elizabeth marched over to the fireplace, well away from the raven and Anne before holding the note over the flames and reading it at the full length of her arm.

Anne made no comment on the fact that this furtive note meant Elizabeth was definitely using spies to keep tabs on her allies Llewellyn and Redthroat, possibly even to keep a more cynical eye on Honkensby's progress. Anne too had been queen once. She knew how the diplomatic sausage was made.

With the mystery note read, Elizabeth dropped the paper straight into the fire, and turned back to the bird. 'Tell Honkensby I want those fugitives, no matter what. She is reminded that her allegiance is not to protocol, not of any country. She is *my* law, and *I* determine when that has been overreached. If she cannot deliver, then I shall get somebody who can. And if *my* fugitives end up under Redthroat's control and command...' Elizabeth trailed off.

'Yes, ma'am?' prompted the raven, terrified.

'I was deliberately leaving the rest of the sentence blank, Constable. For emphasis. It's a threat, you see.'

'Shall... I send word that you trailed off for emphasis then, ma'am?'

Elizabeth nodded, that terrible glint again. 'See that you do.'

Quoth the raven, 'Yes, ma'am, sorry, ma'am, thank you, ma'am!' She left in a flurry of frightened feathers.

'Bessie,' sighed Anne. 'You can't really think it's a great conspiracy?' She picked up another Ming document. Some sad report of a huli jing's attempt to seduce a peasant human boy, ending in horrible murder. 'The existence of the magicals is as natural and chaotic as human life. Even if these fugitives are a new type, they will have been created by accident as much as the rest of them. As much as you, my sweet babe, were made a beautiful girl in my belly by chance, not by magical treason as your father insisted.'

Bessie looked tired and frail again. 'I think... I would be a fool to rule out any thought. I think I am a woman not yet seventy who is still near the end of her life; while a dragon monarch more than a dozen times my age squats and waits, with cities full of her subjects; while the son of the woman I beheaded also waits with his army in the north, with his rabid hatred of magicalkind, ready to pour his spite all over this land. While empires push on every side, and we can't even get a decent trade colony going amongst the Roanoke of the New World. And don't get me started on the Spanish! I think I should leave nothing to chance, and I certainly should leave nothing to bloody Redthroat.'

CHAPTER FIFTEEN
THE BIGGER, BETTER CASTLE

Redthroat's palace was even more imposing close up. It was the scale of the place. While most buildings in Deep London had been constructed at twice the scale of human houses, everything in Redthroat's palace was around four times the size Lazare was used to. The Frenchman was tall, for a human. He was used to looming over people. He quite liked it, in fact. As the giant wooden doors to the palace swung open for them, he had never felt so small or insignificant. This matter wasn't helped by the colossal tapestries lining every wall, depicting Redthroat eating English soldiers. Lazare suspected that that was deliberate. If one were a dragon monarch sharing an island with three different human monarchies, with all of the geopolitical tensions that would cause, would one not wish to put any human visitors on the back foot? Even if it were simply through the medium of carefully embroidered viscera in your decor?

'Wow.' Stunted though she was, Amber seemed in her element in the palace. Likely it was just the fact she was their official escort to the queen, and it was making her feel important for once in a life of darkness and scrabbling over roadkill. Lazare hoped it was just that, and not the gory needlework renderings of broken human bodies and glistening dragon teeth.

Amber nodded to one of the dragon guards in the doorway. 'Did you use copper thread to make all the guts glisten like that?'

The guard shrugged. 'Dunno. Brownies made those for us.'

'Needlework beneath dragonkind, is it?' muttered Nell.

'Well, to be fair, Nell, we don't have thumbs.' Amber flapped along the enormous hall. 'Pretty sure it's this way!'

Tem tried to prise Fang's hand away from her eyes as they all followed Amber. 'I wanna see the dragon pictures!'

'Not these ones, you don't,' Fang told her hurriedly.

Tem had the nightmares too, Lazare reminded himself. Tem, who had endured so much pain and loss and trauma at such a tiny age. And she was able to deal with it all so much better than he – a grown, adult, sexy sexy man – was at dealing with even a fraction of her burden. She had been forced to witness the same horrors he had, been forced to participate in them, and the nightmares followed her, and yet she was still able to hold Fang the way that she wanted to hold him.

Lazare wanted to hold Fang again. He wanted to kiss him again, without seeing horrors and worries, without one of them having to pull away. He wanted to reset his brain to that point before the alchemist's attack, that perfect moment when his thoughts had been of need and want and thighs and arms, rather than fear and inadequacy. Before the alchemist had tormented them, and then the swan and the griffin and the harpies had chased them, driving them ever onwards, always getting away by the skin of their teeth and running headlong into another terrible situation. Why, ever since he and Fang had met, some queen or king or magical being had harried at their heels every step of the way. Driving them westwards, wielding whips of fear. Just as had been done to Fang for half of his life. Did it make any difference that Fang had started trying to put a positive spin on the chase? Acting as if they were running towards a solution, ignoring the truth – that yet again they were just fleeing one problem by running to another potential problem. Fleeing two monarchs by walking straight into the lair of the dragon queen.

Lazare wanted to kiss Fang. He wanted to shake him, and tell him he was a bloody idiot for choosing now of all times to hold out hope. A contrary bloody idiot. A lovely bloody idiot. How Lazare wished he could go back to being the optimistic one, always blithely telling a fatalist Fang that everything would probably be all right. It had been easier that way round. Not least because Fang's desperate hope now only made Lazare adore him all the more.

They left the grand, gory hallway, and followed Amber through a very slightly smaller corridor, where at least the tapestries of Redthroat were more majestic and less bloodthirsty. Fang uncovered Tem's eyes and pointed out one of the nicer, shinier embroideries to her. Her face lit up, and he hurried over to hold her up to the wall so that she could run her fingers over the shimmering needlework.

Idiot. One wasn't supposed to touch the displays. Lazare really, *really* wanted to kiss him.

The upsides of Amber being their official dragon consort were that they knew they could trust her, and she was proud as punch at the appointment. The downside was that she had no idea where she was going. They found themselves utterly lost in the giant castle. They bumped into a dragon guard, but were unable to ask her for directions since she was deep in argument with a wizened zombie.

'As his valet, his comfort is my highest priority,' argued the zombie.

'His comfort is assured; he has our delegate suite as requested,' replied the dragon guard. 'We had to put other visitors up in a nearby guest house.'

'He waits too long for his reception,' continued the zombie. 'He has travelled from the other side of the globe. Did Her Majesty not receive my missive of entreaty?'

'She did, some hours ago, but the queen has a busy schedule and will see your master when she... I'm sorry, can I help you?'

Seemingly just noticing Lazare and his group, both dragon and zombie turned to face them irritably. Both looked formidable – the dragon guard was the size of Lazare's old bedroom, and the zombie was covered in strange tattoos, and stared out at them with an unseeing pearl eye.

'Um,' muttered Amber, 'here to see the queen?'

'Isn't everyone?' asked the zombie. 'Including my master, the first of his kind to travel from—'

'Amber of Deep London and party?' asked the guard, cutting the zombie off.

'Aye,' replied Amber proudly. She turned to the others. 'Guys, they put my name first!'

'This way,' the guard told them in bored tones, turning and guiding them down a corridor as the zombie protested and lolloped in their wake. 'You're early,' added the guard. 'Did you not like your guesthouse? The beds are made of magic clouds.'

'Nah, the manager tried to kidnap us,' explained Amber matter-of-factly.

The guard sighed. 'No doubt you brought it on yourselves, but you can file a complaint if you like.'

'We'd just like to see the queen,' said Fang. He shot an apologetic glance over his shoulder to the complaining zombie valet behind them. 'We can wait our turn.'

'All right,' grumbled the guard, opening up doors to a massive antechamber, 'but I'm not getting you any refreshments. Make yourselves comfortable.' And with that, she disappeared through another, even bigger set of doors, causing the zombie valet to throw his hands up in dismay and skulk off back the way he'd come.

'Making themselves comfortable' was easier said than done, since there weren't any chairs. There were perches aplenty, onto one of which Amber quite happily landed. The closest thing to a seat available to the rest of them were sort-of nests on the floor, filled with rags. Nell tried sitting in one of them, immediately regretted it and had great difficulty hoisting herself up out of it again.

'I wish that bad unicorn hadn't tried to kidnap you,' sighed Tem. 'I'd have liked to sleep in a magic cloud bed.'

Lazare tried not to think about how amazing it would have been to make love to Fang in a magic cloud in a treehouse surrounded by rainbows. He gave one of the floor nests an experimental nudge with his foot and got a sharp twig stuck in the toe of his boot for his trouble.

The door opened again, which took a while because of the whole hugeness of it. The dragon guard stood in the doorway, a faintly confused expression on her face. 'You're in luck,' the guard told them. 'Her Majesty's schedule just cleared up. You can go through.'

Lazare shot yet another concerned glance at the group. 'That was quick.'

'Yes, well,' growled the guard dismissively, 'Her Majesty is gracious and kindly to runts and lesser beings. Be grateful.' The guard nodded them through as she passed. 'And now, if you don't mind, I have to go and find the world's most annoying valet to tell our first ever visiting bunyip that his reception's been shunted.'

'What's a bunyip?' asked Fang.

'Someone who's come all the way from the Wemba Wemba lands, is who,' snorted the guard.

'Where on earth is the Wemba Wemba?' added Fang, incredulous.

'Exactly,' snapped the guard, and she was gone.

They stepped through the colossal door, into a room that was as huge and cavernous as it was sparkling. Amber had recently told Lazare that it was actually a myth that all dragons loved to collect gold. The sight of Redthroat's throne room now led him to believe that Amber had been lying because she was embarrassed by the fact she didn't have any gold of her own. The evening light streamed through windows and danced off the shining mounds that heaped all over the giant floor. Sapphires, rubies, emeralds and diamonds glinted amongst the warm yellow glow. Even following the unfortunate incident of 1324, when Mansa Musa the Alchemist Emperor had, in the twin names of generosity and showing off, accidentally created and handed out so much gold that he'd crashed the value of the stuff for generations, the sheer volume of gold in Redthroat's throne room had to accumulate to an astronomical value. As power moves went, this one was even less subtle than the tapestries. Most of the gold was piled into a giant heap in the centre of the room, a sort of deconstructed glittering throne. On top of it, curled like a kitty cat, was the biggest dragon Lazare had ever seen.

CHAPTER SIXTEEN
REDTHROAT THE INVINCIBLE

The dragon had to be eighty feet from pointed snout to twisted tail, at least. Every scale was as big as Lazare's hand, and all glittered a vivid blood red. Redthroat the Invincible, and yes, that title didn't seem like false flattery to Lazare, on looking at her. The army of the English invasion may have outnumbered their Welsh counterparts two to one all those years ago, but it only took one glance at Redthroat's colossal frame to imagine her bearing down on soldiers in battle, wings blotting out the sky in a veil of blood, every edge of her dagger-sharp. Lazare didn't want to imagine the volume or range of her flame breath, but it could likely wipe out entire battalions in a single exhale.

Redthroat lifted her enormous head and, catlike again, gave a wide yawn. A hundred dragon fangs, each the size of a human child, glistened at them in the gold-light.

'Speak,' she rumbled, in a voice like a distant thunderstorm.

Lazare blinked and remembered that, for all of his misgivings about how swiftly Redthroat had ushered them to her, it was they who had requested an audience with her, and they who sought her favours, not the other way around. He was the orator here, and the charmer; he should be the one to address the dragon queen. Before he could say anything, Tem stepped forward and performed the sort of intricately choreographed curtsey that a small child might come up with when she wasn't really sure what a curtsey should be. It involved several twirls. As Redthroat watched in confusion, Nell also stepped out, in front of the child, and bowed deeply, her hand over her heart.

'Majesty. We, er... we've got a magical problem, see, and the fae can't fix it, and we thought, obviously you're better than the fae... no offence, Tem, and, er... Sorry, Majesty, I'm getting distracted. You are *really* beautiful.'

'That I am,' replied Redthroat matter-of-factly.

Tem scurried back to Fang. 'It's the dragon off the flag,' she told him with an urgent reverence.

Redthroat gave a weary sigh, which came across like a hot desert wind. 'I keep forgetting Llewellyn still has my likeness on that little flag of his. It's the thought that counts, I suppose.'

Nell pulled a subtly concerned expression at the mild irritation in Redthroat's tone. The dragon queen's eyes, like diamonds set in two huge spheres of obsidian, settled on the Welshwoman.

'Oh, no need to look so worried, Miss ver'Evan. The Aberffraw monarchs of Wales are valued allies – as too do I retain friendly relations with Henry of France.' Redthroat turned her sparkling black eyes to Lazare, who responded with his own deep bow, containing no fewer than five hand flourishes. 'And,' continued Redthroat, 'the Wanli Emperor.' Fang, clearly realising he was probably expected to provide some sort of positive reaction to this news, nodded at the dragon and gave her an awkward thumbs up. 'We are even well allied these days,' added Redthroat, 'with the Tudor monarchs of Upper England, doomed as that line currently is.' She shook her colossal, glimmering head. 'Honestly, you develop a perfectly good diplomacy with a human dynasty, and then they go and die out. And that's when they're not murdering and usurping one another. Monarchs and emperors, they're all still so fragile. So short-lived. And a shorter window even still in which to establish an heir and continue the line. What the Upper English Crown is facing now will no doubt be faced by the Aberffraw and the Ming in the blink of a dragon's eye, and I don't need to tell you, Mr Quitte-Beuf, that sort of instability's already been happening in France for some time. And then, what do you get? Uprisings. Massacres. Wars. You get James bloody Stuart riding south, with his ugly little hatred of magicalkind.' Redthroat sighed again, hitting Lazare and the group with yet another gust of hot, dry air. 'Humans, am I right?'

'Uh...' The group exchanged glances.

'Because,' continued Redthroat, 'you're *not* human, are you? Or at least none of you are anymore.'

'I suppose,' muttered Nell.

'It's what we came to seek your guidance on, in fact,' added Fang. 'We thought, as queen of the magicals...'

'But you're not one of us either,' noted Redthroat. 'You're all strange halfway things, all bar your runt dragon, and we tend not to count the runts as they so rarely survive to adulthood as this one has.'

'Was that a compliment?' asked Amber.

'I don't think so,' replied Lazare, his heart hammering.

'Haven't heard of a half-fae surviving past infancy in some centuries, either,' added Redthroat. 'But at least I've heard of them. The rest of you – not undead, not fae, not human, and yet a combination of all three. That alchemist has mixed three elements in you, and created a powerful line indeed.'

'You know about us?' asked Nell. 'About the alchemist, and Tem?'

'Miss ver'Evan, you were magically transformed in my London embassy, in front of a púca ambassador. The alchemist who created you was killed and eaten by several of my subjects. Deep London is my realm – so yes, I know what happened. As I know that my valued allies Llewellyn and Elizabeth both sent agents to intercept you and deliver you to them before you could have your intended audience with me. I know that the griffin and the swan both now circle the walls of Llanelli, awaiting their chance to snatch you up and severely test the boundaries of our alliances. I have eyes on all of you that you know not of.'

'But... wait.' Nell looked perplexed and embarrassed. 'Beg pardon, Majesty, but would the King of Wales truly treat you with the disrespect and lack of grace that Elizabeth Tudor would? He put you on a flag!'

'His ancestor put me on a flag,' replied Redthroat. 'He just kept me on it. I did just say I appreciated the sentiment and his political allegiance. But he's still a king, not a subject. The only concessions I ask of him are for the comfort and safety of magical beings, as much as he likes to privately complain that I've removed Welsh sovereignty, that he's little more than my pet – would that he were; it'd make my life easier. Llewellyn's main loyalty is to himself, and his own limited human power, just like Elizabeth's. The idea of an eternal reign must tempt them so, even though the last human emperor to try undead rule learned it was a bad idea the hard way – right?'

She turned her gaze to Fang.

'But we don't seem to count as undead,' reasoned Fang. 'They would believe they can get around the laws that ban undead rule, with our powers.' He looked around at the others. 'Elizabeth and Llewellyn don't just want immortal armies – they want the spell for themselves.'

Redthroat hummed a little affirmation. It rumbled along the floor and up through Lazare's boots.

'And who knows what measures they'll stoop to to attain it,' she said. 'They may try torture, or cannibalism. Perhaps they've already learned that it is not the three of you they need to force to make them immortal, but the half-fae.'

Tem gasped, frightened, and Fang held the child tighter. 'They're not laying a jewel-encrusted finger on her.'

'Well, they won't now you've made it here,' replied Redthroat. 'Don't look upon them too unkindly – to their human minds, an immortal monarch would herald great stability for their land and their people.'

'And to you?' asked Lazare. 'What would a human monarch with our powers be to dragonkind?'

Redthroat blinked down at Lazare quite calmly, still seeing him through her giant transparent eyelid as it slid back and forth across her black eyes. 'An abomination,' she told them levelly. 'An existential threat, not to be allowed. My Asian brethren buried the last one alive – or unalive; I don't know what one calls burying ten thousand zombies surrounded by a lake of mercury so they can't even claw their way out, but that's what they had to do with Qin Shi Huang. Strange that no human nor undead these days ever question *why* it is always written bindingly in every human land's constitution that undead rule is not just prohibited, but every undead becomes an automatic subject of the dragons. We dragons did that, in the decades of turmoil after Qin Shi Huang. An undead monarch reigning for hundreds of years can only go mad with power. The concept was, and remains, unacceptable to us. As you said yourself, Mr Fang, you people are a loophole. Strange, and new, and unregulated. We don't even know yet just how long you will live for. It cannot be allowed. No matter how noble I'm sure their supposed reasoning is. No matter if it's to keep James Stuart from the Upper English throne.'

'You would rather have another war between humans and magicals than allow Elizabeth our powers?' asked Lazare, as respectfully as he could manage. He tried bowing again, to soften any inferred impudence.

Redthroat didn't seem offended by his question. The mighty dragon sounded more… depressed. 'War with James Stuart may be unavoidable either way. He grows increasingly zealous in his hatred of magicalkind; sooner or later, something will snap. It could be him becoming King of Upper England. Could be him feeling robbed of the Upper English Crown if Elizabeth becomes a magical immortal to retain it. He could cross a line with his treatment of Scottish magicals that I can no longer meet with mere admonishments and threats. I try to avoid it, but… well. It took me four months to incinerate the English army into retreat back in the day; do you really fancy James's chances against me to be any better?'

'They do have muskets now,' reasoned Fang.

'Ooh, gunpowder,' rumbled Redthroat sarcastically. Her flame sacs glowed. Even from dozens of feet away from her huge gold nest, Lazare could feel the heat of them. 'I'm *ever* so scared.' She doused the glow of her throat, and returned to her usual level, if rather hangdog, tone. 'Your concern is appreciated, but I will be fine. Especially now that you are here.'

'I must ask, Majesty,' said Lazare nervously, 'since you have stated that it's in the nature of monarchs to seek eternal life, and you too are a monarch...'

'You believe I'd try to take your immortality for myself?' Redthroat paused, and Lazare could feel the sweat prickle his neck. 'Have I given you any reason to believe that is my goal? Have I attacked you? Imprisoned you? I know that the child is the source of the spell; have I made any attempt to force her magic to my advantage?'

'An alicorn tried to kidnap them earlier, Majesty,' piped Amber, 'and you did move a lot of meetings around to see us quickly.'

'Raynebow Sprynkles will be dealt with, little runty one, and your acknowledgement of my grace in expediting a meeting with a unique new race is appreciated,' replied Redthroat, a soft thunder of amusement in her tone. 'There's nothing wrong with bumping a bunyip every now and then.'

'So you don't want to be immortal then, Majesty?' asked Amber. 'Just 'cause, full disclosure, we still don't know if the spell works on dragons, and as one of your free and happy subjects I do not consent to being the test sample if you were looking to find that out.'

Redthroat gave a small laugh. It sounded like an explosion several miles away. 'I *like* this runt! That sunless ditch of my London doesn't grow them much, but it does make them sassy. I have lived a thousand years already, little runt, and I shall live and reign a thousand more. That is enough life for me. I don't need an abominable spell of muddled fae and human to enhance my greatness. Not least after you all came to me with Miss ver'Evan's heartfelt entreaty for me to help you with your condition.'

'Yes,' stammered Nell, 'um, Your Majesty. Please and thank you.'

'No need to beg and scrape,' Redthroat told her. 'I have told you the stakes, and why I am grateful you came to me first.'

'You can help us?' breathed Lazare. 'Oh, Majesty.' He bowed yet again, even though he'd just been told not to.

Redthroat rumbled another knee-trembling hum. 'It won't be easy – at least, not for you.'

Fang stepped forward suddenly. 'You could make us fae.'

Redthroat cocked her house-sized head at him.

'You have our permission.' He looked around at the others. 'Right?'

'Why fae?' asked Redthroat. 'Was the little one not expelled from their settlement on no uncertain terms?'

'Because of us! Because we muddy her magic. But if we were fae…' Fang floundered, the thin spectre of hope melting away under cursory inspection, and turning out to just be the ghost-shaped hanging jacket of grim reality. Fang tried again. 'Because it's not about Tem's spell; it's about Tem. And all of us, as a… not a "family" as such, but…' He stopped, and tried starting a third time. 'She needs to go home. And she needs people to care for her. And if you made us fae, perhaps…'

'And bring back Mummy,' added Tem, with a rare assuredness.

Fang blinked at the child in his arms. 'What?'

'You said Her Majesty dragon can make fae, like Mummy,' Tem told him. 'And the bad men hurted Mummy and I couldn't bring her back then because my magic wasn't strong enough, but Her Majesty's is the strongest. So, she can bring back Mummy. I can have a mummy and a daddy! And a Lazare and a Nell and an Amber. You'll like her; she's nice. Daddies and mummies are good friends, right?'

Oh, thought Lazare. *Oh, no.* He thought back over the days since they had all discovered Tem's fae mother had been killed during the kidnap. Tem had barely cried over it. A little girl learning her mother was dead – one would expect her to be inconsolable. He'd assumed initially she was still in shock, or too exhausted by her ordeal to weep. But, days on, she hadn't even begun to process it. She had brought three people back from the dead, multiple times; she didn't understand how permanent true death was. And they had taken her to see the dragon queen, telling her that Redthroat could fix everything, put things back, get her home, create more fae. Fang had not been the only one labouring under false hopes. Lazare had a sickly feeling that he was in part to blame for this. One bright thought fluttered irresponsibly through his mind – what if it wasn't a false hope after all, but a perfectly reasonable hope? This was the almighty dragon queen, after all. The being of legends, the bringer of miracles, according to Welsh lore. What if she could make them all fae? What if she could create a new fae, a perfect copy of Tem's mother?

'You know I can't do any of that, right?' said Redthroat.

It hadn't even been Lazare's hope, not really; it had been Fang and Tem's. But the absolute death of that hope still landed a crushing weight on Lazare's chest and stomach. Tem started crying – just a soft cry at first, not the sudden wail of a small child that quickly peters out, but the gentle, broken cry of someone who needs to preserve energy since they will be at it for some time.

'I don't know where this myth that I created the fae came from,' continued Redthroat with another desert storm gust of a sigh. 'Maybe I had dragons deliberately seed it and then forgot; maybe it sprouted of its own accord – honestly, there's so many myths and rumours about me these days, I lose track. The fae evolved perfectly naturally with the rest of the magical folk. Fae, púca, huli jing, aziza and so on – nobody made them any more than dragons or humans were made. They're born, they die. The end. They can't even be made undead. The magic of undeath doesn't work on them.'

'Tem's did, though.' There was an upsetting desperation to Fang's tone. 'It started working on her mother; the fae had to stop it.'

'That was wise of them,' reasoned Redthroat. 'I don't know what it would have created. This child's magic is strange indeed, and likely stronger even than mine. All the more reason to put a stop to her spell now.'

'How?' asked Amber. 'You keep telling us how glad you are that we came to you, that you can help us, and then not saying what you actually want to do.'

'There's a reason for that,' Redthroat told them. 'I want to impress upon you why I have no choice but to do what I am to do, otherwise you might try to run away, and that would just be awkward for everyone involved.'

'What are you going to do?' asked Fang, clenching a fist even as he grasped the sobbing Tem.

'I have only one option,' continued Redthroat. 'I hope you understand the difficult bind I'm in.'

'What are you going to do?' echoed Lazare, stepping defensively towards Fang and Tem, wings raised.

Redthroat stood up on top of her mound, sending golden coins and huge jewels skittering down the pile, her giant, glimmering snout twisted into a roughly apologetic expression. 'I'm going to eat you.'

'What?' chorused the three cursed adults.

Tem's cry grew in volume and urgency, fear and betrayal adding a new sharpness to the broken despair in her wail.

Amber flapped up in front of the group. 'With utmost respect, Your Honoured Majesty, no you sodding well aren't.'

'Charming sassiness or not, my dear little fly, I've been mulling this problem since I first heard of it, and I'm afraid it's the only way – the kindest way.'

'Kindest?' Amber flapped forward as Lazare checked for any exits and found both the door and the large skylight above barred and guarded. 'My friends would survive being eaten, ma'am! Fang got drowned like eight times the other night; he'd pop right back to life. Alive and in agony in your stomach juices!'

Tem wailed even more, in horror. Lazare tried to grab the little dragon's tail to stop her courageous if tactless defence of her friends, but Amber flapped forward again, up towards Redthroat on her mound, a gnat standing up to a hippopotamus.

'If not for my friends, Majesty, then think of your own tummy-ache!'

'I am not a monster,' rumbled the eighty-foot ancient dragon. 'I wouldn't let them suffer. Obviously, I'd eat the child first.'

Tem's screams became hysterical. Fang hurriedly shoved the girl into Nell's arms.

'Sleeping potion, dragonsbane, acid, poison, whatever it takes, get her out of this room,' he instructed the apothecary, before turning back to the dragon, both fists bunched, as if the silly egg would be able to best a giant, flame-breathing dragon just by punching her on the snout.

'The spell comes from her,' continued Redthroat, slowly descending her pile towards them, in spite of Fang's bravely bunched little fists. 'A lonely, insecure child's need for stability and family, realised through magic. A little one's concept of family is eternal, so you will live for as long as she needs you, but without her, there is no need, and no curse, so...' Redthroat stopped, and looked down. Beneath her colossal claws, her mountain of gold was rusting like ancient, damp iron, corroding into lumpen, autumn-coloured nothings. She looked across at Fang.

'Gold doesn't rust,' she told him. 'Sweet of you to try your magic to defend your brood, but you're panicking, aren't you? Making mistakes.'

'We'll stay in Llanelli,' blurted Fang, the gold becoming pristine and shiny again with the exhalation of his breath. 'Let me make a home here behind these walls with my daughter, with the ones I love, please. We will never leave, I promise; you can guard us against giving our powers to other humans.'

Lazare risked a glance at Nell's reflection in a giant-sized golden chalice. She was trying to avoid the dragon guards, undo her bodice and hold a child at the same time. As escape attempts went, she wasn't doing so well, in spite of Fang's distraction.

Redthroat continued her stroll down the pile. 'Three of my subjects already tried to abduct you this afternoon.'

'We avoided them! And if you make an example of them, it'll discourage further attempts.'

'You truly expect me to believe you would contentedly stay in this small city for centuries, Fang of Cathay?' Redthroat continued. 'Possibly forever? You, who have run half the globe?'

'Yeah,' replied Fang. 'I would. I've finally found reasons to stop.'

'And the others? What of Miss ver'Evan, with no customers, no lovers, no adventure? What of your mate, Mr Quitte-Beuf?'

'We're not—' began Fang, but Redthroat cut him off.

'Would he be satisfied with no theatres, no audiences, no applause? Are you reason enough for *him* to stop?'

'I don't need applause,' said Lazare, and he mostly meant it. He would miss acting, of course, but did he *need* it? Did he need it like he needed Fang to be OK? Was love not all about sacrifice? Perhaps this was how he truly showed his worth – not with grand performance, but by quietly giving up the life he loved, for a lost child and a man he adored. 'We all shall stay, for love.'

'Then,' replied Redthroat, 'why is Miss ver'Evan trying to flee?'

Lazare only dared to turn towards Nell as Redthroat hopped easily off her glittering curated mountain. Nell hadn't managed to escape; she hadn't even managed to unlace her bodice. She was trying unsuccessfully to get close enough to one of the dragon guards to rub the dragonsbane dribbling from the inside of her right wrist on it, while avoiding the guards' snarling teeth and warning spurts of flame. She still had Tem held in her other arm. The girl was screaming in absolute horror, eyes fixed on the approaching Redthroat.

Lazare could see Fang already running to throw himself between Nell and Tem and the dragon queen.

'Daddy,' screamed Tem.

'You won't need a daddy when you're dead,' rumbled Redthroat. It wasn't spoken cruelly, but in a faintly sad and deliberately kind-sounding tone. In a way, that made it worse.

The first time Lazare had used his wings, he hadn't been aware of it. They'd just kicked in when Fang had been in danger, flapping towards safety in as much of an automatic bodily response to peril as a flinch or a hit of adrenaline. He wasn't aware of them now either, even though they weren't flapping him to safety at all. He was aware of the approaching dragon queen, opening her jaws towards Nell, towards Tem, towards Fang – the closest to her, his magic useless against her, putting himself between a little one and harm, armed with nothing but his own body to absorb the harm instead.

Just like always. Lazare didn't even have time to get angry at Fang for hurling himself in danger yet again. He didn't have time to feel a thing. His brain was full of white noise. He didn't know he was flying. Just, one moment he was standing a few feet away watching helplessly and the next, Redthroat's vast, wide, glistening maw was upon him, and the white noise of the screams had Fang's voice and it screamed out his name, and then there was nothing but heat and darkness and pain.

CHAPTER SEVENTEEN
AND YOU'D BETTER HIDE VERY SOON

'**L**azare!' Fang watched helplessly as the Frenchman flew between him and the dragon queen's open mouth, and the mighty jaws closed around him, easily gobbling up his Lazare, his funny, preening, annoying, lovely parakeet of a man, in a single bite.

'Lazare,' he screamed again. Redthroat chewed. He heard a muffled wail of pain from inside the dragon's mouth, matched by a new wail behind him. He felt a burst of Tem's magic from behind him, streaming over to Lazare trapped between teeth as big as the child herself, shoving the life back into him. Redthroat chewed again. Lazare screamed again. Tem's magic exploded again.

'Stop that,' ordered Redthroat, through a full mouth.

'She can't stop it,' argued Amber, flying right up to Redthroat's eyes. 'Trust me – we've been through this before. I *warned* you about this, ma'am!'

'You're just prolonging the suffering, child.'

Fang screamed a wordless scream of rage and despair. The walls of the room dripped dragon blood and excrement and rot. He knew it wouldn't make Redthroat stop; it wasn't a tactical illusion, it was honestly more of an extension of the scream. His friends! No – his family. His daughter. His Lazare. His sweet, wonderful Lazare. Suffering, screaming, hurt and traumatised, again. All those fears that if he dared grow close to someone again they would get hurt, now realised. And Fang had led them to this! He had led them into the dragon's mouth on a false hope, because he hadn't known what else to do. It was all his fault. Again. Why did he keep doing this? Why was he doomed to take the people he cared for most in the world by the hand and lead them straight into torment and violence, over and over again? The dragon chewed again, and he heard the crunch and at once he was watching helplessly both in the dragon's lair and back in his home village, held back, seeing the blood on the stone in his mother's hand. Repeating the same mistakes, again, and again, and again with his endlessly recycled dregs of life, and it was always the people he loved who suffered for his stupidity.

He still had no plan. No idea how to get them out of the situation he'd put them in. He wasn't even thinking straight enough to begin to come up with a plan. He did the only thing he could. He lashed out and punched the dragon queen on the snout. It was incredibly hard and pointed, covered in sharp ridges. The upshot was, not only did he fail to deter Redthroat in any way, he also sliced a gash in his own knuckles.

'Take me,' he cried, his fist now streaming blood. 'Eat *me*.'

'I'm going to,' Redthroat told him, her mouth still full. 'Soon as I manage to eat... eurgh, it's like gristle.'

'Your Majesty,' called Amber urgently, still up in the dragon queen's face as Redthroat tried chewing yet again.

'No,' screamed Tem. Her magic was a constant torrent now. Her magical panic matched the panic in Fang's own heart, stomach and head. He didn't know what to do. Was he crying? Yep, he was crying. How was that going to help anybody? He wasn't helping! Tem was keeping Lazare alive, Nell had stopped trying to get past the guards at the back and was at Fang's side, holding the child in one arm and desperately waving her dragonsbane-dripping wrist at Redthroat with the other, and here was Fang just standing there and crying. Even little Amber was trying her best to talk sense into the queen.

'You're just making everything worse,' cried Amber in Redthroat's face. 'That poor kiddie already gets nightmares; you want to give her more?'

'I'm trying to end her sorrow; that's why you wretches and runts came to me, isn't it?'

'Yeah, pardon us for thinking the Queen of Dragons would have a solution that wasn't just eating us,' railed Amber. 'Clearly we overestimated you. You're an idiot, ma'am!'

'Living in a hole has made you *too* sassy,' replied Redthroat, and chewed again. 'And Miss ver'Evan, *do* stop waving dragonsbane at me; it's not helping.'

Even as Lazare screamed and Fang screamed and Nell screamed and Tem's magic gushed, Amber reared up in mid-air, and breathed one of her little plumes of fire. Redthroat's right eye was almost as large as Amber's whole body, and right up against the queen's face, the little dragon hit the giant eye dead-on.

Redthroat hissed through clenched teeth, shrinking back in pain. 'There is "sassy" and then there is "treason", runt.'

'Well, like you say, I've been in a hole all my life, ma'am,' Amber told the queen hotly. 'Living off scraps. Living with others. Not hoity-toitying it about in a place where everyone acts like we're best, making people bow to us, hurting people deliberately.'

'You hurt *me* deliberately, runt!'

'You started it. And stop calling me "runt", please.'

'I am your queen!'

'Are you actually, though? Deep London's *very* different to Llanelli, you know. If Llanelli's your idea of what your kingdom should be, my hometown is nothing like that. When's the last time you even visited, let alone did any sort of active ruling down there?'

This seemed to give Redthroat food for thought. Still wincing from the irritation to her eye, the scales around her brow creased in a frown.

'Around a century ago,' the dragon queen admitted. 'I meant to visit once a decade, but the Emfor is just the worst. Mean you to say all the dragons in Deep London are as belligerent as you? Even the bigger ones? Could they form some sort of insurrec— GLAH!'

The 'GLAH' was the sound of an eighty-foot dragon having her mouth forced open from the inside by a shaky, bloodied but generally intact actor. Fang's breath caught in the back of his throat as he mentally counted two arms, two legs, two wings and a head that was still attached to the

Frenchman's body, a face that was annoyingly good-looking as ever, if dripping with petroleum.

'Lazare,' screamed Fang, clambering up the dragon's open jaw to help him out

'Eurgh,' managed Lazare, his arms straining to keep the mouth propped open.

With Fang's help holding up the roof of Redthroat's mouth, both men were able to slip and slide down her petroleum-covered pointed tongue, past her colossal teeth and onto the floor, where it was at least comparatively safer. Fang kept a tight grip around Lazare's waist with one hand the whole way, as if the Frenchman would be swallowed away from him if he dared to let go.

'What in God's Tail was that?' complained Redthroat, her mouth freed again.

'It was my flame; it distracted her so Lazare could escape,' called Amber over her shoulder cheerily.

'Hello? Torrent of dragonsbane?' Nell shouted back. 'I weakened her!'

'Either way,' added Amber, 'I think we might both officially be traitors now. That's exciting, innit!'

Lazare just gazed at Fang. 'You're bleeding,' noted Lazare, looking at Fang's hand. He met Fang's eyes, and wiped the saltwater away from Fang's cheek with a thumb, which, since Lazare's own hands were covered in petroleum, only made it worse. 'You're crying.'

'How are you still in one bit, *monsieur*?' asked Redthroat, annoyed.

'I don't know,' Lazare admitted. 'My intestines came out three times in there...'

Fang couldn't help letting out an ugly moan at that.

'But Tem's magic kept slurping them back in,' continued Lazare. He risked a quick glance at the child, whose gushes of sobs and magic were petering out. 'It's OK, sweetie,' he told her. He raised his ripped shirt over his stomach. 'Look.'

Fang looked. There wasn't even a scar on Lazare. That was new. There were usually scars, even after Tem had brought them back. Was she getting stronger?

'You're even more dangerous than I thought,' Redthroat told the child.

The dragon queen took another mighty step towards Tem and Nell. Nell, her wrist still boldly aloft as it continued to dribble a sad little line of dragonsbane down her arm, made a less than graceful retreat from Redthroat, in a strange sideways run, trying to keep an eye both on the approaching dragon queen and on the unmoved guards by the barred escape. Fang, still holding Lazare's waist, ran over to join them, all trapped still, but at least all together.

'No part-human should have the power to do that to a dragon's food,' growled Redthroat, 'definitely not a stupid kid. "Happy ever after" is a curse on all, but it's all you understand, isn't it, child?'

'Leave her alone,' warned Amber, unheeded.

'You mustn't be allowed to foist forever on others just because it's the only thing your tiny brain comprehends,' railed Redthroat. 'Understand transience! Understand death! Your mother is dead! Understand that. These adults are not your parents, and they too must die.'

'No!' shouted Tem. She'd stopped crying for now. She just seemed angry.

'They must. Like your mother. She is gone. Things need to die.'

'No,' shouted Tem again. 'You need to be nicer!'

This stopped Redthroat. She gazed down at the child, an oddly worried look on her expression.

'Dragons are supposed to be nice,' scolded Tem. 'Like Amber.'

Redthroat took a small step backwards. 'Don't you change me, half-breed. Don't you dare use your cursing will against me.'

Willpower – a child's stubborn will, combined with her inability to countenance the deaths of those she loved. Was that truly the source of Tem's magic? The source of their immortality? If so, how long could it truly last? How far could it spread? Had they been going about it the wrong way, journeying to find another powerful enough to break or change the spell? Could it be broken simply by helping Tem to let go – of her mother? Of them? Perhaps Redthroat had supplied them with the answer after all – even if it was not one they had been wanting or even expecting. Fang pushed those thoughts aside for when he'd have time to deal with them, and concentrated instead on the extension of this new idea that was causing Redthroat to back away. The dragon queen believed that if Tem's magic came from childlike willpower, then she might have the ability to bend others to her will – provided there was a concept she was certain enough about, such as her certainty that dragons were supposed to be as nice as Amber. Having her personality reshaped in the form of a scrappy little urban sweetheart was likely Redthroat's own idea of a terrible curse. He gave a tiny nod to Nell, communicating that they should use the hesitation now.

Still with his bloodied hand around Lazare's waist, Fang pushed on towards the barred and guarded gate. The dragon guards took their cues from Redthroat's cautious hesitation, and held back. There was still the considerable matter of the barred doorway. Amber flapped past them all, and with an almighty huff, breathed fire on the iron bolt.

'My door,' roared Redthroat, although as Fang, Nell and Lazare grabbed the lowest handle of the giant door and pulled, Fang did notice that the dragon queen and her guards were still hesitating, staying out of Tem's way. Instead, Redthroat addressed Amber, enraged. 'Are you out of your mind, underground runt? Literally – does the fae control you?' She turned her glittering, angry head to one of the guards. 'Gwyrddlas, fetch my fae ambassador! And my Deep London attaché! I need to know how far the rot has spread, when we make an example of this treacherous... Also, obviously arrest them before they escape, Gwyrddlas, for pity's sake!'

Amber's flame wasn't enough to melt the bolt, but as Fang and the others pulled at the door, after a few seconds of intense heating from the urban dragon's fire, it was at least soft and damaged enough to break the thing. Fang and his group opened the door enough of a crack to slip through, which they did, at speed.

'Seize them,' cried Redthroat, who was still, Fang noticed, not seizing them herself.

'But what if the fae changes us with her will?' asked one of the guards.

'I don't know,' came Redthroat's voice as Fang's group sped through the nest-filled antechamber away from the golden lair. 'What if you get fired for not doing the pretty bloody basic job of guarding the queen's throne room?'

Amber flew ahead of them, turning corners, guiding them back out through the palace, which Fang would have appreciated more had she not got them all quite so lost trying to find the way in. As oversized and intimidating as the palace had felt as they'd walked through it the first time, it felt even bigger now that they were trying to escape it as fast as possible. Various dragon guards and palace staff watched their conspicuous flight through the huge, echoing halls with concern and suspicion. After a few seconds, Fang noticed a heavy scrabbling behind them. One of the guards – the one addressed as Gwyrddlas – was chasing after them.

'Seize them,' called Gwyrddlas to a dragon up ahead. 'Don't worry, the child won't alter you if you do.'

'Why would you say something like that?' called the other dragon as Fang and his group rushed past, as yet unseized. 'What did the kid do in there?'

'Nothing,' replied Gwyrddlas unconvincingly.

Amber guided them around a corner into another huge hall, lined with multiple balconies to upper storeys. At the end of the hall was, mercifully, a side door. Unfortunately, a huge, familiar blue dragon flapped angrily from one of the balconies and landed in the middle of the hall, right in between the group and their exit.

'Do you mind?' bellowed Bluejohn. 'I have been *trying* to placate a very important bunyip all evening; he's annoyed enough as it is without this hubbub interrupting his rest.'

'Seize them,' called Gwyrddlas, behind them.

Bluejohn bared his fangs. 'With pleasure,' he growled. 'Bloody troublemakers.'

'The kid might do something weird to you,' warned the other dragon.

'What?' asked Bluejohn.

Fang concentrated. He'd had an idea, but he had no idea if he was able to pull it off.

'Uhhhh, Bluejohn?' asked the third dragon. 'Are you all right?'

'I'm annoyed,' Bluejohn told the other dragons, 'and over-worked, frankly, and I don't speak a word of Wemba Wemba, which makes explaining schedule changes to a bunyip very hard and— Why do you two look so worried?'

Bluejohn was no longer blue, nor huge. He had become a sandy beige, and shrivelled to a size no bigger than an adult sheep. Or, at least, he looked that way. Fang feinted sideways with the others to run around the dragon, giving him as wide a berth as they would if he were still his original size.

'Aww,' noted Tem, looking at the shrunken Bluejohn, 'cute.'

'You've gone all small,' fretted Gwyrddlas.

'I don't *feel* small,' replied Bluejohn. He checked one of his claws, and reeled back a little in horror. 'Argh! Why aren't I blue? Gwyrddlas, aren't you meant to be turquoise?'

Gwyrddlas, now the colour of cobblestones and the size of a dog, gazed at her own claws. 'God's Flame Sac. She's turned us *urban*. She's turned us "*cute*".'

'What fae magic be this?' panicked the third dragon as Fang and their group reached the door out of the palace.

Fang exhaled a desperately held breath, and lost control of the illusion. It was not 'fae magic' at all, but Fang's own twisted-up backwards glamour. It was also the exact opposite of Fang's usual illusions. It wasn't easy to maintain, but it turned out he could use his reverse glamour to make something big and dangerous look small and cute after all – as long as the smallness and cuteness disgusted most of those observing it. Fang added this to the growing list of details he would deal with if they could just get out of Redthroat's realm without anyone else getting eaten. He still had his hand around Lazare's waist. He didn't move it. He couldn't let go; he didn't want to let go ever again. That was probably issue number one if they got out of here. A slightly more extensive range of illusions than he'd previously assumed paled rather into significance, compared to the realisation that he... that he couldn't bear to let go of Lazare's waist.

They ran through the door, into a walled-off garden with a large pond, and gorgeously intricate balconies overlooking it. There was a huge gate not far away, but it looked firmly shut.

'Lazare, you unhurt enough to fly us over?' Nell called.

Before Lazare could reply came a deep and booming voice, speaking a language that in all his travels, Fang had never come across before. A dark, man-sized shape slithered down from a first-floor balcony and lolloped towards them at speed, still speaking at them in that utterly alien language. It seemed partly animal, partly bird, and made the strangest sounds Fang had ever heard.

'The... bunyip?' guessed Fang.

'Why isn't his valet with him?' noted Lazare as they all backed away from the creature's approach.

'Here!' called another voice. It was the bunyip's valet, at the gate. He opened it. 'He says "hurry".'

Fang risked another little glance at the bunyip as they all ran towards the opened gate. The bunyip was just getting into the pond for an evening dip. Perhaps that was all he had wanted; Fang had no way to tell. One other thing Fang noted was that the bunyip didn't seem to register or recognise the valet at all. It struck Fang as odd. But there was no time to be suspicious. They were getting chased, and he could see that beyond the open gate was Llanelli's beach, and relative freedom. Fang made sure his group were all together as they ran through. He would never know the valet's reasons for helping them, since as soon as they were out, the valet slammed and bolted the gate behind them.

CHAPTER EIGHTEEN
SEIZE THEM

They burst onto a shore that glittered in pink and gold with the final rays of a beautiful sunset. Out at sea, mermaids and morgen frolicked in the gentle waves created in the wake of the lazily splashing tentacle of a resting kraken. There was no time to appreciate the magical beauty of it all. They turned towards the land and kept on running. Fang suspected that his illusion wouldn't have distracted the dragons chasing them for very long. He also suspected that making a run for it out in the open like this would only invite more attention and, with it, more trouble. He was immediately proved frustratingly correct on the second issue.

'Xanthippe, it's the pretty boy again,' called a familiar voice from above. The two harpies wheeled overhead.

'Doesn't look like their meeting with Redthroat went too well after all,' added Megara. 'What's the matter, pretty boy? Dragons turn out to actually be big fiery bossy-bums and not the gracious magical marvels they were made out to be? It's OK, we can relate to that.'

'Leave us alone,' shouted Nell up at them as they ran.

'Or what?' called Megara. 'You'll give us the sneezes again? Oh, we're trembling in our feathers.'

There was a crash behind them, and the two dragon guards burst from the palace's front gate, with Bluejohn close behind them.

'Ohhh, looks like you're in trouble,' called Xanthippe in a sing-song tone of mockery. 'Why don't you come with us?'

'Don't you worry about that alicorn, either,' added Megara. 'It'll just be us friends.'

'What's this?' called Raynebow Sprynkles, flapping into view.

'Oh look, it's our good friend Raynebow Sprynkles,' shouted Megara conspicuously. 'We were just about to fetch you.'

'Raynebow Sprynkles? Harpy sisters?' One of the palace guards took flight, heading not towards Fang's group, but to the bickering would-be abductors. 'You're under arrest by orders of Redthroat the Invincible, on suspicion of sedition most foul.'

'We didn't do anything,' cried Xanthippe. 'And we're not fowls. She's not even my sister; she's my cousin, my second cousin – I barely know her.'

'And anyway, how could we even do a sedition against someone if they're "invincible"?' shouted Megara. 'Right, Xanthippe? Raynebow Sprynkles…? Where'd they go?'

Both Xanthippe and Raynebow Sprynkles were already flying at great speed away from the dragon guard chasing them. Megara turned on her tailfeathers and also fled, with the dragon guard in hot pursuit. Fang would have been relieved, were it not for the fact that his own group were still being chased by a dragon guard and the massive Bluejohn. He also had absolutely no idea how they were supposed to get out of Llanelli. The walls surrounding the city were scores of feet high. This was where hope got you, Fang! It got you trapped in a gorgeous magical city with shimmering dragons hot on your heels! For all his self-admonishment about the perils of hope and trust, he still hadn't let go of Lazare. He clung to Lazare, and he clung to Tem, and he clung to the possibility that they could somehow escape all this, as they had escaped before.

They were smaller than their pursuers. They could use that. Nell, seemingly having the same thought as him, sprinted ahead, and released a cloud of thick but pleasant-smelling smoke from her left ear. In the smoke cover, she indicated for them to duck into a passageway, beautifully carved but only four foot high. Fang had to crouch to fit, and set Tem down, but still didn't let go of her or Lazare's hands, dragging the Frenchman along behind him as the actor struggled to fold his wings tight enough, and apologised to every annoyed-looking púca, brownie and coblyn that they hurried past in awkward, hunched shuffles.

'Sorry, sorry! Beautiful place you have here,' Lazare called. 'What is this, some sort of market?'

'It's a school, you big clumsy bastards,' shouted a female brownie at them hotly.

'God's Tonsils,' groaned Lazare. 'I am *so* sorry. Could I offer you a soliloquy of condolence?'

'No,' called the brownie, which was fair enough.

'We should probably find a cover that doesn't put kiddies in danger,' admitted Nell.

'There's a way out,' noted Tem, pointing to an exit off to the right. They scrabbled towards it, but just as Tem got to the doorway, it was filled with the snarling, sharp mouth of a huge, grey dragon. The little girl shrieked, and Fang pulled her back into him, as the dragon snapped his jaws.

'Her Majesty very strongly requests that you return to resume your audience with her,' Haearn growled.

Tem wasn't the only screaming child. A handful of baby brownies and púca pressed themselves against the walls of the little stone passageway, squealing in fear at the glistening dragon teeth in the doorway to their school. Still apologising profusely, Fang's group turned themselves around with difficulty, and hurried off a different way.

Haearn snapped in the doorway again, making the children scream once more. 'You! Children! Seize them! Orders of the queen!'

The tiny children were too terrified to do anything, let alone seize a group of large intruders.

'Seize them, I said,' roared Haearn, in a voice so terrible and booming that it only made the frightened squeaking worse.

One adult coblyn grabbed Nell by the sleeve. 'Here,' she told the apothecary, leading her down towards a less busy corridor. 'Staff and workmen's entrance. Takes you right to the wall.'

'Why are you helping us?' asked Fang.

'I'm not,' replied the coblyn angrily. 'I'm getting you and those bloody dragons away from our kids.' She seemed to soften a little, noting Tem's fear. 'Redthroat's dragons are always scaring the poor littluns, and they've no respect for us fae-folk. Even less so for half-breeds.' She shot Fang a glance. 'You the da, I take it?'

'Yes,' replied Fang, and it wasn't really a lie.

'Well,' she said, leading them past staff rooms and store-rooms, 'you take care of her, love. Dunno what you came to Llanelli looking for, but take it from me – the only answer you'll ever get from Redthroat is what's best for Redthroat.'

She led them to a small door, only just big enough for Lazare to squeeze through, and opened it up. At this end of the school, the city wall was much closer and their various pursuers nowhere in sight for now. They thanked the teacher and hurried through. As they ran towards the city wall, Fang made a mental note that there had been female pupils at that school. Fae culture educated its girls. If he were to be caring for Tem in the longer run, he'd have to find a good school for her. Wait, why was he even thinking about something like that, instead of the far more pressing issue of how they were all supposed to get over a colossal, guarded boundary wall? He tried to file 'school for Tem' away with the bulging metaphorical cupboard of many, so many, other things. And continued to not let go of Lazare.

'Big wall in the way between us and getting out of here,' puffed Nell to the others. 'Any ideas?'

'No plan,' called Lazare, 'just wings.'

'Yeah, that'll probably do it,' added Amber.

'There are dragon guards,' Fang reminded them.

'We'll cross that bridge when we get to it,' blustered Lazare, 'even if the bridge is an angry dragon,' and Fang couldn't exactly grumble that it wasn't the best idea to go running head first into a situation, fuelled by nothing but blind hope that it would be all right, considering it was how Fang had got them all in this mess in the first place. He had very nearly lost Lazare to his own blind hope. And yet, the hope still fluttered. It had been dormant in him for so long before he'd met Lazare and Tem, and now even after the Redthroat plan had gone so immediately, horribly wrong, the butterfly of hope still danced around Fang's belly like a gossamer idiot. Even when crushed, it had popped right back up again, still alive, mysteriously indestructible. Like Lazare. Maybe they *could* avoid the wall guards. Maybe it would be all right.

They reached the wall, and Fang set Tem on Amber's back.

'You boys go first,' Nell told the men.

'Will you be all right down here alone?'

'Yeah, sure.' Nell darted anxious glances behind herself, looking incredibly not sure about being all right down there alone.

Lazare scooped up Fang and took off. 'I'll be three minutes,' he reassured her. 'Five at the most. Ten if we get in a fight. Fifteen if it's a big fight...'

'Just get on with it,' shouted Nell, worried. Fang concentrated on her, and after a couple of seconds, the Welshwoman noticed that her flesh was sloughing off her bones. 'What are you doing?' she called up to Fang.

'Making you look inedible,' he cried down.

'Ah. Good shout. Yuck, though.' Her jaw appeared to fall off. 'Sake.'

Lazare flapped harder, and they overtook the laden little dragon in scaling the huge city wall. It was hard to believe from the Frenchman's strength and agility that only minutes earlier he'd been minced between the teeth of a dragon.

'Are we not just immortal anymore?' Fang asked. 'Are we invulnerable as well? Redthroat said Tem's magic reforges us to her will. No little girl wants to see the ones she loves get killed, but nor does she want them hurt.'

'It did definitely still hurt,' Lazare informed him. 'And we all still have our vulnerabilities. I really don't want to test the scope of her powers; it upsets Tem so. But I'll tell you one thing.' He flapped again, hard. 'Getting eaten really shook me out of my doldrums. I haven't felt so alive in days. I'm still troubled by the memories of you being drowned, but the worry of it all has gone. Maybe because the worst-case scenario just happened and I came out the other side of it? And it was so much easier being the one who got hurt, rather than the one pathetically having to watch.'

Fang thought about getting repeatedly drowned, and compared it to the screaming misery of watching Redthroat chew, hearing the mangled crunches. 'You're right. It *is* easier.'

'And now we're even stevens,' Lazare told him, gazing down at Fang in his arms. The wind whipped his dark curls, and his eyes shone with an ease that Fang hadn't seen since before the alchemist had tortured them all. He'd missed that light in Lazare's eyes so much, the irritating cheesiness in his easy smile. It made Fang's heart feel even lighter, made the fluttering idiot butterfly of hope inside him beat its stupid bright peacock wings even faster. The flurrying air caught the edges of Lazare's loose shirt collar, undulating them over his clavicles like silken waves.

'Don't get a ruff,' Fang told him.

'What?'

'Back in London, you wondered if you should buy a ruff,' Fang reminded him. 'I don't think you should. You have a nice neck.'

Lazare's smile increased in cheesiness by at least *trois fromages*. 'Why, *merci, mon coeur*. So do you.'

'So it's agreed – neither of us get ruffs.'

Lazare snorted a laugh. 'Your neck would *not* suit a ruff. A beard, on the other hand…'

'I'm rubbish at growing beards,' Fang admitted. 'Comes out all patchy.'

The cheesiness cheesed even cheesier. 'And who said I meant *your* beard?'

'Oh!' Fang realised he should probably act annoyed that Lazare's heavy-handed flirtation had also returned, but honestly, he'd missed that, too. He'd missed it, and he liked it. It wasn't just flattery with Lazare; it was… real. Loaded with a promise that felt tangible. A promise not just of attraction. Not just of sex – although that would be nice. A promise of lips on his lips and a hand in his hand, and of days where they could stop running and stand still together, and of nights where there was only one bed and that one bed was a warm and comfortable thing. It still wasn't how Fang had felt before, with Flower. Maybe nothing would feel like how he'd felt with Flower. But this… this wasn't lesser. It was just different. And there was still a chance it could end as horribly as it had done all those years ago in his village. But that was then and this was now, and this was the other side of the world, and this was not a huli jing but a winged man so indestructible that the queen of Dragons couldn't break him in her jaw, and Lazare had been right: the worst had happened and they'd come out the other side of it, and there was stupid bloody bright hope in his belly, flapping its wings in time with Lazare's, and telling him with every flap that perhaps he deserved this, perhaps he deserved to allow the hope a home once more, perhaps—

'Watch out,' cried Amber, beneath them.

Lazare spun in the air, narrowly dodging a plume of fire. Three dragons bore down on them from their guard post at the top of the city wall. Fang yelped, startled, before doubling down his concentration on Nell. He couldn't leave her unprotected down there, and he couldn't focus any backwards glamour on the dragons while he was still concentrating his magic on her. Lazare and Amber would have to dodge them without his distracting images of unexpected grossness or cuteness.

'You are a guest of Queen Redthroat,' called one of the guard dragons. 'You are being very rude!'

'*She's* rude,' shouted little Tem in reply.

'You'll regret that, mongrel,' growled the guard dragon, even as Amber reared up and puffed her tiny flame sacs to defend the child.

Fang didn't even have to warn Lazare to intervene; the Frenchman was already swooping towards Amber and Tem. Fang tried to think of a way to defeat four dragons without losing focus on Nell, and discovered to his distress that even thinking too hard about the imminent problem made the illusion over Nell begin to fade.

'We could really do with weapons,' Lazare told him as he sped them both towards the little ones.

'Do you know how to use a weapon?'

'Not really,' admitted Lazare.

Amber and the guard dragon blew flame plumes at one another, both of which missed as the dragons dodged in the air. The other two guard dragons rushed towards them. Fang silently apologised to Nell, and shifted his focus – only to see two huge, feathery shapes soar through the air. This was not one of his illusions – he hadn't had time to fully switch the magic from Nell.

'Is that—' managed Lazare before an adar llwch gwin and a giant, annoyed-looking white swan charged at a dragon each, beaks open. Gruff got a good peck at one dragon with his sharply hooked predator's beak. The dragon roared in outrage, and tussled at the adar llwch gwin with his claws, only for Gruff to reciprocate with his own talons.

The dragon guard attacking Amber stopped to address the bird and the griffin angrily.

'How dare you! No puppet of a human monarch has authority within these walls!'

'A Welshwoman is in danger,' cried Gruff, flapping and scratching in battle.

'Where?' asked the dragon.

'Er...' Gruff, still desperately flapping, spotted Nell, watching with anxiety from the ground. 'Down there. And where'er she may be, it is my duty to the Welsh Crown to protect her.'

'But she's fine,' railed the dragon. 'And what's your excuse, swan? I was under the impression that Elizabeth's guard-bird actually cared about rules and protocols. What possessed you to set a feather this side of our wall?'

Honkensby momentarily stopped hissing and snapping her fairly intimidating flat, toothless bill at the other dragon.

'This part of the wall was built in the wrong place,' she announced hurriedly. 'Redthroat built the wall thirteen yards over the agreed boundary of Llanelli. Yet another example of her overreach. Gruff showed me the documents in Carmarthen, didn't you, Gruff?'

Gruff paused for just half a second too long before replying. 'Yep.'

'And he gave me special permission to pursue my royally mandated quarry in the Kingdom of Wales, including this thirteen yards beyond the wall.'

'Well, hang on a minute,' protested Gruff.

Fang patted Lazare's arm to communicate and made intense eye contact with Amber to follow them. This was the distraction they needed. If they hurried, it might be enough to get them over the wall and go back for Nell. Lazare and Amber began to flap upwards, as quickly and surreptitiously as they could.

'You're lying,' gasped the lead guard dragon.

'I do not lie,' replied Honkensby, affronted.

'You both just got frustrated with prowling the out-skirts of the wall and waiting, didn't you? Thought you'd chance it.'

'I never chance anything!' Honkensby wheeled around the dragon trying to fend her off, and deliberately flicked a huge wing at one of the dragon's legs. The dragon roared in agony.

'And now you've broken my lieutenant's leg,' cried the lead guard dragon. 'Typical Upper English magicals, surrendered all your majesty to serving humans, just like Llewellyn's lackeys, and this pathetic little underground runt of a dragon...'

'The one that's getting away, you mean?' asked Honkensby.

Uh-oh. Lazare, Fang, Amber and Tem were still a good ten feet from the top of the wall. Honkensby and the lead guard dragon jostled one another to give chase, and Gruff used the moment of panic to get in a good scratch at the wing of the dragon he'd been fighting. The dragon screeched, wheeling downwards for a controlled landing, and Gruff hurried to join the chase.

'You said you'd hand me the quarry,' Gruff shouted at Honkensby ruefully.

'No,' called Honkensby, '*you* said I should hand you the quarry. *I* just said, "Leave the talking to me".'

'So you *did* lie,' noted the dragon guard.

'They're mine,' seethed Gruff. 'This is Wales! It's the law!'

'Sod the law,' cried Honkensby desperately.

Swan, griffin and dragon were all almost upon them. They weren't going to make it. They certainly wouldn't have time to get Nell, and Fang couldn't bear to leave one of his little family behind.

'Lazare?' he asked.

'I get it,' said Lazare gently. 'If all of us can't escape, none of us can. Who's safest to surrender to? Elizabeth or Llewellyn?'

Now there was another wretched question Fang had no answer to. He felt the guilt stab at him again, even as the wretched hope that would not die whispered to him that maybe, just maybe, against all the odds, salvation was just around the corner...

Against all the odds, a carriage flew over the top of the wall, and rushed to their salvation.

CHAPTER NINETEEN
MAGIC CARPENTRY

The top three quarters of the carriage looked like a perfectly normal wooden passenger carriage, albeit one with no horses drawing it, and one that was many yards up in the air, which is not where one could expect to find a perfectly normal wooden carriage. Its bottom quarter was far less run-of-the-mill. It had no wheels, but a dozen carved wooden horse's legs were adjoined to the bottom of the carriage, galloping away against the air. It – quite understandably, given the situation – absolutely jangled with magic. Before Fang could even think too much about how this was the second time in the past few days that a speeding carriage had appeared from nowhere and yoinked them to relative safety, a strong hand shot out from the carriage, grabbed him by the ankle and yoinked him and Lazare to relative safety.

Confucius's Pancreas, he thought as he was pulled, *I hope it isn't Christopher Marlowe again. I bet it's Christopher Marlowe again.*

It was not Christopher Marlowe again. Instead, Fang found himself blinking at a face he certainly hadn't expected to see on a magical flying carriage.

'Aren't you Nell's little brother?'

Rees ap'Evan gave them a grin. 'Her ex and Jenkin here told me and Mam and Dad she was in trouble again.'

'Hiya,' called Jenkin, wrangling reins that seemed to be directly attached to the base of the carriage itself.

'*Noswaith dda*,' added Sioned, catching Amber and Tem in both arms.

Rees shook his head fondly. 'Always getting in scrapes, that one. Some old crone with a wooden eye said she'd spotted Elizabeth's no-good swan tailing you to Llanelli – always trust a crone. You seen Redthroat yet?'

'Yes,' replied Lazare, 'really very close up.'

'Cor,' breathed Rees. 'Jealous. Home, then? These majestic magicals are looking, for all their wisdom and grace, a little bit bitey.'

The dragon, swan and griffin pursuing them fluttered and flapped for a moment in surprise at the galloping horseless carriage, then, as one, turned their attentions to Nell, still stuck on the ground. All three dove towards her.

'Oh no you don't,' cried Jenkin, pulling the reins to tilt the carriage straight downwards.

'Magic carpentry?' Fang managed to ask Jenkin, grasping tight on to Lazare with one hand and reaching to grab Tem with the other.

'Magic carpentry,' replied Jenkin proudly.

The galloping carriage outpaced the three flying beasts descending on Nell. The Welshwoman timed a leap towards her brother, who hoisted her up onto the carriage. Jenkin yanked the reins again, and carved hooves on the carriage's legs lightly galloped once across the ground before springing to lift them off again.

'Hiya, stinker,' Rees cried cheerily to his sister. 'Your fancy-pants London friends leave you behind, then, did they?'

'No,' Nell told him certainly, 'they don't do that.'

'Besides,' added Amber, 'Lazare's the only one out of us London friends who has fancy pants.'

Tem nodded in agreement. 'Amber doesn't have pants at all.'

'I would never leave you, even if my pants are fancy,' Lazare told her. Fang found himself squeezing Lazare's hand a little tighter.

'How good's this carriage at outrunning winged magicals?' Nell asked Jenkin.

Fang risked a glance behind them. Honkensby, Gruff and the guard dragon were lagging behind them and losing ground.

'Pretty good, probably,' Jenkin replied confidently.

'How "pretty good"?' asked Nell. 'Because, um.' She nodded over in the direction of the rest of the city. Haearn, Bluejohn, the harpies and really quite a lot of alicorns were headed in their direction at some speed.

'Easy squeasy,' said Jenkin, rather less confidently. He pulled at the reins again, steepening the angle of their climb.

'Really?' asked Sioned archly.

'Well, no. Difficult squifficult, but I reckon we can make it.'

Rees donkey-scrubbed his sister's head, worried eyes dancing beneath a mask of sibling mockery. 'Always a drama with you, isn't it, Eleanor? You know if all this messing about with Fancy Pants and pals isn't working out, Mam and Da'll let you come back home; you can have my old room.'

'For the last time, Rees, I am *fine*.'

'You're being chased by a bunch of dragons and various assorted bird chimaera,' Rees reminded her.

'So what? I'm used enough to that by now.'

'You mean to tell me this sort of thing's the norm in London?' Rees shook his head. 'Da was right: it *is* dangerous in the big city.'

'I'm *fine*,' Nell repeated, in spite of all the immediate evidence to the contrary.

'He's got a point, Nell,' Sioned told her. 'You should at least stay for the Eisteddfod, take a break from all your dashing about, reconnect with your roots…'

'Reconnect with you, you mean?' asked Nell. 'Go back to being a supportive girlfriend who watches you recite poetry?'

'Would that be so bad?' Sioned asked. 'It's really good poetry.'

'It would be a little bit bad,' said Jenkin, 'as she already agreed to go on a date with me.'

'That was an accident,' replied Nell. 'Look, I think you're both really great, but I just don't have time to stop and smell the flowers and date the hot bard and carpenter right now. I have a quest! And a curse! And a fancy-pants London friend, and a shabby-pants London friend and a no-pants dragon friend, and a cute little girl to take care of – look how cute she is!'

Tem smiled shyly down at her own knees as the three Carmarthenites acknowledged her cuteness.

'Well, maybe once all this is over,' said Sioned hopefully. 'Not just the "getting chased by dragons" bit. Find a way to end the curse, then come home. I'll be waiting for you.'

'Um, excuse me, so will I,' added Jenkin.

'So will your bedroom,' Rees told her. 'By which I mean my old tiny bedroom, obviously.'

'Oh, come *on*,' Nell sighed testily. 'I like being a big city businesswoman! I worked hard for it; why would I give that up?'

'But what about home?' Rees asked.

'Camarthen's not my home anymore,' Nell told him, not unkindly.

'And what about love?' Sioned asked.

'I have love! In abundance!' Nell gestured around at the group. 'What do you think this is?'

Yes, thought Fang. Nell was right. This was love. All of this was love. It wasn't the love he'd known before, whispering pet names in the dappled shade of the peach tree, but this love was all-encompassing in its own beautiful, terrible ways. This was love, and he wanted to cling to it. This was love, and he deserved to feel it. And, just as Nell loved and had no wish to change her life in Upper London, Fang knew he liked his own life too, just as it was. Curse and all, if it even was a curse. Perhaps he should stop seeing it as a curse, and simply view it as Tem's spell, cast by the love of a young child's heart, capable of being undone if given enough time for that heart to grow older and more independent. Perhaps the solution had always been for Fang to seize this second chance and live a life, with these people who he loved. The thought wasn't merely a flittering butterfly hope; it felt solid. For the first time in many years, living life didn't seem so bad anymore. Being there for people, and letting them be there for him. Perhaps that – the desire to continue with the life he had right now – was the reason he hadn't let go of Lazare since the actor had escaped Redthroat's jaws. No, he thought, since he was being honest with himself at the moment, he really should admit that that wasn't why he was still holding on to Lazare.

'I think what this is,' called Jenkin, shaking Fang from his thoughts, 'is a dragon's dinner, unless you let me concentrate on escaping.' And honestly, thought Fang, that was pretty unfair of Jenkin to say, since he'd been wheedling Nell for a date multiple times, instead of keeping his focus on the escape.

The galloping carriage cleared the top of the wall and raced over it to the other side.

'Ha,' called Amber to their various pursuers. 'Welsh side of the wall. We're no longer in Redthroat's domain, so back off!'

None of the pursuers backed off, or even slowed down.

'Oh, wait,' added Amber, 'I forgot about magicals getting to act like they own the place in the rest of Wales.'

'How could you have forgotten about that?' Fang asked her.

'I think I wanted to because I was a bit embarrassed by it,' Amber admitted. 'I mean, living underground and eating roadkill and scraps is far from ideal, but neither's this whole situation.'

Jenkin made the magical carriage gallop through the air to try to get some more distance between themselves and all of their pursuers. Behind them, Gruff flapped into the paths of Bluejohn and Haearn, declaring that since this was King

Llewellyn's territory, the adar llwch gwin had authority here, so they should all do as he said and return to Llanelli. Haearn ignored him entirely, while Bluejohn's response to Gruff's demand was to flick him out of the way with a huge claw. Gruff fell into Honkensby, their wings tangling in the air. In the flurry of feathers, they managed to accidentally block the way of an alicorn and both of the harpies.

'It's a political pickle, all right,' sighed Amber, watching the chaos in their wake.

'Are we going to have to outrun these fellows all the way back to England?' Lazare asked.

'That would be difficult for several reasons,' admitted Jenkin. 'Not least because' – and here he nodded to the final rays of the setting sun ahead of them – 'we're currently flying west. England is the other side of quite a lot of dragons right now.'

'You might have to hide out in Carmarthen for a bit,' added Sioned hopefully.

'God's Ovaries,' snapped Nell. 'I said no!'

'Just til the heat's off,' Sioned continued. 'Your French friend applied for the Eisteddfod, after all; do you not want to show off your poems, *monsieur*? I'm sure I can do a Welsh translation since you're a friend of my Nellie.'

'I think I'm over my poetry phase,' replied Lazare. 'It's not as if I was going to win, and...' He caught Fang's eye. 'My Calliope does not consent. It's not fair on a person to force musehood upon them.'

'We wouldn't be safe in Carmarthen, Sioned,' Nell told her. 'Redthroat's lot would know to look for us there; so would Gruff and Honkensby. It would put you in danger too – and

Jenkin, and Rees.' Here, she turned to her brother seriously. 'Mam and Da.'

Rees's brow furrowed and he nodded in understanding and agreement.

'Thanks for coming to our rescue; that was seriously cool of you,' continued Nell, 'but once we've found a way to lose the rest of our tail, you set us down and we'll take it from there. I'll write to you once we're back safe in London, and then maybe *you* lot can come and visit *me*. Catch a show – I can get you in backstage with Marlowe or Shakespeare – and actually buy something from my shop, of course. It's a really good shop.'

Sioned and Jenkin exchanged glances.

'Upper London's quite crimey, though, isn't it?' asked Jenkin. 'And expensive? I'm but a poor widowed carpenter, you know.'

'And the Emfor's *so* long and boring,' added Sioned.

'It's fine,' replied Nell, 'I get it. Just makes me feel better about saying no to you both – it's not personal, just London Me is the real me, and I deserve to date people who want the real me.'

Fang came to a another realisation – one so sudden that it was blurted from his mouth before his brain could have chance to taste it.

'Don't quit the poetry,' he told Lazare.

'You hated the poetry,' Lazare reminded him.

'I didn't *hate* it. It wasn't *that* bad. I mean, I wouldn't quit your day job…'

'I'm also far from successful at my day job,' murmured Lazare.

'But you love your day job,' argued Fang.

'Is that enough?'

Fang actually laughed a little at that. 'That's always enough. *You* liked your poems; that's the important bit. That's why you have to keep at it. Plays and preening and big silly overblown poems are just... what you are.'

And Lazare deserved someone who loved the real him, who wanted the real him. Embarrassing poetry and all.

Fang loved Lazare. Fang wanted Lazare, all of Lazare, with his exasperating poems, and his desperation to get bit parts from Christopher bloody Marlowe, and his ridiculous, dangerous gallantry.

'Are you sure?' Lazare asked him. 'Just, I have a *lot* of rhymes lined up for describing your eyes.'

Fang nodded bravely.

'You think I'm good enough for poetry *and* acting? You don't find me vapid? Mediocre?'

'I think,' replied Fang honestly, 'you're good enough for anything you set your mind to. And you are anything but vapid or mediocre. Mediocre people don't leap unscathed from Redthroat's mouth.'

'Guys, this is all great,' Amber told them, 'but could we maybe save the poetry chat til after we're safe? Because we're still being chased by two massive dragons and a fair number of alicorns.'

Fang looked over his shoulder. Bluejohn, Haearn and five alicorns were still in pursuit. They weren't right on their tails, but neither had the rushing carriage widened the gap between them. They were certainly far too close for the gang to land without immediately getting captured, and Bluejohn and Haearn at least were showing no signs of tiring.

'This the fastest this thing can go?' Fang asked Jenkin.

'Mr Fang,' replied Jenkin, 'did you think we were only keeping this pace because it hadn't occurred to me to go any faster? Yes, this is its top speed. And it can probably only keep it up for another few hours.'

'Because you'd run out of magic?' asked Lazare.

'Because we'd run out of Wales,' Jenkin told them. 'West coast is about three hours in that direction – can't fly it over the sea.'

'Why not?' asked Amber.

'It just can't! Could you all stop criticising the very well-constructed magic flying carriage that saved your lives please?'

'It's a pity you don't have your potions on you,' Rees told his sister.

'What,' asked Nell, 'the potions from my failed shop that was a big failure?'

'It was a good shop, OK,' Rees snapped. 'I saw what some of your potions could do at Da's farrier's. Stuff that could tranquilise a horse. Bet you'd have something to slow those big buggers down.'

'I do,' admitted Nell. 'Jenkin – pull back a bit.' She started unlacing her bodice. 'I'll show you something cool.'

'Ooh,' cooed both Sioned and Jenkin.

'Eurgh,' cried Rees.

Fang put a hand over Tem's eyes.

Jenkin slowed down, and Haearn and Bluejohn swiftly flanked them.

'Finally realised you can't outfly us?' Bluejohn snarled. 'Better turn this thing around. You're coming back to Queen Redthroat's palace – *all* of you. And this contraption. I'm sure Her Majesty will have suitable punishments for such intruders from the Welsh sta— gggll...'

Bluejohn's diatribe was cut off by a wet gurgle as Nell suddenly stood up, her navel exposed through her unlaced bodice, and shot a jet pressured stream of clear liquid from her belly button, arcing the few feet into Bluejohn's open mouth.

'What in God's Tailspike— wa-kkkll...'

Nell turned swiftly to the other side of the carriage, shooting a second stream into Haearn's mouth right as he asked what she'd just done to Bluejohn.

'Belly button,' she cried triumphantly. 'Horse tranquiliser!'

'Will that be enough?' Fang asked. 'They're considerably bigger than horses.'

'Won't knock them out, but we don't want two massive dragons falling on Wales anyway,' Nell told them. 'It'll slow them down, though.'

Indeed, Bluejohn and Haearn really were slowing down considerably. The flaps of their huge wings were becoming so ponderous that with a slap of the reins, Jenkin was easily able to pull right ahead. The last alicorn still chasing them landed on Haearn's back, galloped along the struggling dragon, and with a leap from the dragon's head and a strain of effort, was able to pump her wings fast enough to catch up to the carriage.

'Whatever it was you did to those big stupid dragons, I'm not falling for it,' she shouted, 'I— glack...'

She was hit straight in the mouth with Nell's belly-button juice, and immediately began fluttering jerkily downwards like a stunned bird.

'She'll be fine,' Amber told Tem as the child peered over the side of the carriage at the alicorn's graceless but gradual descent.

'Magic powers,' Nell told her brother smugly, sitting back down again. 'Told you it was cool.'

'Will you please do your corset back up,' Rees told her, shielding his eyes from her. 'I don't want to see my sister's duckies.'

CHAPTER TWENTY
THY FATHER LIES

Even with Jenkin turning the carriage north, still the dragons fell away. They waited til night had fully fallen and there was no trace of the two giant dragons to be seen until Jenkin considered it safe enough to land. Even then, he decided not to stop, but now turned them southeast, and rode the carriage across the land at a canter. The road was quiet at that time of night, but not completely devoid of other travellers. Fang's group were treated to some odd looks from those that their cantering magical horseless carriage passed, but honestly not as many as Fang had expected.

'Wales, innit,' replied Jenkin with a shrug, when Lazare brought this up. And, yeah, that was fair enough. 'I can get you to Swansea tonight. If Redthroat's after you, she'll likely have blocked the Emfor, but from Swansea, you can get another route to somewhere like Oxford. Maybe the astrologers there can help you.'

'Been there,' replied Nell. 'Slept with the most senior astrologer I could find – she just sent me to Wales.'

'You slept with an astrologer?' huffed Jenkin. 'But not me?'

'Or me?' added Sioned.

'She was very helpful,' Nell told them both.

'So were we,' argued Sioned. 'Jenkin made a getaway carriage, and I wrote poems. I should charge you for my poems!'

'You can have my poems for free,' Lazare told everybody gallantly.

Fang couldn't help but smile at that – his ridiculous chivalrous fop being his old ridiculous chivalrous self. He ran the knuckles of one hand gently over the edge of Lazare's hose, and with the other hand, smoothed down Tem's hair as she drooped sleepily into his side.

'Dragon; little girl,' he said softly.

'Lover, beard of curls,

Chemist – a potion.

This mix. My whole world.'

The others stared at him.

'What was that?' asked Lazare.

'That was a poem,' Fang told them.

'It was a bit short,' said Sioned. 'And the scansion was weird. And one of the lines didn't rhyme.'

'It's a jueju,' Fang told them. 'From the Great Ming. At least, I think that's how you format one. Didn't you like it?'

'I loved it,' Lazare told him, stroking the back of his hand. 'Especially the second line. Is this… did my getting eaten by a dragon fix us, somehow? Do you…'

'*Why* does the third line not rhyme, though?' interrupted Sioned.

Fang huffed a small, frustrated laugh. 'I think we deserve to talk about this when we're not on a magic carriage surrounded by poetry critics,' he told Lazare, 'who don't understand,' he added, raising his voice, 'that the third line isn't *supposed* to rhyme.'

'But that just doesn't make sense,' Sioned argued. 'I need another poet here as an arbiter.'

'I'm another poet,' Lazare told her, 'and I think it's good.'

'One that *isn't* clearly tupping with Mister The Third Line Isn't Meant To Rhyme,' Sioned replied.

'Stop taking my rejection out on the lads, Sioned,' Nell told her. 'You're being ridiculous; it's not like we're going to stumble across another poet on the Swansea road at this time of night.'

'You never know,' Sioned replied. 'It's nearly Eisteddfod; poets'll be coming from all over – to meet the Star Bard.'

'Lazare?' called a familiar voice from a similarly familiar cart passing them the other way.

'God's Halitosis,' breathed Lazare. 'Bill?' he called.

William Shakespeare pulled Wulfric's cart to a halt. 'Fancy stumbling into you guys.' Wulfric, Fang noted, was nowhere to be seen.

Sioned gave Nell a smug smile, holding out a hand towards Bill. 'See? Shakespeare. After my autograph, were you, William?'

'What's *he* doing here?' grumbled Nell.

'Again,' replied Jenkin, 'Wales. Poets everywhere you turn.'

'I was sort of looking for you guys,' admitted Bill. ''Tis true, I came to Carmarthen for the Eisteddfod, but I heard you'd run afoul of trouble. You helped me in London, so I wanted to return the favour.'

And yes indeed, kindness for kindness' sake, and kindness returned were all fine things, and trust and hope in his friends – his family – remained in Fang's heart, but his head couldn't help but point out to him that not only was this a terribly convenient meeting but also that if Bill were travelling from Carmarthen to find them, he'd be going the opposite way.

'I thought your son was sick,' noted Nell.

'False alarm,' Bill told them hurriedly. 'He's been sickly for years; he'll be better in no time.'

'B—' began Nell.

'I hear the fowl that runs you foul is in league with the eagle-eyed,' added Bill in that same hurried tone.

'What?' asked Fang.

'He means he's heard we're being chased by Honkensby and Gruff,' explained Lazare. 'Is this really the time for your puns, Bill?'

'Being around the Star Bard can make lesser poets nervous,' noted Sioned.

'I'm saying, you are being chased by airborne pursuers with very good eyesight, and surely your remaining in a magical carriage is a dead giveaway,' Bill told them.

'He's got a point,' noted Nell. She turned to the three Carmarthenites. 'And the longer you three stay on the run with us, the more danger we're putting you in. I can't get my baby brother arrested – Mam'd kill me.'

'Shurrup, dickhead,' replied Rees, with absolute love.

'There is space and safety in my cart,' Bill told them. 'I can take you from here; they won't be looking for a poor mummer's wagon.'

'Isn't that Wulfric's cart, though?' asked Lazare.

'Good Wulfric lent me it after our night in Oxford,' Bill told them quickly. 'Kit wandered off and Wulfric had to return to London on an urgent business matter, as the work of keeping inn does always so keep him in work.' Another awful pun, Fang noted. Hmm.

It made sense to switch carriages, as much as Fang was troubled by the discrepancies in Bill's tale. Nell was the first to get down from the magical carriage, bidding a swift, and rather relieved, farewell to her brother and failed suitors. She hopped on with Bill. Fang followed, carrying Tem – more out of a desire not to split the group again than anything else. Amber flapped over to the cart, nodding one last thanks to the Carmarthenites. To Fang's surprise, Lazare seemed the most wary to join Bill's cart. He sat at the back with Fang as Bill turned around to trot east. The magical carriage turned and sped off back to Carmarthen, and Fang was made aware of just how slow and plodding an ordinary horse-drawn cart was by comparison.

Nell made a little cushion for Tem and Amber with her skirts on the cart's wooden bench. 'May as well get comfy, kid; it'll take us a while to get back to London.'

'Oh,' said Bill. 'I don't think you should go back to London. Was that really your plan?'

Fang had to admit, he didn't actually have a plan now, besides the one to simply live, somewhere quiet and safe, and let Tem grow until she no longer needed them to do so forever. He didn't care where that was, so long as it was with Tem, and Lazare, and Nell and Amber, and they could all remain themselves and be happy with what was left of their lives.

'My shop's in London,' argued Nell.

'As are the Queen's Guards,' Bill reminded them. 'The feathers will be looking for you. Elizabeth wants you, really quite urgently. There are posters.'

'I'm finally on a poster?' asked Lazare.

'You will be found and arrested if you go back now,' said Bill. 'However, I was thinking. Stratford is quiet. It isn't "the sticks", no matter what that codpiece Marlowe says, but it's quiet enough to be safe, at least for the while. You were kind to me when those ruffians attacked, and Lazare, you have always been a fine companion. I feel guilty that I never thanked you for your good company by giving you more of a chance upon the boards. Allow me to make it up to you. The house I was able to buy my family is of goodly size – large enough to shelter you all until you're self-sufficient. I am certain Anne would be pleased of the company, and would hide you from the authorities well. For where there is a Will, she Hathaway, haha?'

Lazare gave Bill an odd, worried frown. 'Was that another nervous pun?'

'I'll admit to nervousness, good Lazare; I'm offering to shelter fugitives from the queen! It may have escaped your attention, but my fortune is rather dependent on staying on the queen's good side; we can't just all do a Marlowe and get zombified to escape her wrath – some of us have families to think of.' Bill paused. 'You have your own family to consider as well, of course – the little one. Tell me – while Redthroat clearly couldn't break her spell, did she at least shed light on how it works?'

Fang liked neither Bill's expression nor this new line of conversation, but before he could stop her, Tem answered the poet sleepily. 'I don't like when my grown-ups get hurted, so magic unhurts them. Hasn't worked for Mummy yet; I think I just have to wish harder.'

Fang's heart sank slightly at Tem's words. Every time the child was told her mother was dead, she still refused to fully acknowledge it. Perhaps it would take weeks, months, years for her to properly come to terms with her loss. He resolved to guide her through it, no matter how long it took. She had gifted him the time to do so, after all. Cutting through that soft, sad thought came another thought, sharp and urgent – none of them had told Bill that the immortality was due to Tem's spell. Fang exchanged glances with Nell and Lazare. They'd picked up on that, too.

'What are you hiding, William?' asked Lazare.

'Nothing,' the playwright insisted. 'Tem will fit right in back home. She'll have other kids to play with – Hamnet and Judith and Susanna. And I'm sure once you've all found your bearings, Stratford would embrace an exotic new apothecary shop, Miss Nell. And Lazare will be heartened to know I plan to set up a Stratford arm of my theatre company. Marlowe's not the only one who can branch out of Upper London, you know! I would be delighted to take you on as one of the main players of the new group.'

Lazare blinked. 'Can I play Oberon?'

'Of course!'

Lazare squeezed Fang's knee and shot him a glance that screamed 'yeah, this is definitely another trap'. Fang did not enjoy having Lazare confirm his concerns, but the feel of the hand on his knee was at least a consolation. He rested his own fingers gently on top of Lazare's. He really needed to find them a room, so that they could... talk. Talk it out. They still weren't fixed, if one could even 'fix' a person. They were just both elated that Lazare had got through being eaten unscathed, but he could use that elation to talk about what had been broken between them by the alchemist, and what had been broken before they had even met, and what of that they could reasonably hope to mend. Yes. He would find them a room together somewhere private, where they could... talk. Talk, with Lazare kneeling over him, unlacing his breeches, soft skin and beard, strong arms and mighty magnificent wings...

Bill, at the reins, glanced over his shoulder anxiously, and noted the hand on Fang's knee. 'You two are courting? Congratulations, Lazare! Love comforteth like sunshine after rain.'

Oh, yes, thought Fang, dragged from his sexy reverie. *The blatant trap. Damn you, William Shakespeare.*

'That's pretty,' Nell said to Bill lightly. 'One of Kit's, is it?'

'No,' replied Bill, in the careful tone of someone trying hard not to show he was annoyed, in order to keep everyone happy. 'Mine.'

'That's nice,' added Nell. 'You're a much better writer than an actor, you know. Fancy telling us where you're actually planning to take us?'

Bill gave them all a quick, guilty glance, and drove the horse to trot a little faster. 'As I told you – home.'

'And who is waiting for us at your home, Bill?' asked Lazare, the disappointment in his friend cutting through his usual veneer of friendly charm.

'My family! It is no trick or trap, Lazare, you'll see. Under my care, your family will flourish! I ask but for that kindness back for me – kindness returned that every soul doth nourish…'

'Bill,' snapped Lazare, 'you've slipped into iambic pentameter. You've been working on that speech for ages – what are you hiding?'

'Hamnet's sick,' blurted Bill. 'Really sick. The plague left him in such a state, he's been barely holding on for years now. The doctor says we have weeks left. Charms and physick can help him no longer; my family needs a power that can undo death.' He turned again, and gazed pleadingly at Tem. 'A young boy needs you, little one. Will you help? And then I shall keep you and your daddy safe.'

'You are friends with a vampire and a zombie,' Fang reminded him. 'Get Wulfric to turn your son, or Marlowe. Why drag Tem hundreds of miles under a pretence?'

'Don't you think I've tried that? They won't do it; none of my undead associates will. I take them to the boy, and he tells them… he thinks he does not want to be turned, you see. And so, without his consent, they refuse to do it, even though he's too young to understand, and *I* am his *father*…' Bill nodded down at the worried-looking Tem frantically. 'But *she* cannot help her restorative powers; they just pour out of her.'

Fang held out a hand for Tem, who scooched away from her seat to Fang's lap, as far from Bill as he could get her without leaving the moving cart.

'Who told you that?' Fang asked.

'Word gets around fast,' replied Bill, 'especially when magical and theatre circles intersect.'

261

'We really can't go home to London,' muttered Lazare. 'Too many know about her. This is going to happen every time anyone has a loved one get sick.'

'I'm sorry,' fretted Tem.

'Don't be sorry,' Bill told her. 'Be glad! Everything will be fine, as long as you do this one simple thing for my boy!'

'If your son doesn't want to be like Wulfric or Kit, then I'm sure he doesn't want to be like us, either,' Lazare told Bill.

'I don't want my magic to change anyone else who doesn't want to be changed,' worried Tem, clutching Fang's arms. 'It's caused so much trouble already. And sometimes it doesn't work properly, like it still hasn't brought back Mummy yet…'

'Because you let her die,' said Bill hotly, 'and once you've let someone die, they can't come back so that's why you have to hurry to save my Hamnet, and—'

'Don't talk to her like that,' snapped Fang. 'Tem is not a thing to trade back and forth, nor a puppet for your manipulation! You do know we can just easily hop off a trundling cart like this? I was willing to hear you out as a friend of Lazare's, but I think, William Shakespeare, this is where we say goodbye.'

'Well, I wasn't going to abduct you all without a gun, was I?' Bill pulled a pistol from his hose, causing Tem to yelp and cower. 'I'm sorry, but you're staying put.'

'Oh, Bill,' sighed Lazare, disappointed.

'Why are your friends like this?' asked Fang, concentrating on the gun until it turned into a severed and rotting bull's penis in Bill's trembling hand.

Lazare shrugged apologetically. 'I have a thing for drama queens.'

'Don't mock me,' quavered Bill. 'I'm not fooled by your illusions; I've heard of fae magics you people wouldn't believe! Men, with the heads of donkeys!'

'You're not going to shoot us, Bill,' Lazare told him softly, letting go of Fang and clambering over towards the driver's seat. 'And even if you were, what good would it do?'

Fang noticed that, even in Bill's desperation, he had not levelled his gun at Tem, the only member of their group who was neither immortal nor able to flap away.

'I beg you,' cried Bill to Fang. 'We are both fathers, sir. You understand there is nothing we would not do for our children!'

'Which is why,' Fang told him, getting between Tem and the penis-gun, just in case, 'you already understand I will not have my child used against her will. Not even for a friend.'

Bill let go of the reins entirely and stood up, levelling the obscenely transformed gun at Fang's head. The only real reaction from the group was Nell muttering, 'Oh for pity's sake,' and making a dive for the reins so they didn't crash.

'And what about for love?' cried Bill. 'If you will make me see my Anne weep for our son, then maybe I should make your dear Lazare wail for you!'

'You can't kill me, you egg!'

'Aye, but I can hurt you! I can... blind you? Ruin that face? Shoot away your fingers and toes, and...'

Lazare put a hand on Bill's shoulder. 'But you won't. You're a good man; you're just going through something I have never had to endure.'

'If it helps, Bill,' added Fang, 'I *have* had to endure seeing a loved one die. Sometimes it can't be helped, and while the pain never leaves, over time, it can be managed.'

Bill's hand trembled again, and then he slumped, lowering the gun with a sob. 'You're right. Just... why'd you have to be so fucking *smug* about it?'

'Fang is a surprisingly smug git, for a man who's always mooching off mates and dresses like an explosion in a used rag depository,' Nell told him sympathetically. 'Also, I think I might have commandeered this cart? In my defence, you're the one who let go of the reins. Did you want dropping off somewhere, love?'

'We should take him home,' said Amber. 'Least we can do, and Stratford does sound nice?'

Bill shook his head miserably. 'No, 'cause you can't trust me now, can you? Still got this gun.' He waved around the gun uselessly. At least it just looked like a gun again now, since Fang's illusion had had no effect whatsoever. 'God's Nostril, what if someone back in Upper London worked out my stupid plan and told the feathers? Stratford may be swarming with ravens and swans by the time we get there.' He sighed. 'Sirs, I am vexed. Bear with my weakness; my brain is troubled. *Adieu.*'

And with that, he clambered off the side of the slow trundling cart harmlessly.

'Oh, don't be like that, Bill,' called Lazare as they very slowly rolled away from him.

'Come on, hop back on,' Nell told him. 'Let us drop you off at Brecon; you can catch a coach east from there.'

'What's the point? You were my last hope.'

'There's always more hope,' Fang told him. 'Even when you think it's dead, it just keeps on coming back, like magic.'

'Bill has a point; you really do sound smug, Fang,' Amber noted. 'I'm happy you're trying to be positive and all, but this is a mess. We've stolen the cart of a man just trying to save his kid—'

'We can't help him; her magic doesn't work like that...'

'God's Claws, would you let me finish? We've got a cart, but what now? Upper England's not safe, neither's any of Redthroat's domain, and we can't stay in Wales; that griffin'd find us. And we're no closer to untangling the curse or getting Tem back home.'

But Fang didn't want to undo the curse anymore. He just wanted to live, and be wherever this family was.

'I mean,' continued Amber, 'where are we headed to right now?'

'For now,' replied Fang, 'we're running away. From everyone chasing us, from the man with the gun.'

He pointed back at the aforementioned man with the gun. Bill was still perfectly visible, only a few dozen yards behind them, standing forlornly in the middle of the road: a sad, balding, human droop. It seemed rather pathetic claiming to be running away from him.

'You can't just keep running away, Fang!'

Fang smiled brightly at the dragon. Anything was possible, when one had hope. 'Yes, we can! There's a whole world out there to run to!'

Lazare reached out and squeezed Fang's hand. 'I get it, Fang. You have the little one to protect. But I can't do this.'

And, as fast and brutal as a rock inside an angry fist, the hope was bludgeoned out of him again.

CHAPTER TWENTY-ONE
CHÉRI

'I don't understand.' As much as his heart was plummeting, Fang continued to grasp desperately to Lazare's hand. 'You said you loved me! You got so angry whenever I questioned if you truly meant it, but now that I believe you – what – you've changed your mind?'

'Oh, I love you,' Lazare told him emphatically. 'I meant it the first time and have meant it every time since, more than I believe I have ever meant anything. Not merely for your prettiness – and yes, you are pretty, Fang; I know it annoys you to bring it up – but for the ugliness you try to create, as a mask. There's a loveliness in that too. The fake ugliness you wrap around yourself just accentuates the real beauty within.'

'It *does* annoy me when people call me pretty,' blurted Fang. 'And make out I'm some prize to be won. Because have they seen you? Come on, you're beautiful. Why is nobody ever creepily possessive towards *you*?'

Lazare stared back at him, eyes shining in the moonlight, his silly perfect beard ever so slightly out of place in the breeze. 'What a terrible way to tell me you think I'm hot.' He smiled, and there was such genuine love in that smile, and gladness, but also a wistfulness that Fang really didn't like the look of at all. As far as grand proclamations and heartfelt entreaties went, Fang could tell he was Fanging this one right up.

Fang tried starting again. 'I know I've been unkind to you. I was trying to be cruel to be kind, but it came across as just cruelty, and it came from a place of cowardice. And I know I've hurt you. Caused you those nightmares—'

'That was the alchemist's doing,' interjected Lazare, but Fang shook his head.

'We can't blame him for everything. I never wanted to hurt you, Lazare, but sometimes it's like I can't help it. Is… is that why you "can't do this"?' Yes, thought Fang, that would make sense. 'I'm sorry,' he continued even as Lazare tried to speak. 'I had this silly idea that Redthroat could fix us, that Redthroat *did* somehow fix us by accident, but that's stupid. Stupid! Stupid as ever!'

Lazare stopped Fang's self-admonishing rant by reaching out to his face and squeezing his cheeks together, pushing Fang's mouth into a surprised fish pout.

'Since we were attacked by the alchemist,' Lazare told him levelly, 'I've been having what one could call "a wobble". It wasn't "you hurting me". I'm just not used to heroics, and I couldn't stand seeing you get hurt. I couldn't stand that I'll never be able to stop it, because you getting yourself in danger is just sort of what you do.'

That was fair, thought Fang, but he feared what was coming next. If Fang putting himself in danger hurt Lazare's heart too much, gave him nightmares, made him miserable, and Fang couldn't help how much danger he always ended up in, why would Lazare want to be with him? Wouldn't it be better for Lazare if they weren't together?

'You would not have me quit acting and poetry,' continued Lazare, 'and I would not have you stop getting into scrapes, for the same reasons. I love you for you, as you are.'

Fang pulled Lazare's hand off his face, and cradled both Lazare's hands in his own, as if they were newborn kittens.

'I understand,' said Fang. 'I finally understand this kind of love. This perfect imperfect love, with faults that shine. Because I love you in that same way.'

There! He had said it! He had said it, and he meant it, with an absolute leaden certainty. This was love, real love, it was different to before, but he recognised the weight of it. A heavy anchor that could either hold him fast and safe, or drag him down to drown. Perhaps *this* was what he had needed to fix them, all along. Just three magic words. Perhaps everything would be all right now.

'Oooh,' crowed Amber in an annoying sing-song voice even as Nell tried to shush her, 'Fang loves Lazare.'

Yes, the back of a commandeered poet's cart in front of an audience probably wasn't the best place to be doing this. But Fang still had a horrible feeling that it was now or never. He risked a glance up at Lazare's expression. Those warm brown eyes danced in the moonlight with utter adoration and yet, upsettingly, still a dash of sad.

'Get you, Mister "Perfect Imperfect Love", Monsieur "Faults That Shine".' Lazare smiled. 'Sounds like something I would say.'

'I know.' Fang tried to chase that last smidge of wistful sadness in Lazare's loving gaze away, with a spot of bravado. 'You're a horrible influence.'

'*You're* a horrible influence. I got eaten by a dragon today; that's the sort of nonsense *you* would pull.'

Somehow, Lazare's reminder that he'd recently been eaten managed to brighten the atmosphere. When he smiled again at Fang, that smidge of sadness was chased away by a hit of exhilaration.

Lazare pulled his hands from Fang's, pushed his fingers up into Fang's hair, cradling his head, and kissed him. Fang could still feel the smile on Lazare's lips as they were pressed, parted, against his own. This kiss was different to those that had come before – those frustrated, angry expressions of feelings that were still too tangled up in his belly to be given words. This kiss was a giddy celebration, and an exhalation of relief, if one that still rather stank of petroleum. For just a second, he felt as if everything was finally in synchrony. For just a second, a cacophony of worries and rages and disappointments that had been blaring in his head for years fell silent, and there was only Lazare's smile against his mouth, the tip of his tongue against the inside of Fang's lower lip, the hands against the base of his skull...

'Yeah, that's right, kiss him,' came a gravelly voice from Fang's knees, completely ruining the moment. 'Kiss him good.'

Fang shot an annoyed glance down at Amber staring intently up at him.

'Yucky,' whispered Tem.

'I know it is, kiddo, but it's how this lot mate and, trust me, this has been on the cards for ages; they kept dancing around it and it was getting annoying.'

Lazare pulled out of the kiss, his irritating, glorious grin marred once more by that strange, wistful sadness to his eyes as reality came rushing back. Lazare pressed his forehead against Fang's. Fang couldn't even read the other man's expression now. All he could see was nose. He hadn't fixed anything by declaring his love, had he? Lazare still 'couldn't do this'. The anchor of Fang's love, only just realised, was about to drag him deep yet again.

'God's Liver,' breathed Lazare against Fang's head, 'Fang, I love you so much, but our love can't be at the expense of others. It can't make us selfish. I can't leave my good friend in the middle of the road with no hope and a loaded gun, just because you want to run away.'

Fang pulled back. 'No. No no no, this isn't fair! Not after everything, not after I just said... Nell offered him a lift; he said no! And just because of that, that makes our love "selfish"? Just because of that, you're leaving me?'

Lazare tried to grab Fang's hand even as Fang yanked it away. '*Chéri*,' Lazare entreated, 'why would you think I was leaving you?'

'You just said you can't do this!'

'Yes, but that doesn't mean I'm leaving you! Well. It sort of does mean that, but just for a while, OK?' Lazare gave up on trying to catch Fang's hand, and settled for placing a palm on Fang's jaw. 'I would never force Tem to try her magic, nor would I force her spell on a boy who seems to have already made his choice, but my friend is in crisis. I can at least fly Bill home in time to say goodbye to Hamnet. It's his child. You would want someone to do the same for you.'

'What if there are guards like Bill said?'

'I can outfly them if it's just me.'

'What if you can't?'

'What if I can?' Lazare put his other hand on Fang's cheek, so he was cupping Fang's face. Fang could see the absolute determination twinkling in Lazare's warm eyes. How Fang loathed it. 'Come on. I know you understand this. You're the man who got beaten to undeath saving a kitty cat – the man who risked everything to help a little girl, and a silly, frightened actor.'

'Oh, now you're using *that* against me?' complained Fang.

'I'm doing this, *chéri*,' continued Lazare with that same terrible determination. 'Don't wait for me, Nell; you'll get caught in that slow cart. I'll catch up to you, OK?'

'How would you even find us?'

'I take it you'll be going west? That's been your instinct so far, Fang.'

Fair enough, thought Fang.

'There's a lot of west, though,' replied Nell, troubled. 'Ireland, Iceland, a whole ocean…'

'If that swan keeps finding you, I know I can find you, too. I'll just watch for the trail of drugged ruffians and reports of highwaymen getting beaten up by a ridiculously handsome man.'

'It's still not fair,' Fang told him. 'When I split from the group, you shouted at me for being reckless. Now you're calling me selfish in love and flying off to do the same thing? You only just got eaten by a dragon!'

Lazare grinned at him. 'Maybe I caught reckless heroics off you.'

'But your nightmares…'

'Were not helped by my inaction before, and will not be helped if I don't do the right thing now.' He kissed Fang again swiftly. 'I can do this. Writing poems is all well and good, *chéri*, but maybe I should be the sort of person who has poems written about him.'

He took a folded piece of parchment from his doublet and tucked it into the pocket of Fang's britches. And with that, he took off.

'Lazare, wait!'

Lazare turned his head back to face Fang as he flapped, but Fang knew he had his mind set on helping Bill.

'Is *chéri* your new name for me or something?' called Fang.

'Yes, I'm trying it out,' replied Lazare. 'Do you like it?'

'Not really!'

'Too bad.'

And he flapped to Bill, scooped him up and flew away. Fang watched him go, clutching tight to Tem.

'Lover, flying free.

Reckless, leaving me.

You're gone. I ride west.

Your Fang – *not "chéri".*'

Nell slapped the reins again, trotting them westwards. 'I'm still really not sure about that poem structure, Fang.'

It took thirty seconds or so for Bill to get his breath back after being scooped into the air by Lazare. Once he had, the only word he was able to squeak out at first was 'Why?'

'Because,' replied Lazare. 'Put that gun away, Bill; I'm still all petrol-y – it's a hazard. Or better yet, dispose of it. If you're

273

to have only a few weeks with Hamnet, make the best of them; don't waste time arguing with your family about why you showed up with a pistol.'

'You really won't bring him back?'

'He doesn't want it, dear Bill.'

Bill drew breath to make another argument, then gave up before even putting voice to it. 'I suppose I shouldn't expect you to understand. You don't have to know death, for you or your lover.'

'Oh, I do, *mon ami*. I know death and pain and suffering. This is how I know that the fear and helplessness it foments cannot be allowed to rule us. And I know a lot about second chances, and making every moment count.'

'Then why are you not with your love right now, "making it count"?'

'This is how I make it count, right now.'

'Being in love's made *you* quite smug as well, you know, Lazare.'

Lazare laughed lightly. 'Perhaps. But then, I survived being eaten by a dragon today. That will make one rather smug, and predisposed to heroic acts, and optimistic about one's prospects of beating all odds.'

'Even though I just proved that you can't trust anyone?' asked Bill glumly.

'I still trust some,' replied Lazare. 'Not queens nor kings, not Welsh dragons, certainly not harpies. Not you, I'm afraid, old friend. But my trust is not dead. There are kind strangers still, and I firmly trust my love, and my family. As should you, Bill. You should trust in Hamnet, and what he wants his life and death to be.'

Bill nodded sadly, and, as they flew over a river, dropped the gun. He missed the water entirely, causing the gun to discharge as it hit the riverbank below, and kill a duck.

'Bollocks,' said William Shakespeare.

'We'll take tracks through the valleys,' Nell announced. 'We're less likely to be spotted there, but still keep a watch out for Honkensby, Gruff and... well, anyone, I suppose.'

'Lazare's pretty fast on those big wings,' added Amber, already anxiously watching the night sky. 'At the rate we're trundling, he should have caught up with us by the time we reach the coast... right?'

'If not,' reasoned Nell, 'we'll head for Cardigan, get a ship west from there. If we're going to make it easy for him to find us, we should take the most obvious route.'

'Won't making it easy for him to find us mean it's easier for everyone chasing us to find us too, though?' asked Amber.

'Well, yes,' Nell conceded, 'but it's worth the risk. Got to let the big prancing dandy get back to us.' She snuck Fang a little glance over her shoulder. 'He *is* coming back,' she proclaimed firmly.

Fang lay on the back bench of the cart, the sleeping Tem in his arms, looking up at the stars as they slowly clopped along. The child seemed untroubled by nightmares tonight. That was something. He worried, still. He still had to find her a home, somewhere safe, somewhere quiet, where nobody would try to snatch her or threaten her into using her magic against her will, no matter how desperate or tragic the would-be kidnapper was. Had he done right by poor Bill? Wouldn't he have done the same as the playwright, were their situations swapped? Had he not rejected Bill's plea outright, might Lazare still be by his side? Fang tried to get his mind back on track to concentrating on Tem's wellbeing, rather than his own racing thoughts about Lazare. Lazare *would* come back, right? Why had Fang let him go? Had Fang gone from having no trust to having dangerous, irrational levels of the stuff? No. It was fine; it would be fine; this wasn't like losing Flower; Lazare wasn't dead, just giving a lift to a ridiculous, sad-faced playwright. He could trust Lazare; he loved Lazare. He loved Lazare!

He loved Lazare. The thought of a soft, over-manicured beard, and warm, dancing eyes made his heart leap even as it twisted his stomach at the memory of those magnificent wings flapping away. And the last thing he'd said to Lazare had been 'not really' – who says that on parting with the man they love? Idiot.

'He's coming back,' Fang replied, echoing Nell's firmness of tone.

He'd better come back. Fang touched the folded up, unread note in his pocket. Fang had a lot more to say to him than 'not really'.

'Too right,' grunted Nell. 'I mean – you two haven't even managed to have sex yet, have you?'

Fang's eyes widened as he looked at the stars. No, he hadn't! He hadn't even so much as loosened Lazare's stockings, and thanks to Nell's reminder, now he *really* wanted to feel that skin against his own, slick with sweat, those hands grasping his thighs, those hips, those arms, those wings that had now flown out of his reach.

'Bollocks,' he whispered.

In an inn just outside Llanelli, a poet sat at a writing desk in his room. He scratched out a note by candlelight. He didn't use ink, but urine. He hoped that his queen would not mind receiving a letter writ in piss, but it was safer that way, the message being unreadable until heated – an old spy's trick. Worse still than the unsavoury nature of the invisible ink were the contents of the note – a report that the queen's favoured swan guard had been observed bungling her mission on multiple occasions.

I fear that Cpt Honkensby, while competent enough patrolling her comfort zone of Upper London, is tragically out of her depth in the broader field, being interrupted by a passing traveller at the Welsh border and thus failing to arrest her quarry there, and on pursuing them to Carmarthen causing immediate suspicion amongst the locals, sabotaging her own endeavours. Indeed, I was forced to surreptitiously intervene, successfully disguised as I was, to pass on warnings that King Llewellyn's pet griffin was approaching to apprehend them for the Welsh king. It is only thanks to my hand and, dare I say, a touch of kismet, that they are not now in a dungeon of Dolwyddelan Castle. E'en so, Honkensby then allowed your fugitives to be taken to Llanelli. I felt duty bound to follow, Majesty, as your captain for some reason prioritised arguing with the griffin at Llanelli's walls over entering the city to keep them from Redthroat's jaws. 'Twas child's play to disguise myself as the manservant of one of Llanelli's visiting foreign dignitaries and help the fugitives flee Redthroat's guards. That Honkensby neither entertained such a ruse herself nor even suspected I was watching and assisting reflects poorly on her abilities indeed. As matters stand, the immortal fugitives remain on the run. Nobody is any closer to obtaining the immortals' powers – multiple chances have sadly been wasted.

I do detest to bear such ill tidings to you, Majesty, but allow me to also bring succour. I have thus far followed Honkensby's pursuit out of goodwill towards my former queen and patron. It truly was a pity how miscommunication caused me to fall from your favour those few years ago. Indeed, I have many times asked the Royal Guard to revisit my case as I'm sure further inspection of the evidence will prove my exoneration, yet they refuse. Apparently the swan officer who back then accused me of being a double agent working against you has since risen to a lofty post amongst their ranks, and will not have her word questioned. 'Tis misfortune furthered that my sudden and unexpected demise put such a terrible end to my service of you. These past years I have been bereft, my queen, fallen from the grace of your favour. It is my desire to put this right. You know my skills in espionage remain unmatched. Grant me your assent to trail the immortals in an official capacity. I have spent some time working my way into their affections already. They trust few now, but they are simple folk and they view me as a friend. They are no match for the wits of the greatest spy in Upper England. Allow me to present them to you, my queen, and perhaps then you will see once more that I am worthy to bow to you in your royal chamber.

He set the quill down and shook the cramp from his hand. Goodness, that had used up a lot of piss. Brevity was not exactly his thing, but at least he made up for it by being a big drinker. He opened a drawer beneath the one full of false beards, wigs, ink for temporary tattoos and a multitude of false eyes in wood, copper, pearl and various materials besides. The more startling the false eye, he had found, the less attention people paid to the rest of the face around it. A handy discovery indeed.

He rifled around in the papers, taking a moment to look again fondly at his sheaf of architect's designs for his new theatre. Twice as big as the Globe itself, the artist's impression of the new theatre dominated the south bank of the Thames. The Queen's Theatre. Yes, that had a lovely ring to it. He slipped the urine-covered note in between sheafs of folio, to be safely sent off first thing next morning, and stretched in his chair. What a day! Over in his lodging bed, one of that night's lovers shifted beneath the sheets, causing the other two to mumble sleepy complaints.

'Well,' crowed the poet, pulling his shirt up over his head. 'Sounds like you lot are ready for another round of cock from the late, great Christopher Marlowe.'

In the room beneath his, the lodger who had only just got to sleep woke up again, and clamped their pillow over their ears.

'Bollocks!'

CODA
AT SEA

O n the Atlantic Ocean, dawn was just beginning to break. This was Anarouz's favourite part of night watch – the first rays of the rising sun colouring the sky and sea dark blue, before those smudges of pink and orange began to daub the waterline. Just him, and the sea, and the sky and the sun peeking up from the east to meet him.

'Morning, Anarouz!'

He jumped a little at his crewmate's voice. She was incredibly good at sneaking up on people – Anarouz supposed that's what one could expect when one sailed with magicals. The captain's tendency to welcome all sorts on board as long as they could make themself useful had certainly changed Anarouz's life for the better many times over, so he certainly wasn't going to complain about sharing quarters and duties with magical and undead folk from all over the globe. It was an unwritten rule aboard the *Dendan* that you respected your crewmates equally, and didn't ask what had brought them to a life of piracy. The result was a very happy ship. Albeit one where ghouls from the other side of the world would some-times pop up from nowhere and make you jump – which was not ideal when you were up in the crow's nest.

'You're up early,' he said.

'Up late, more like. I'm nocturnal, mostly.'

'Because of the, uh…' Anarouz pointed to his crewmate's pointed, ginger furred ears.

'Because of the whole fox spirit thing, yeah.' She smiled. She sprang with a light agility into the crow's nest, her long, white-tipped tail held out to aid her superhuman balance, her mane of bright orange hair catching the first rays of the new day's sun. She sat down next to Anarouz, curling up her limbs so they could both fit in the cramped space. 'Thought I'd keep you company for a bit,' she announced, 'because I like a pretty sunrise, and I like pretty boys.'

'Oh!' Well, this shift was getting better and better. 'That's very kind of you to say, Flower.'

CHAPTER ONE
The Unundead

It begins where it should have ended, in an alleyway at the rough end of Upper Blackfriars. It was night, not that there was much distinction between night and day beneath the tight-packed buildings that loomed over the cobbles in this part of Upper London. Be it sunshine or moonlight, whatever natural light dared to peek through the glorious English clouds or the smoke of the city tended not to venture all the way down to an alley like this. Tiny candle flames in windows overlooking the alley faintly illuminated the scene below in timid orange flickers, as if they were afraid of what they might see down there.

And, well they might be afraid. There in the gloom lay something that was very nearly, but not quite, a corpse. For now, it was still technically a man, but it was a mess of a man. The cobbles around him were slick with dark red. The man slumped in the blood and the filth, waiting for the inevitable.

After a while, there came a soft, heavy sound. Padded paws on stone, the faint click of claws, the dragging of a long, thick tail of scales along the muddy alleyway. It stopped close to the man. The creature sat next to him and waited.

'Don't mind me,' said the creature in a husky, friendly voice after a while. 'I'm not going to start until... you know. I would never. Just, I smelled the blood, and wanted to get here first and call Baggsie.'

The man managed to turn his head a little and opened an eye, to squint at the creature. She was small, for a dragon. Either a lone juvenile or a runt who had somehow managed to scrap it out and survive to early adulthood. Whichever it was, this dragon clearly needed a decent meal, and as soon as he was dead, his fresh carcass would provide one. His death would help her survive. That was something, he supposed. And, he did appreciate her not starting to eat him until he was dead. He knew that the law expressly prohibited killing, or eating living humans on the Upperside, but he also knew that times were hard, criminality was rife and that a crafty dragon could drag him down below to Deep London where it was legal to kill him. One could even argue that the laws agreed with the Tudor throne to protect the people of Upper England shouldn't apply to him, because he was foreign.

'Besides,' continued the dragon, 'thought it might be nice for you to have a bit of company at this difficult time.'

The man huffed a painful sigh. He really had been hoping to die alone. It was what he deserved. Oh well. Maybe there were some other upsides. He spat out a glob of blood and gritted out a question.

'Did you see a cat?'

'A cat?' asked the dragon.

'With an injured tail,' added the man.

'Um,' replied the dragon, 'hang on…' She sniffed the air, then snuffled over to a barred basement window a few yards along the alleyway. 'There's one in this basement,' she announced. 'Don't know how she's injured, but I smell cat blood.'

'She going to be OK?'

The dragon gave another sniff. 'She isn't losing enough blood for it to kill her, and she's safe and warm down there.' The dragon came ambling back to the almost-corpse. 'Unlike someone I could mention. Why'd you ask about her?'

The man didn't answer.

'Don't tell me that's how you ended up getting all beaten and stabbed?' asked the dragon. 'Stepping in to help a little street cat?'

Still, the man didn't answer.

'That's adorable,' added the dragon, 'I mean, as far as fatal beatings can be adorable.'

The man groaned a groan that he hoped conveyed an emphatic 'just let me die in peace'.

The dragon sat down again, and they both waited – the dragon exhibiting rather more anxiety than the dying man. The dragon kept looking around, nervously. Clearly, the rules of Baggsie didn't count for much in a city full of crime and hungry dragons, vampires, zombies and so on. The man had no doubt that this dragon was starving and that she stood no chance of winning a fight if any bigger creatures came to steal her meal before he was dead.

He tried dying faster, for her. It didn't work.

'Is there anything else I can do for you?' asked the dragon. 'Any last words you want me to pass on to a loved one?'

The man snorted, derisively. The dragon shifted anxiously again.

'Would you mind if maybe I took you down to the Deepside?' she asked after a while. 'The tube's not far at all, and once we're in Deep London, I can make it instant and painless for you... oh, hang on, actually...'

The darkness was closing in, now. Not the darkness of the alley; a different darkness. A more final darkness. A darkness that silenced sound, and made pain dwindle to nothing. He couldn't even smell the stench of the alleyway anymore. Here it came. No more running, no more guilt, just the peace of death. And, perhaps, at the other end of the peace, someone would be waiting for him. He was coming! He embraced the absolute darkness.

And then, in the darkness, a spark. A spark! Oh no! It hurt. His heart... his lungs... they were working again. Heaving, pumping, painfully. Stop it, you horrible organs, just let me die, he wanted to cry. The darkness fell away from him, insubstantial as a shadow. The alley was still there. The dragon was still there, her mouth open, glistening fangs inches from his face, her expression frozen with guilty embarrassment. She pulled her head back.

'I am so sorry, I could have sworn you were... you know.'

The pain was searing. He could hear the blood in his ears, and it all hurt so much. 'What happened?'

'I don't know! I swear, your heart stopped, all of you stopped. And then you just... restarted.' She anxiously looked around herself again. 'I should go.'

'No... wait.'

'No. I shouldn't be here. You're not dying, you're not dying at all! You used to smell of death, but now you smell all weird. This is wrong, this is bad.'

The dragon started hurrying away, waddling along the narrow alley as fast as her little reptile legs could take her. The man tried to get up, tried to follow her. Everything hurt so horribly. He just about managed to push himself painfully onto all fours before the dragon disappeared into the gloom, in the direction of Blackfriars tube.

Great. Now he was alive and in horrible pain and stuck in an alley. He didn't feel like he was dying, anymore. It was nothing as peaceful as that. This felt worse. And, not dying meant that he now had to deal with the problem of how he was supposed to get all the way to Upper Southwark. South of the river, in this state, at this time of night. He managed to get some purchase on the wall of one of the nearby buildings, pushed himself onto his wobbly legs and began to make slow, aching progress along the alleyway, dragging himself along from beam to beam like a nervous first-time ice skater. This was going to take forever.

He persisted, step by shuffling, painful step. Left foot. Right foot.

But then, he thought to himself as he made his slow southbound trek, hadn't his whole life been a slow, painful journey, step by terrible step? He'd really thought the journey had come to an end, tonight. He should have died. It didn't make sense. This was yet another problem for him, right when he'd hoped his problems may have finally been over.

Typical, thought Fang.

Left foot, right foot, left foot, right foot.

Fang was already five thousand miles away from the only place he'd ever called home – give or take a few hundred miles or so, honestly he'd stopped counting somewhere in the Ottoman Empire. What was another mile or two, on bloodied, bruised and shaking legs?

Left foot. Right foot. Left foot. Right foot. Left.

*

'Well, then.' Lady Alice Feignshaugh paused, cleared her throat and started again. 'Monsieur Quitbeef. Yes. Well, then.'

Lazare de Quitte-Beuf smiled winningly at his employer and tried to pretend that he couldn't read from her tone that she wasn't going to be his employer for very much longer, at all.

Lady Alice clapped her hands together with a pretence of pleased satisfaction. 'I must commend you, Monsieur, on your tutelage. After a mere nine months, I must say that Cuthbert's command of the French language has come on in leaps and indeed bounds. He speaks it as if a native of your land, I have no doubt!'

Cuthbert Feignshaugh could not speak French as well as any Frenchman, and it didn't take a Parisian to know that. Cuthbert could speak French as well as a bored child with a thick English accent, and even then was only able to tell you whether the boulangerie was on the left or the right, and that on Tuesdays he enjoyed riding horses with his cousins.

'And Cecily plays the flute like an absolute cherub following your months of instruction,' continued Lady Alice, with a cheer as thin and as hard as varnish.

Lazare had never seen cherubim, nor heard whether they were known to be proficient flautists. There was, he supposed, a chance that cherubim were only capable of squeaking out a tune that occasionally veered into something like

Greensleeves, the way Cecily Feignshaugh was after nine difficult, patience-straining, if reasonably paid months.

'So, I do believe your mission has been a complete success,' concluded Alice. 'Bravo, Monsieur.'

She smiled at him, expectantly. Lazare smiled back, mentally unpicking what she'd said to locate the meaning she'd buried deep amongst layers of flattering lies.

'Are you,' he hazarded, his smile never dropping, 'firing me, Madame?'

Lady Alice beamed at him. 'Goodness, no! We're setting you free! To pursue other avenues! You have your acting career to concentrate on after all, you don't want to waste any more of your time after achieving what you temporarily joined our household to do.'

Lazare continued to smile politely. 'Is this because I'm French?'

'Monsieur, you're so delightfully amusing, why, we *hired* you because you're French!'

He nodded, aware that his smile was losing its lustre. 'Is it because of the wings?'

And there was the glint in her eye. 'Noooo,' she cooed, 'goodness, no. We Upper English do not discriminate against our friends from the other side. Why, you saw for yourself, Mr Peaks was taken good care of, even though he was a zombie.'

Lazare didn't reply. Mr Peaks had been kept as a footman in Lady Alice's employment for a mere six weeks after being turned into a zombie. Lazare had had his little misfortune only a month ago.

'I'm sure that, as with Mr Peaks when he felt it was time for him to move on, you'll find London to be simply packed with fresh opportunities for a talented young vampire such as yourself.'

'I'm not a vampire, Madame,' Lazare replied, ensuring she could see his normal human teeth through his renewed smile.

'Or whatever it is that you actually are,' continued Lady Alice, smoothly, and Lazare had no answer to that. He knew that the one thing he very definitely was, was fired.

Lazare wasn't a vampire. That much, he knew. To become a vampire, one must be turned by another vampire. It hadn't been a vampire attack that had started Lazare's recent troubles, but humdrum, run of the mill human muggers, with boring old cudgels and knives. Vampire attacks were actually very rare in Upper London, in spite of all the lurid rumours and whispers about their kind, and it was even rarer for a vampire to revive a dying human by turning them without their consent. No, none of this was a vampire's doing. In fact, the only vampires that ever bothered Lazare even now were...

'Sir? Good sir? Excuse me?'

Lazare sighed inwardly, and painted his smile on for the approaching vampire.

'I couldn't help but notice that you appear to be afflicted, sir.'

The vampire seemed to be a boy of around ten or eleven, although his eyes, like the eyes of any vampire, were old and tired. Like Lazare, the boy had a large pair of leathery wings, the same shade as the skin of his face. There was something familiar about him that at first Lazare couldn't quite place.

'Wulfric, sir,' continued the child, holding out a hand for Lazare to shake.

Lazare accepted, politely. 'Lazare de Quitte-Beuf, at your service. Um... have we met?'

'Possibly?' Wulfric shadowed Lazare's own expression as they tried to place one another. 'Do you frequent the Moon and Werewolf? Upper Deptford?'

'Guilty as charged.' He clicked his fingers. 'You're a pot boy there.'

Wulfric looked offended. 'I'm the owner.'

'Of course you are, Monsieur,' replied Lazare, hurriedly. 'Forgive a poor mummer's foolishness.'

'You're that French fellow who drinks with the actors,' said Wulfric. It was the vampire's turn to look apologetic. 'Your affliction must be very new, in that case. I truly hope your vampirism isn't down to any of my clientele, I've been *very* firm with undead customers that they are not to—'

'They did not,' said Lazare, cutting the boy off, 'as I am not "afflicted" as you think.' He flashed another wide, deliberately toothsome grin.

Wulfric noticed the teeth, and Lazare watched the by-now familiar expressions of surprise, confusion and disappointment flit over the vampire's face.

'Oh,' said Wulfric.

'*Oui*,' replied Lazare, smoothly.

'So, you're... you're not actually...'

'I am not. Same old human teeth, same old human appetites, I was able to go outside that one afternoon last week when it was sunny.'

Wulfric sighed. 'That's a pity, Monsieur.'

'I know.'

'I was hoping to invite you to join our support network.'

Lazare nodded. He'd had this conversation before and yes, he agreed, it truly was a pity. One vampire had managed to get a good five minutes into trying to sell the support network to him before noticing that he wasn't actually a vampire. It sounded marvellous.

'We have lawyers and everything,' continued Wulfric, 'we could have helped you get a base in Deep London, keep your connections Upperside, or help with any discrimination cases, in terms of employment, or lodgings...'

Wulfric gave a meaningful little glance to Lazare's bags of belongings.

'I am indeed between jobs and lodgings right now,' Lazare admitted, 'at least nobody chases one with flaming torches in these enlightened days.'

Instead, thought Lazare, in the forward-thinking and ever-so-civilised Upper London of 1599, they waited a few weeks so that it didn't look like they were sacking you because of the wings, and then turned you out of a live-in tutoring position so that you were immediately without income or board and under threat of being arrested for vagrancy. In many ways, that was worse than a lit torch – it was insincere and cowardly. You weren't allowed to fight back. You just had to say 'thank you, Madame' for the insipid letter of reference and politely be on your way.

Wulfric's smooth little face creased with a bewildered frown, and the vampire's top lip curled up slightly as he gave Lazare a good sniff. 'So... what *are* you? Where do you belong? Are you undead, at least?'

'I don't know,' replied Lazare, truthfully. He didn't *feel* undead, but how else could he possibly describe the sudden change that had happened to him a month ago? He had almost died... no, that wasn't quite it. For the briefest moment, it had felt as if he *had* died. And then, there had been a sort of spark in the darkness, and a searing pain, and then he simply hadn't been dead anymore. He wasn't dead, but he wasn't entirely alive, either. He definitely wasn't human anymore – the massive wings he'd woken up with made that pretty clear – but in the past month he'd discovered he wasn't a vampire, a ghoul, a zombie or any of the known magical demographics of Deep London either. As for the question of where he belonged, he definitely didn't know the answer to that either, but certainly hoped it wasn't 'in the gutter'.

'Before you ask,' added Lazare, anticipating what usually came next whenever a vampire respectfully approached him, 'I don't want you to take me Deepside and finish me off or fully turn me, either. I just feel like that would make things more complicated.'

'No.' Wulfric stopped sniffing and stood back again, with a troubled expression. 'I don't think I could, even if you did want that. You smell... off.'

As an enthusiastic consumer of the finest perfumes available on a tutor's wage, Lazare couldn't help but feel a little affronted at that. '"Off"?'

'Off,' repeated Wulfric, still frowning. 'I'm so sorry, Monsieur. I don't think I can help you, at all.'

Lazare tried another smile, even though his heart really wasn't in it. 'That's all right.'

'And I certainly can't try turning you or drinking you, because you really do smell...'

'Off,' replied Lazare with forced cheer. 'Yes. I get it.'

'I should get back to it,' continued the vampire, turning back the way he'd come, 'there was a dead fox in the gutter over there that should make a decent meal for a couple of... oh, for pity's sake!'

Lazare gazed over the little vampire's head to see what had annoyed him so much. There was indeed some of a dead fox lying in the gutter, although the back half of it was a cleanly picked skeleton by now. A stumpy, brick-brown runt of a dragon was making fast work of scavenging the carcass.

'I was going to have that,' cried Wulfric. 'I called Baggsie!'

The dragon looked cowed. 'You were chatting, I didn't think you'd mind. D'you want me to save you a leg?'

'No! I wanted...' Wulfric sighed. 'Fine, I'll have a leg. And the heart, unless you've snaffled that, too.'

The dragon backed away from the fox corpse, before sniffing the air and staring at Lazare.

'*Bonjour*,' said Lazare, politely.

'We don't have to share with him,' Wulfric told the dragon, reaching into the cadaver's chest cavity. 'He's not one of us.' The little vampire pulled the heart out easily and tucked into it as if it were an apple.

The dragon approached Lazare with a combination of trepidation and wonder, still sniffing. 'I recognise that stink.'

'I don't stink...' Lazare complained. He was wearing his second best pomander, for crying out loud.

'I can smell it even under all that lavender you're wearing.' The dragon sat down in front of him, the fox corpse seemingly forgotten. 'God's Scales,' she exclaimed, 'it happened again. I found another one!'

'Lavender is very in fashion right now,' argued Lazare, before breaking off suddenly. 'Wait... what do you mean, "another one"?'

'Another one,' repeated the little dragon, brightly, like that was enough of an explanation.

'Another... not-quite-a-vampire?' asked Lazare.

The dragon turned tail and started waddling off. 'I'll show you him. C'mon.'

Also available

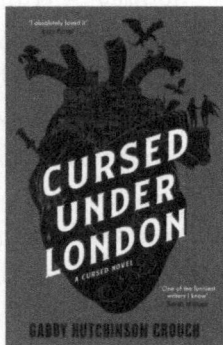

About the Author

Gabby Hutchinson Crouch (*Horrible Histories*, *Horrible Science*, *Newzoids*, *Homeschool History*, *The News Quiz, The Now Show*) is a BAFTA awarded comedy writer with a background in satire and an unexpected niche in historical comedy, both of which make her uncannily good at pub quizzes.

Born in Pontypool in Wales, and raised in Ilkeston, Derbyshire, Gabby moved to Canterbury at eighteen to study at the University of Kent and ended up staying and having a family there.

She is the author also of the acclaimed Darkwood trilogy, a modern fairy tale series for grown-up and younger readers alike and The Rooks trilogy, a supernatural horror comedy about a family of ghost hunters.

About Cursed

Cursed is a fantasy rom-com series following Fang, Lazare and Nell, three humans who are struck with the curse of immortality. As they set out to reverse the curse with the help of friends they've met along the way – Amber the urban dragon, and fae child, Tem – they realise that although they can no longer die, their newfound powers make them targets for criminals and the law alike. And surely, when in grave danger, falling in love should be off the agenda, shouldn't it?

Also by Gabby Hutchinson Crouch:

The Cursed series
Cursed Under London
Cursed in the Lost City

The Darkwood series
Darkwood
Such Big Teeth
Glass Coffin

The Rooks series
Wish You Weren't Here
Out of Service
Home Sweet Hell

Acknowledgements

Huge thanks to Pete, Matt, Daniela and everyone at Duckworth for giving life to the stories in my head, and putting them in such gorgeous books. Thanks to my agent Dom and everyone at JFL.

Thank you to everyone who said lovely things about *Cursed Under London* and generally helped me shout about it, especially Lucy, Jess and Paul. Most of all, thank you to my wonderful family, especially Nathan, Violet and Alex, the best three people in the world. I would also thank my colleague Spooky, but she can't read because she is a cat.

This book is a love story, and a love letter to bisexuality, and to Wales, and to fanfiction. Thanks, bisexuality! Thanks, Wales! Thanks, fanfiction!

Note from the Publisher

To receive updates on new releases in the Cursed series –
plus special offers and news of other humorous fiction
series to make you smile – sign up now to the Farrago mailing
list at farragobooks.com/sign-up.